CONSERVATIVE AFFAIRS

RILEY SCOTT

Bella
BOOKS
2014

Bella Books, Inc.
P.O. Box 10543
Tallahassee, FL 32302

Printed in the United States of America on acid-free paper.

First Bella Books Edition 2014

Editor: Medora MacDougall
Cover Designer: L. Callaghan

ISBN: 978-1-59493-402-5

About the Author

In addition to having published poetry and short stories, Riley Scott has worked as a grant and press writer and holds a degree in journalism. A chunk of life spent in the Bible Belt has given her a close-up look at the struggle for balance between love and church, home and state. She is a proud New Mexican with a strong love for green chile, dogs, and lively literature.

Dedication

For every girl who has ever felt like she couldn't share her story, for all the loved ones who have given me the courage and strength to live my own, and for all who have supported, inspired, and encouraged my dreams.

Jo stared at the screen of her laptop, fingers hovering above the keys, yet unable to strike.

In three hours, she had written one word. "Bullshit." It stared back at her from the screen, seeming to resonate within her. It summed up her life pretty well—certainly her job at least.

She finished the last few gulps of her beer and crunched the can, satisfied to have something fold under her pressure. Lately she was the one folding and giving in to whatever her boss wanted.

Most days she got along fine, pretending and dancing on the tightrope that everyone in politics had to manage, but today's assignment was simply too much.

Maybe that's why she had put it off until after her trip to the bar. Nonetheless, Jo had to find some way to write a speech for her boss advocating for the so-called "Defense of Marriage Act."

How great would it be if her ultraconservative boss just got up and recited what Jo had written? "DOMA is bullshit." Jo grinned, picturing the agape mouths of reporters, supporters and everyone else present. It would be a glorious day—but also her last one as an employee of the mayor's office. Unfortunately, Jo had to stick to the guidelines she had been given.

Not that they were really guidelines, she thought. They were more like the spewings of a homophobic monster frothing at the mouth and uttering Tarzan-like phrases: "Man and woman, good. Man and man, perverted. Woman and woman, abomination." Add in some lines from the Bible and maybe a line or two about how gays are out to destroy the universe and families, and she'd have the speech written.

Time to channel your inner judgmental church girl. Shouldn't be that hard for a preacher's kid whose mommy is still praying and pushing for a white wedding.

She thought about her upbringing in the church, the exposure to the judging and being judged and sighed. "Hate the sin, not the sinner."

She clasped her hands over her mouth, realizing she had spoken the words aloud.

"Shit," she whispered. The sounds emanating from her bedroom told her that her latest mistake had woken up and was getting ready to leave. The night's events came blaring back with the speed and force of a giant semitruck. Not only had she decided to blow off steam at the bar after work, ignoring her deadline, but she had also brought home a one-night stand. She closed her eyes, wishing away the conversation that was impending, as the noise of footsteps sounded again in her bedroom.

She had to stop doing this. Sooner or later, it was all going to come back and bite her in the ass. When it did, there'd be hell to pay. Headlines shouting the news, all her secrets laid bare, no job…and no family.

At twenty-seven, people were supposed to be a little more at peace with their lives, weren't they? If so, she was certainly an exception.

Her thoughts were interrupted by the opening of her bedroom door.

"Uh, hi..." The gorgeous blond spoke awkwardly. "I didn't know where you had gone to, so I thought I'd take off."

Lauren...or Laura...or maybe Lisa. The name just simply would not come to Jo's mind.

"All right. Have a good night," Jo said instead.

"Thanks, I had a good time," the blond continued. "What are you doing up, by the way? It's four a.m."

"Just working on some stuff for the morning."

"Oh, that's right. You said you were a law student, right, Sarah?"

Jo simply nodded and forced a smile. "That's right."

"Okay, well, call me." With that the blond was gone.

"Sarah, the law student..." Jo laughed to herself. She was getting too old to play these games. She wasn't a law student; she was a professional liar. Camping out in the closet did that to people. Not that she had much choice, given how high-profile her family was and her job. She couldn't have girls running around telling people they'd slept with Jo Carson.

Still, everyone needed a good lay every now and again, so she had perfected the art of deception, just as she had perfected the art of attracting just about every woman she'd ever desired. Sometimes, she silently joked to herself, she could basically talk a girl out of her clothes. With eyes that dazzled and words that dripped of sweet honey, she had had her way with as many women as she wanted—but never for more than one night and never out in the light of day. Jo wasn't sure if that made her a superhero or a super villain, but either way, she'd take it.

Stretching her neck from side to side, she tried to think back to the sex she'd had with the blond or the buzz still rolling around in her head from the beer. All she could think of, though, was that stupid DOMA speech and what a hypocrite she was.

She had to write the speech. She needed this job to prove herself professionally. If she wanted a future as a writer in any shape or form, this was her foot in the door. Besides which, people like Jo Carson didn't just come out of the closet. There was too much at stake. There was always too much at stake for the offspring of Michael Carson, who didn't dare be anything but perfect cookie-cutter children.

She was reminded of that every time she called home. Her sisters, Tori and Alli, had dutifully acquired everything a good little Carson was supposed to have—the dashing husband, the kids, the nice little suburban house—and her mom never let her forget it.

Blah, blah, blah. Jo had heard it all before—and it was getting worse. Last time they had spoken, her mom had thrown her for a loop. "You're going to meet him this year, I just know it."

"Who, Mom?" Jo had asked, hoping that she didn't already know the answer.

"Well, your Mr. Right, of course, darling. I just have a feeling. You'll meet him this year, and then we can plan another wedding. Now I've been thinking, turquoise would be a beautiful accent color, and you could use black for the bridesmaids' dresses..."

Jo had stopped listening. Martha Carson had gone into overdrive while planning both Tori's and Alli's weddings and was dying to see her middle child walk down the aisle. Nothing in the world was worth having to listen to her planning yet another wedding.

Would she have any interest at all if she knew the person I wanted to marry was female? Jo couldn't help but wonder, though she knew the answer. Of course she wouldn't. It would roil the empire her family had worked to create, and it would divide the Carsons forever. She had a pretty solid feeling that even her sisters would turn their backs on her if it ever came to that.

With a sigh, Jo ran her fingers through her long dark hair.

"Well, Jaws," she said, reaching down to pet the shih tzu half asleep at her feet. "It looks like it's time to spread some hate."

CHAPTER ONE

The all-too-familiar ding of her work-issued BlackBerry produced a stinging pain in Jo's right temple. She craned her head to the side to crack her sore neck, then opened the email.

"Meet me in my office in 5. Need to discuss DOMA speech.–M"

Unable to do anything else, Jo burst into laughter. *Whatever could good old "M" want to discuss about the DOMA speech?*

For a brief moment, she fantasized about coming out right there in her boss's office. "Ma'am," she'd start. It was always best to be polite and recognize authority—or so she'd been taught. "The reason your DOMA speech isn't quite up to your standards is because you asked me to write it and I might possibly be the biggest vagina lover on the planet."

Stifling her laugh and shaking her head, Jo gathered up a notebook and headed off to receive a list of rewrites.

Calm, steady and collected, she knocked lightly on the door and prepared to turn on the charm.

While she waited for permission to enter, she ran her fingers over the elaborate brass nameplate on the solid oak door.

"Madeline Stratton, Mayor of Oklahoma City." It wouldn't have been out of place in a European palace; like almost everything in the office, it was over the top. Although the ornate décor was largely a holdover from the previous administration, anyone who had observed Madeline's air of authority and her ability to captivate an entire audience at first entrance into a room could have easily assumed she was the one who had decreed it to be so extravagant. Jo knew that was not the case, though. Reflecting upon her boss's true demeanor made her smile, despite the uncomfortable task awaiting her.

"Josephine?"

"Yes, ma'am," Jo replied, sticking her head in the door. "Are you ready to see me?"

The Honorable Madeline Stratton waved her hand welcomingly and nodded. "Of course. Come on in and have a seat."

Jo cleared her throat and took the offered seat. "So, about the speech…" she began.

The mayor held up her right hand to silence Jo. "First things first, Josephine. I liked the overall tone of the speech. It flows nicely. Ups and downs in the right places, good message points, everything."

Mayor Stratton was known for her dramatic pauses when speaking, personally as well as publicly. The time she was allowing to elapse now was painful. Jo was sure everyone within a ten-mile radius must be able to hear her heart pounding out of her chest.

Could she know? Was this the end? She forced herself to breathe, cringing when the exhalation came out loud and anxious-sounding.

Quickly the mayor spoke up. "It's all right. I liked the speech. There was only one thing I wanted to address."

Jo nodded, giving her the go-ahead.

"It doesn't quite pack the punch I would like for it to, especially when dealing with such an important issue."

When Jo didn't reply, the mayor added, "What I mean is, you use all the right messaging and wording, but it has the propensity to appear to some—your father's friends, the conservatives on the city council, for instance—as though I'm accepting of this lifestyle. Not supportive, but accepting—and you and I both know that we can't let our opponents use trivial stuff like this to torpedo our reform agenda. I can't stand the thought of all our hard work being in vain. The people are trusting us to do what we said we would. If we let a marginal issue like this distract or divide us, we'll lose the support of half of the city council and some very important donors. If that happens, we can kiss reelection next year goodbye and the last of our reform agenda with it."

The cold calculation behind the words hit Jo like a slap in the face, but she didn't let on. Her stomach churned, as she battled internally with the words. The mayor seemed to be coming from a place of legitimate concern for most of her constituents—to the detriment of a minority. Though the words stung, she couldn't help but admire the strategy behind them. "Yes, ma'am. I will make some edits, but may I ask one question?"

"Go ahead."

"How would you like me to go about making these changes?"

"Josephine, you're a brilliant writer. I'm sure you'll figure it out. Just make sure that you are crystal clear about my disapproval of the gay lifestyle. Also, include information on the importance of preserving the sanctity of marriage and how gay marriage, even civil unions, will undermine family values."

Biting her tongue, Jo smiled and nodded. "Will do."

She stood and turned to leave.

"Oh," the mayor exclaimed fervently. "And put something in about the actions that I plan to take to prevent gay marriage..."

Jo spun on her heel. "What type of actions?"

"Right now, we'll work to support civic and city groups that want to protect traditional marriage. We'll also stand behind the city council if it needs us to put forth any related proclamations. And...and...and..." Madeline tapped her fingers on her desk as if trying to drum up the perfect answer.

"Burning gays at the stake?" Jo offered and silently cursed herself for the answer.

Her boss broke into laughter as if this was the most humorous thing she had ever heard. "Oh, you truly do have a wicked sense of humor. Your father was right about that one."

The mention of Jo's father still stung—as if she could never have landed a job such as this one without his help. She forced a smile and nodded in agreement.

"That'll be all, Josephine. I'll look forward to reading through it again when you've finished the rewrites."

The piercing blue of Madeline's eyes captured Jo's gaze for a second longer than was necessary—or advisable. Quickly, she exited, afraid of making the moment awkward. Well, more awkward.

As her heels clicked slowly down the tiled hallway leading back to her cubicle, Jo mulled her job situation over in her mind for the millionth time. She was, she had been told, the best speechwriter the office had ever had; reviews of the mayor's speeches were off the charts. It was more than being good at her job, though, that was keeping her chained to a place she should want to leave. She had always loved politics. It was fast-paced, ever-changing, exciting. She was actually doing things to make a difference in the world.

Politics was where she had always wanted to be. But... did she really want to be working *here*, for Mayor Stratton? It hadn't felt as if she really had a choice, thanks to the "Daddy connection." Her heart wrenched. As much as she wanted to fight it, she let out a sigh of acceptance. This was her life, and she was who she was.

If only Mayor Stratton didn't hate the one thing Jo was sure that she was...Jo would have liked her just fine. She was a good boss, fair and loyal. She was a strong woman, and Jo loved strong women.

Hell, if the woman weren't so damn conservative, she might even have considered taking Ms. Madeline out for a spin. She let her mind contemplate that thought for a little while. No doubt about it, with that blond hair, those long legs, and those gorgeous blue eyes, Madeline Stratton was hot. She also possessed an incomparable intellect, something that Jo always found so enticing. Accomplished, beautiful and sharp as a tack—

she was the full package. Forty-two, but with the body of a twenty-five-year-old, she could have been the poster child for a "Republicans Are Sexy" campaign.

"What the hell, Jo?"

Gabe, the mayor's scheduler, had popped out in front of her while she was walking and moved quickly aside now to avoid a collision. She gasped; she'd nearly plowed into him. She blushed, thinking that somehow he had read her mind. What was she doing, anyway, thinking about sleeping with her boss?

"Oh! You scared me!" she finally sputtered.

"Chill out, man," Gabe said, laughing. "Did you seriously just make a joke in Madeline's office about burning gays at the stake?"

A sheepish grin spread across Jo's face. "Maybe," she replied with a shrug. "But, in all seriousness, Gabe, I think she'd take it almost that far if that's what was needed to get her programs passed."

"Do what we all do," Gabe said. "Just go with it. Take it to the extremes she wants to take it. If we need to rein her in before the speech, we will. But it's her career."

Jo never tired of this—the team ethic the mayor had engendered in the office. She was the new kid on the block—she'd been working for the mayor for less than a year, replacing someone who'd left for a job in DC—and most of the others had been there since the beginning of her term over three year ago, but people were still looking out for her. It felt good knowing they had her back—just as she had theirs. "Okay, thanks, Gabe. I'm going to 'go with it.'"

He patted her on the shoulder. "Go get 'em, tiger. Or attagirl. Or some cliché that's supposed to make you want to grab the bull by the horns and seize the day."

She shook her head, laughing and thankful for phenomenal co-workers. "Thanks, crazy."

"Wait, they didn't tell you?"

"Tell me what?"

"You're in the nuthouse, sweetheart." Gabe laughed at his own joke.

"No, they didn't mention it," Jo quipped. "But the padded cell gave it away." She gestured to her cubicle as she walked in that direction. Most days, it did feel like a psych ward here. Being overworked, underpaid and typically underappreciated was enough to drive any group of people insane.

"One more thing, Jo." Gabe had followed her to her desk.

"Sure, what's up?"

"I like the speech as it is. I wish she didn't want it to be more hateful." His eyes were sincere, and suddenly Jo wished she could hug him.

She didn't think she could manage words, so she just nodded.

"My brother is gay, you know?" He pitched his voice low, too soft for anyone else to hear.

"No, Gabe, I didn't. Does anyone else here know that?" She responded out of curiosity, hoping that her question didn't come out sounding as judgmental in any way.

He laughed. "No, ma'am, and they won't, I trust."

"Oh, of course not. Your secret is safe with me. But I think it's awesome that he has a supportive brother."

"Yeah, they don't look too highly on that around here, unfortunately."

She felt like she was being issued a warning, even though she knew there was no possible way Gabe could know she was a lesbian. Still, she heard the message loud and clear. DO NOT SLIP UP.

As the day passed, she felt the tension in her shoulders ease somewhat, but not enough. There was something unsettling about discussing "the gay lifestyle" with her boss and Gabe suddenly opening up about his gay brother. Jo wished it were a normal day—one in which the word "gay" never came up in conversation. Things were so much more comfortable in her nice little closet on days like that.

She reviewed the computer screen in front of her, making last-minute edits and reading for tone. "The Bible defines marriage as between a man and a woman...As our society has become more accepting of the homosexual lifestyle, we have seen the traditional family dissipate...Gay marriage is not only wrong; it defies the principles upon which this nation was founded—and which still hold true today."

With each word she typed, a little piece of her heart chipped off and fell away. If only she could write what had come to mind when she was first crafting the speech: "BULLSHIT!" Instead she was choosing to save her job. She hit the print button and grabbed the sheets of paper as they shot out of the printer. Silently begging for this to be the last time she would have to look at it, Jo carried the revised speech to the mayor's office and handed it to her.

There was a "hmm," an "mmhmm," a "yes" and a "how about that?" Stratton was scanning the document as if she were sifting grains of sand on a beach.

Finish the damn thing, Jo screamed inside her head.

After what felt like an eternity, the mayor lifted her gaze to meet Jo's. The deep blue in her eyes sparkled, and Jo's heart turned over in her chest. Pretty eyes had always been Jo's weakness. Come to think of it, though, Madeline Stratton also had a beautiful mouth. Full, soft lips and with perfect, impeccable, shining teeth that lit up a room any time she smiled.

"Did you hear a word I said?" The mayor's voice snapped her back to reality, only to make Jo realize she was biting her lip.

SHIT!

"Sorry," Jo recovered quickly. "Long day." She tried to get her emotions under control, hoping that her face didn't show the panic going on in her head.

The mayor laughed a genuine laugh, the kind Jo rarely heard escape from her lips. "I understand. We've all had those days."

Being rundown and overworked in a place like this was so common that everyone was able to get away with acting a little crazy now and then. Jo was thankful for that, especially in this moment.

"So what was it you were saying?" Jo asked innocently.

"Well, I said that I hope you are enjoying this speech because you get to spend another night with it."

"But it's everything you asked for." Normally, Jo wouldn't challenge her boss, but she couldn't bear the thought of writing one more homophobic sentence.

"And what is that?" the mayor asked.

"It affirms the constitutionality of defining marriage as solely between a man and a woman, the biblical basis for this definition, and most importantly it affirms your disapproval of the 'gay lifestyle' and the concept of same-sex marriage. It quotes the original Defense of Marriage Act and many other prominent figures who share your position. I really don't know what more we can add without sounding like we literally want to burn gays and lesbians at the stake."

The mayor threw her arms up in mock surrender. "Easy, girl." She smiled, and Jo felt her breath catch in her throat.

"That's all I wanted," she continued. "I wanted you to claim it, to own it and to sell it to me. You did a damn good job on this one, Josephine. I'm proud to call you mine."

Like a child who had been chosen to receive a gold star sticker, Jo beamed, unable to speak. Madeline Stratton was not known for giving out pats on the back.

Finally, words came. "Thank you" was all she could muster.

The mayor winked. "By the way, you stopped just short of the burning at the stake." She laughed and shook her head. "I appreciate that. I'd hate to get into more trouble with the progressives, who paint me as too far right on the political spectrum as it is. I hate that label. And as you all know around here, I hope, it's not necessarily accurate. Now, go home and get some rest."

CHAPTER TWO

Drumming her fingers on the steering wheel, Madeline wished for the millionth time that day that she still smoked—or at least that she could sneak one.

Unfortunately, though, she was deemed a fireball by the media. A no-nonsense woman in a man's game. And the cameras seemed to find her wherever she went. There would be no sneaking a smoke, just like there would be no letting on that her life was even slightly imperfect.

"Everyone had secrets." That's the motto she had lived by in her younger days, and she still believed it. Everyone had secrets, that is, except for those in the spotlight. Not for very long, anyway. These days she felt like nothing more than a target of the city's paparazzi, constantly running and ducking beneath the bushes for cover. It was inevitable: one day her baggage would be discovered and displayed all over the Internet, all over the tabloids, like Britney Spears' crotch had been. Until then, however…

Madeline glanced at the clock on the dashboard—she was already twenty minutes late. Hanging her head, she was moments from tears. Couldn't one thing go right? How could her life be circling the drain in such a dramatic, yet furtive fashion?

Finally, the traffic budged slightly, allowing her to slip off the highway and exit. She would have to take a back road to get to the restaurant with a prayer of receiving a small bit of understanding.

"Please, John, give me a break." She whispered the words, wishing there was a way to telepathically signal him. She tried his cell one last time. Nothing. Straight to voice mail.

When she finally arrived, she was an hour late. Scratch that. An hour and seven minutes. She knew there was no way that John would let her forget the extra seven minutes.

She sighed and slammed the door on her Suburban. When John caught her eye through the restaurant window, she could swear she saw complete indifference in his expression. Hoping for a sign that he still cared, she probed deeper but found nothing.

It was the look she got every morning over breakfast, the look she got as he pulled his car out of the drive, the look she got as he walked past her each night on the way to his room down the hall. The look that she got everywhere but in the public eye.

Then, and only then, would he turn on the affection. Under the examining eye of the photographer's lens, he was Mr. Charming, holding her hand, smiling lovingly at her, twirling her around the dance floor and placing his hand protectively on the small of her back while he led her through a crowd.

Sometimes she wasn't sure she could take even one more second of the lies. In the back of her mind, though, she knew it was her only option. Being mayor was not only a dream come true for her, it was what she was meant to do in life. She could make the tough decisions. She was a leader, and at last she was right where she belonged.

She was a Republican and as such had long known she would need a ring on her left hand to get votes. Her party seemed to think there was something downright scandalous about a single woman being in politics, although she could not figure how anything was more sordid than the sham of a marriage she was parading in front of the press.

Gracefully, she straightened her shoulders, put on the camera-ready smile she was known for and strode elegantly into the restaurant.

Our restaurant, she thought. *At least it was, once upon a time...*

Where she and John had come on their first date, where he had proposed, where he had taken her to celebrate her election as a city councilor years before, where they had celebrated her mayoral race victory just three short years ago and where she had always envisioned they would celebrate her statewide and even national election wins. Where their dreams had come true and then crumbled. All of it had happened in that corner booth by the window.

He stood and took her coat. Kissing her on the cheek, he hissed, "Where the hell have you been?"

She smiled and leaned in for a long, lingering hug. She stole affection whenever possible and knew that he would give it here.

"Sorry, honey." Her voice was too chipper, she noticed. She hoped no one else did. *Let's not spoil the show for anyone now.*

"I simply couldn't get out of the office until late. We're planning for the unveiling of the new education plan, you know?"

As if scripted, he smiled perfectly. "I'm just glad you're here now."

He directed her to her seat, always a gentleman.

"I've already put in our order." He smiled at the waiter as he walked past. "Good old Geoff here always remembers your order."

She smiled at Geoff, hoping it would calm the waves of pain surging through her heart. Was this what they had become? Were they really just two strangers—people who once knew each other who now could only talk in public?

They talked animatedly over wine, which she limited to one glass. Never let the public see you weak, single or drunk was a rule she stuck to hard and fast. It was all a show, and, though she hated to admit it, they were becoming very skilled at acting in it.

For a moment or two, she allowed herself to wish that it were real. To wish with all she had that, even for an evening, she'd see that smile of his cast in her direction in the dark, loveless halls of their home.

But as soon as dinner was over they walked arm in arm out to the parking lot.

He kissed her on the check tersely.

"I'll see you at home?" she asked hopefully, longing to extend the show of harmony into something less public.

"That's none of your business," he hissed back so low that anyone watching from the restaurant or parking lot would have no chance of hearing.

"John?" Her voice came out sounding like a plea, and she cursed herself for showing weakness yet again. She was always too soft where he was concerned.

His smile was perfect, but there was no disputing the fact that their discussion was over when he whispered, "Have a good night."

So that was it. She'd drive home alone and climb into an empty bed, where she'd toss and turn and wonder where he went when he didn't come home. She hated it when he slept in the room down the hall, but at least then he was home.

She exhaled loudly once in the safety of her vehicle.

"It's over."

It was the first time she'd allowed herself to actually speak the words, although she had thought them for a long time.

"It's over," she repeated as the tears began to fall.

Glancing toward the restaurant, she realized she was being watched from the windows of the restaurant by other patrons. It was time to go. She put the Suburban in gear and drove away, to the one place she could fall apart without being in the public eye.

CHAPTER THREE

The wind whipped around outside, driving torrents of rain against the bedroom window. Lightning crackled and thunder boomed. The heater clicked on, doing its best, but fighting a losing battle against the cold that was seeping in. On a street somewhere in the distance a siren wailed.

Jo sighed heavily and moved Jaws off her feet. She had a lot on her mind, and Oklahoma's blustery October weather wasn't helping. She doubted anyone in the tri-state area was getting any sleep. They knew all too well that such winds could be portents of much more ominous weather. She checked the time. It was going on four a.m. The one thing she longed for—a deep, peaceful slumber—was clearly not going to happen. As she rose from the bed, Jaws peered out from under the covers, both confused and irritated to have been woken.

She lovingly patted him on the head, thankful that at least one of them was unbothered by the crazy weather of this area. "I'm sorry, buddy. Go back to sleep."

He wiggled out of sight, nestling back into the covers. At least one of them would be getting some rest.

Normally, Jo slept through even raging winds. In Oklahoma, nights like tonight were a dime a dozen. But she had been awake long before the storm hit.

As she began to prepare herself a cup of tea, the dream that had woken her earlier came back to haunt her. It was a simple dream, but it had unnerved her. Even though she wished the image would go away, she knew that every time she closed her eyes, it would visit her again.

Jo shook her head, trying to make her memory an Etch A Sketch. In search of distraction, she grabbed her BlackBerry. Even though it was four in the morning, maybe there was something she could work on until it was time for work.

She unlocked the screen. There was something happening today, Jo thought, as she looked at the date. She wracked her brain until it came to her. When it did, she wanted to cry.

Columbus Day, a federal holiday. The office would be closed today.

She scrolled through her inbox. Nothing pressing.

She had to get out of the house. Days off of work meant time alone, something she increasingly disliked.

It may be true that no man is an island, but I think at least one woman is, Jo thought.

As if hearing her silent plea for company, Jaws stumbled into the kitchen. She scooped him into her arms and kissed his fluffy head. "Want to come to work with Mommy today?"

He licked her cheek as if in reply. Her heart swelled with love, then plummeted. That was the most genuine affection she had felt in months. The emptiness of her little apartment reverberated off the walls, coming back at her, reminding her constantly that she was all alone.

An hour later, dressed in her favorite pair of ripped, faded jeans and a simple red sweatshirt, she strode into the office, Jaws in tow. The storm had blown through, but, as she had expected, the place was deserted. Anyone in their right mind would be at home, fast asleep and planning to relax all day.

She settled at her desk. Jaws laid down at her feet, preparing to finish the night's sleep that had been taken from him. Now she could breathe easier. She had her computer, her cup of coffee and her favorite companion snuggled at her feet, and she could find tasks to keep her busy.

She booted up her computer and, opening her Brandi Carlile station on Pandora, let the sultry sound of a bluesy, folk song take her away. She leaned back in her chair and began to sing. Her voice, deep and sensual, hit all the right notes, rising and falling to the perfect rhythm. It felt good to sing. She hadn't done so in a while.

She closed her eyes and let the music take her to a place where things like love and happiness weren't a myth. To a place where it wasn't all about one-night stands and secrets. In her mind, she saw the silhouette of two beautiful women, kissing openly on a starlit street, sharing a love that went beyond the bedroom. Then, from out of nowhere, appeared the haunted blue eyes from her dream.

The image brought her out of her daydream, out of her song, and sat her straight up at her desk.

"That was beautiful."

Jo yelped, caught off guard by the voice emanating from one of the side offices.

A deep laugh rang through the office, followed by the sound of footsteps.

"Oh…um…hi," Jo said as Mayor Stratton came into view.

"Good morning to you as well." The mayor was obviously amused.

Jo stuttered and stammered, trying to put together an intelligent sentence. Not only was she embarrassed to have screamed in front of a boss whom she assumed already found her inexperienced, but the eyes she was staring deeply into were the ones she had seen in her dream. Eyes that held the same expression as the ones that stared blankly back at her from her mirror each morning. Eyes that were haunted, guarded and beautifully sad.

"I thought I was the only one here," Jo finally said.

"As did I. Tell me, Josephine, what on earth are you doing here at five a.m. on your day off?"

"I didn't want to be at home." *Dammit!* Jo chided herself for speaking the words aloud, but the sudden appearance of her boss had unnerved her, leaving her susceptible to making stupid statements like that.

Once again, Jo looked up to meet the mayor's gaze. She swore she saw in her eyes an understanding of, almost an agreement with, Jo's statement.

"I see," the mayor responded, her words dancing around the subject, seemingly careful not to probe too deep.

"That's not what…I mean…well…" She'd dug this hole. She might as well figure a way out. "What I meant is that I needed to get some things done here before I can relax."

The mayor sat down in the leather chair across from Jo's desk. "Do you have anything that's pressing or unfinished?"

Madeline Stratton was the kind of boss who paid attention to everyone's assignments. She knew Jo's workload, her schedule and every project she had in the works. There was no point in lying to the woman.

"No," Jo conceded.

To Jo's surprise, the mayor shrugged and offered a smile. "Me neither."

"Why are you here so early on a day off?" Jo asked, then remembered to add, "if you don't mind me asking, that is."

"I asked you first, remember? So I guess it's a fair question."

"True."

"I guess I'm just more at home here than anywhere else lately."

The answer came after the mayor had weighed her response for a while. It was followed by a startled hop. Jaws had not only woken up, Jo realized, but he was also sniffing the mayor's shoes.

"Oh, my goodness, I am so sorry. I brought him in with me because I figured I'd be alone. I'm so sorry."

The mayor reached down and scooped the shih tzu up. "Don't you worry. He's a cute little guy. What's his name?"

Slightly embarrassed, Jo wished she had given her dog a more respectable name—one worthy of sharing with someone as serious and dignified as the mayor. "Uh, his name is Jaws." Jo gave a half smile.

"That is just too perfect," she exclaimed, petting his head. She turned back to look at Jo. "Do you want to grab some breakfast?"

A casual breakfast with the boss hadn't exactly been in Jo's plans, but there was a vulnerability in Madeline Stratton's eyes this morning that she had never seen before.

Jo's heart hammered in her chest. This was the most normal conversation she'd ever had with her boss, and she was worried it might jeopardize her job. She was getting ready in her head to politely decline the offer when her mouth blurted out, "I'd love to."

"Great! I know this little place where I can usually avoid an early morning photo shoot."

Jo glanced over at Jaws, who was still enjoying the love the mayor had to offer. "Let me drop him off and I'll meet you there."

She walked over to get him, then stopped, momentarily flummoxed by the awkward scenario in front of her. Before she could overanalyze how to scoop Jaws up without brushing against the mayor's lap, Madeline picked him up to hand him over. Their fingers brushed as Jo took him, and every nerve in her body tingled at the slight contact. Composing herself, she held her dog in her arms and turned away to refocus on more pressing issues. She felt as if she had just gotten in way over her head. What on earth could she discuss with this woman over breakfast? Would she share too much? Appear too cold and disconnected?

Half an hour later, as she pulled into an alley and double-checked the directions the mayor had given her, Jo was even more uncertain. She knew she should call and cancel. She was preparing to throw the car into reverse when she saw Madeline get out of a Suburban parked near a small brick building.

"Shit," she muttered, smoothing the shirt she'd changed into and stepping from her vehicle.

"I'm glad to see you found it." There was an unfamiliar note—*happiness?*—in the mayor's voice.

"Me too. I didn't even know this place was back here."

"That's the beauty of it," Madeline Stratton smiled again, a look that before this morning had seemed so uncharacteristic. "I know the owner, and she gives me a little booth in the back that's secluded from the rest of the dining room. It's one of the few places I can go to unwind a little."

The words hung in the air, like nakedness exposed. Jo had never stopped to consider what it must be like to be the mayor—to constantly be scrutinized and thrust into the spotlight. Her empathy for the mayor grew; being in the spotlight of public office was probably even more intense than undergoing the scrutiny of a church congregation.

All of her nervousness had cumulated to make her hands shake in a way that they hadn't since she had been on her first date. She followed the mayor as they entered the restaurant and found their way to a hidden back table.

They placed their orders and made small talk over coffee as they waited for their food. Madeline Stratton might be a woman of power, Jo soon realized, but she was also human. Jo's heart had nearly settled into a normal rhythm when she turned her deep blue eyes in Jo's direction.

"So, why don't you tell me a little about yourself? I mean, beyond the interview stuff, we haven't really had a chance to get to know one another."

Jo forced a smile even though her heart was once again beating like a kick drum. "Well, you know my family, so you know most of my background—where I'm from and everything like that."

"Yes, you come from a good family, Josephine… "

"Jo." Jo decided this was as good a time as any. "You can call me Jo. It's what pretty much everyone but my parents call me. Josephine just seems way too formal. I insisted on the shortened version as a kid after watching *Facts of Life*."

Jo watched as the mayor's eyebrow shot up in question, but then she cleared her throat, moving on from the mention of the show.

"Very well, Jo. You're also free to call me by my first name when we're not in the office or at a public function. Now, why don't you tell me more about yourself—something not related to your family? What do you like to do? What are your dreams? You know, what makes you, you?"

Jo wasn't entirely sure what to tell her. "Well, I like to write. For fun, that is. I'm not sure what my dreams are these days. They seem to change regularly."

Madeline appeared to be taking in the words slowly and savoring every nuance, as one does when taste testing a fine wine.

"I envy that," she responded quietly.

"Which part?"

"That you can still change your dreams."

Jo hesitated but asked anyway. "Do you want to change yours?"

Madeline averted her eyes, as though she'd shared too much. "No, not really. I just miss being young I suppose."

"You're still young enough to chase another dream if you have one," Jo pressed. "I think you should do what makes you happy. Embrace that freedom."

"It's not that easy. Besides, I think you might need to heed your own advice. I did find you at the office this morning as well, remember?"

"Touché," Jo said with a wink and immediately chided herself. *You don't just wink at the mayor, idiot!*

"So, how did you like the crepes?" Madeline smiled, but something had changed. It was no longer the open smile that had allowed Jo to see briefly into her soul. It was the smile that the news cameras received. Jo's window into the heart of Madeline Stratton had officially been closed.

CHAPTER FOUR

Gabe carried two cups of coffee from the break room. He had arrived thirty minutes early today, aware that Jo always showed up twenty minutes before she had to be at work. It was a nonetheless endearing quirk.

Hell, everything about Jo was endearing. Those long legs that were muscled and toned in all the right places, her perfect figure and her intense green eyes. Her intelligence, her quick wit and the way she could handle anything that the mayor or other staff members threw at her with grace and poise. It was all too much some days. Her voice cascaded in his mind, like a waterfall caressing every parched inch of it.

Even more intriguing was the wall she had built around herself. It was so high it seemed as if no one would ever be able to scale it. Since she had begun working in Stratton's office, though, it had been Gabe's goal to be the one who finally did so.

He wanted to know more about the raven-haired beauty in the corner cubicle than he had heard in the interview answers she had given. Sure, he knew all about her education, previous experience, writing for press outlets and working on various campaigns around the area and the boatloads of money her family had dumped into Stratton's campaign fund. But he wanted—no, he *needed*—more.

He needed to know what made Jo come alive, what she feared, what she wanted. He needed to know how she liked to be kissed, how to make her smile and how to win her heart. It wasn't the most romantic move, but he figured getting her coffee was a starting point. If nothing else, it would give him a chance to start a conversation.

Good morning. How are you? Too generic.

Hi there, Jo. How was your night? No, too creepy.

Hey, Jo. Did you enjoy the holiday weekend? Maybe.

What an idiot! I mean, standing by her cubicle, rehearsing my opening lines? How dorky is that?

Deciding it was best to retreat and try again tomorrow, Gabe let out a sigh. Almost as soon as he had admitted defeat in his head, though, he heard the front door open.

Damn!

The world seemed to freeze as Jo strode into the office. It was a casual walk for her, he was sure, but somehow she managed to make it look like she was walking a runway. Quickly, before she turned to meet his stare, he looked her up and down. Her skirt hugged her in all the right places and stopped just above the knee to show off her incredible legs. As she moved, her hair fell perfectly and the light danced in her eyes.

"Morning, Gabe," she called, heading to the break room.

"I got you coffee." *Why do I even plan these fucking things out?*

Not the opening line he wanted, but it would have to do for now.

The confusion in her eyes shook his confidence even more. They seemed to be asking, "Why?"

"I was here early and thought you might enjoy some when you got here."

"Thank you." She smiled and accepted the cup.

He wondered if the gesture seemed as odd and out of place to Jo as it did to him. She had never shown any interest in him, but despite the urging in his head to cut his losses and try again another day, he continued standing by her cubicle.

"So, did you have a good weekend?"

"I did," Jo said simply, taking her seat in front of her computer.

She glanced back. "Is Stratton in yet?"

"Not yet."

"Oh, okay." He thought he sensed disappointment, but then Jo added, "I had breakfast with her this weekend."

"Really? Did I forget about an event?" The thought that Madeline Stratton would spend time with her staff outside of work hours was so preposterous it didn't even occur to him.

Jo laughed, and the sound made him weak in the knees. "No. It was just the two of us, a casual breakfast." Gabe wrinkled his brow and frowned slightly, and she quickly added, "But don't mention it to anyone."

"Don't worry. I'll keep under wraps the fact that you're the boss's favorite."

They both laughed, but Jo's laugh sounded suddenly nervous to Gabe's ears.

"Thanks," she offered. "And thanks for the coffee."

With that, she turned back to her computer and focused on the screen.

Good job, man. Struck out again, Gabe thought to himself as he sulked back to his office, defeat weighing down his slumped shoulders.

* * *

The exchange with Gabe left Jo contemplating the life she could have had. Since her first day in the office, she had felt his eyes follow her every time she moved, and she knew that the interest he showed her was far more intense than the interest he showed most new employees.

Momentarily, she allowed herself to envision the life she could have with someone like Gabe Ellison. There they were, she in the white dress, he in his black suit. Her mother would be beaming, her father proudly telling everyone how they had met while working for the esteemed mayor. What a good little conservative daughter they had produced! Mr. and Mrs. Ellison (because of course she would take his last name) would go on to have children, dazzling political careers and a fabulous house. Everyone would be happy—except Jo.

If only she were attracted to men, life would be so much easier, albeit less entertaining and certainly less fun. It would give her the chance to hold hands with someone in public, go out on dates and occasionally receive an approving glance at family holidays. No, these were not necessities in life; they would have been nice, though…

She was popped out of her dream world by the realization that getting her coffee this morning was only the beginning. Gabe was building up a head of steam and would soon be moving ahead at full speed—which really was a shame. He was a friend and one of the best co-workers she had ever had. After she turned him down, that would surely change.

Of course, she could always go out with him a few times, just to have something to report back to her mother. Maybe she'd play it cool, go out to dinner a time or two and then tell him she didn't really have time for anything serious.

It was a game she had played a million times. She liked to refer to it in her internal monologue—as she sadly had to do with most of the details of her love life—as "throwing the family off my tracks." If she occasionally dated a man—even casually—then it would prevent them from suspecting that she liked women. All she had to do afterward was tell them that she hadn't found "the one" yet or that work was keeping her busy, but she was trying.

Maybe she'd agree if Gabe asked her out.

She was allowing herself to ponder living the "straight life" a little too often these days. True: It would mean that she wouldn't spend all of her days hiding away. Actually, it would be more like wasting away.

She was still mulling this over when lunchtime came. Rounding the corner to the break room, she almost smacked into Gabe again. No doubt he had been waiting there for her. Jo forced a smile, but it did nothing to stifle the sigh that escaped her lips. He was everything she should want, but she felt nothing when she looked at him.

"How's your day going?" Gabe's smile stretched across his entire face.

Before Jo could answer, Jacquelyn, the communications director, burst into the break room, looking as though she might break into tears. "I need to talk to you right now!"

"Which one of us?" Gabe calmly asked, placing a steadying hand on Jacquelyn's shoulder.

"You," she pointed to Gabe, then glanced in Jo's direction. "You too, I suppose."

Nervously, she glanced over her shoulder. "But not here. We need to step out of the office for a few."

They made a hasty exit, although it was not apparent to Jo where they were headed. Jacquelyn's face was ashen and she seemed to be holding her breath. Jo couldn't imagine what could have shaken her so badly. She was always so poised, professional and in control of situations.

"Here. Get in here." Jacquelyn pointed at her SUV.

Without questioning, Gabe and Jo climbed into the vehicle. Jacquelyn locked the doors, and if the air hadn't been so tense, Jo would have laughed at the gesture.

"What's going on?" Gabe and Jo asked simultaneously.

"I just got a call from Channel 15 news," Jacquelyn's hands shook as she spit out the words. "They want a comment from Stratton about her husband. They want to know why he was out to lunch with a woman and why he had taken the same woman to a hotel room two nights ago. They are breaking the story tonight at five. I don't know what to tell them—because I can't just walk into Stratton's office and break the news to her that her husband is a cheating son of a bitch."

Gabe looked as if he had been punched in the gut. Jo figured that was a normal response. But it was so unlike the response she was experiencing. For reasons she couldn't explain, she felt red-hot anger and a fierce need to protect Madeline from feeling the pain that was coming. To kick John Stratton's sorry ass, hold Madeline in her arms and wipe away her tears.

She had to get it together. Try as she might, though, she couldn't see any easy answer to this situation. And that had nothing to do with being new to the staff. Looking at Gabe and Jacquelyn, she saw that, despite the wealth of political experience between the two of them, they not only didn't have a clue how to proceed, but were also deeply reluctant to be the bearer of the bad tidings.

Jacquelyn tried to call Ian, the mayor's chief of staff for the fifth time, slamming down her phone in exasperation when she was sent to voice mail again.

"Our fearless leader picked one hell of a time to disappear off the face of the earth," she said, her words coming out as a frustrated hiss.

Gabe's eyebrows shot up. He reached out to touch Jacquelyn's shoulder, then quickly pulled it back, realizing how bad an idea that would be under the circumstances. She looked like a rattlesnake, ready to strike.

"It's not like he could plan it." He looked at his watch. "He's likely in the middle of the funeral service now and has his phone turned off. He's due back tomorrow and I'm sure he'll phone us as soon as he's able." Jacquelyn narrowed her eyes at him but shook her head, as if pushing the anger to its rightful recipient instead of unleashing it on Gabe and Ian.

"What do we do until then?"

Jo's mind raced, and she wanted to close her eyes and wish the whole thing away. How could anyone break the news to Stratton?

Sure, Madeline was a bitch some days. She was intense and a little severe at times, but there was a softness in her eyes and she had a good sense of humor. And, as Jo had seen at breakfast, she was human. Jo knew that if this had happened to her—if she ever gave someone the chance to hold her heart and she betrayed her like this—she would be devastated. And, of course, she'd probably want to rip the messenger's head clean off.

As she glanced from face to face in front of her, it was clear from Gabe's furrowed brow that he had too many questions to be a supportive participant in the discussion Madeline might need. One look at Jacquelyn's pursed lips signaled to Jo that she was, as always, considering her career above all else.

Her heart raced as she considered what she was about to do. Jo sighed, knowing she shouldn't get involved but also knowing that there was no way she could walk away. "I'll tell her."

The puzzlement on Jacquelyn's face was evident, as was her abject relief.

"Are you sure?" she asked, unable to stifle the sigh of relief that escaped her lips. Jo saw the tension drain from her body and a brightness return to her eyes.

It was clear that she was happy to see Jo take the fall, should there be one.

Drawing another long breath, Jo nodded her head, even though her hands trembled in her lap. She wasn't sure, really, but somehow it felt like the right thing to do.

"Jo? We can tell her if you'd rather." Gabe's shaky voice offered her a way out, but his mousy expression seemed to beg her not to take him up on the offer.

"No. I've got it," Jo insisted. "I'll even draft the statement. I can have it to you before five," she said, offering Jacquelyn a professional explanation for her actions, and got out of the car.

Before she could close the door, Gabe stuck his head out. "Thank you, Jo," he said, offering her a smile that didn't quite hide his frazzled expression. "I know this is a big thing to take on, but we're happy to have you on the team."

Pursing her lips to keep from letting out a half-amused laugh, she shook her head, shut the door and walked away.

It's no wonder Gabe was so alone in the world, she thought. He was a good person, but weak. If he couldn't muster the backbone necessary to step up in a situation like this, there was no way he could be seen as loyal to anyone.

CHAPTER FIVE

Could you pinpoint the moments your world changed forever? Madeline believed you could. For her, there were a number of such moments, happy ones that left her heart soaring as well as devastating ones that had left her feeling as though everything she knew and loved was being picked up by an Oklahoma twister and spun around in the sky until it plummeted back into the earth at breakneck speed.

Take the moment she was elected mayor. Although that had been a happy life change, something she had worked hard for, it had left her with the feeling that nothing would ever be the same again. She had been correct. It had turned everything upside down, thrusting her headfirst into a world filled with trade-offs, games, cameras and public scrutiny.

That life-changing moment had led to the others too. The moment John told her he didn't love her anymore. The moment he announced he would be sleeping in a separate bedroom. The moment she realized for the first time that he wouldn't be coming home for the night.

That day had been like any other. They hadn't spoken until she got home from work. Then they had fought. He threw a bottle of wine across the room and walked out the front door. He had done all these things before. And, as she had each night when he left before, she had left the outside light on for when he drunkenly stumbled home and then had laid in bed as usual, waiting to hear the sound of the front door open and slam before allowing herself to fall asleep. That night, though, the door had never opened. Finally, at 3:15 a.m., she forced herself to admit that he wasn't coming back. Everything around her felt as if it had turned to quicksand, shifting beneath her and trying to pull her into its depths.

It was a moment she replayed often, evoking it whenever she needed an extra surge of strength to get through a particularly difficult day. *If I got through that*, she would remind herself, *I can get through anything. I can get through this.*

As she caught the words falling reluctantly from Jo Carson's mouth, though, she felt as if she just might stop breathing.

Hotel. Affair. News channel. The words repeated in her mind, a vortex leading to the swirling and haunting world of her inner demons.

She had assumed for months that John was cheating. Without any evidence, though, it had been easy enough to ignore. That was the way she wanted it. She didn't want to think about her husband sleeping with another woman. It was much easier to get through the day pretending that everything would be all right when she got home.

"Do you want to comment on the story, ma'am?"

The compassion in Jo's voice broke through her distress, finally capturing Madeline's attention. She looked up to tell her to tell the press John was a lying, cheating asshole, but when she opened her mouth, a choked sob came out instead of words.

Jo was by her side immediately, pulling her into an embrace as the tears began to fall. Madeline wanted to be strong, but it was as if someone had opened the floodgates. She leaned into Jo's embrace and quietly sobbed.

Jo continued to repeat, "I'm so sorry," as she stroked Madeline's hair.

Madeline was not big on showing emotion in the first place and crying in public could be disastrous for female politicians. But being here with Jo was oddly comforting. She was thankful that she was the one who had come into her office to tell her the news. She was even more grateful that Jo had had the foresight to lock the door. No one needed to see the mayor bawling like a baby. Not even Jo Carson, she decided.

Sniffling, Madeline did her best to regain her composure. "I apologize, Jo."

"No, don't apologize. I'm here if you need anything."

The sympathy was too much. For reasons she couldn't explain, it triggered another sobbing fit.

* * *

As Madeline Stratton sobbed quietly in her arms, Jo felt her own heart breaking. She fought off tears of her own, continuing to stroke Madeline's hair, trying to channel her empathic reaction into an alternative outlet.

What kind of jackass would crush the heart of such an extraordinary woman? Would walk out on someone so beautiful, someone whose blue eyes held within them both intelligence and sweetness, especially when they were crying? It didn't make sense that someone this incredible should be crying her eyes out, wondering what she had done wrong.

Then again, it didn't make sense that Jo was the one who had rushed to her rescue, who had *needed* to be there when Madeline got the news. She didn't have an established relationship with the mayor like some of the other staff members did, but a tornado could not have ripped her away from Madeline's side in that moment. If Madeline needed her, she would be there, even if she couldn't explain why.

"Do you want to get out of the office?" Jo asked carefully, deciding that if she were having a breakdown of her own, she wouldn't want to be here.

Madeline nodded her head weakly. When she looked up at Jo, the raw pain in her eyes was enough to make Jo's eyes pool with tears.

"Wait here for a minute. I'm going to shuffle some things on my desk, and I'll drive you."

"I'll be fine," Madeline insisted.

"No. I'm not going to have you driving yourself anywhere right now. Please, just wait a moment."

For a woman who was usually filled with enough fight to take on an army by herself, Madeline's concession came too easily. "Okay," she agreed in a voice barely above a whisper.

Before Jo was out the door, she added, "Please tell the reporters 'no comment.' I don't know what else to say."

Jo nodded, feeling every bit of Madeline's pain as if it were her own.

Quickly she walked to Jacquelyn's office and shut the door behind her.

"Holy shit, you're as white as a ghost. How'd she take it?"

"I'm taking her home and getting her out of here." Jo had to focus harder than normal to make the words come out calm and collected. "Also, her response is 'no comment.' She figured it would be easier that way."

"Okay, are you coming back here after you take her home? I want to know all about it, what she says."

"Have a fucking heart, Jacquelyn! This is her marriage, not some topic of petty gossip," Jo shot back before opening the door and walking to her desk to grab her things.

Her blood was boiling by the time she got back to Madeline's office, so she took an extra minute outside of the door to calm down. Tensions were running high, and she needed to be the strong, steady one right now. She knocked lightly on the door. "It's me." Entering quickly, she gathered everything Madeline might need if she decided to lose herself in work this evening and then draped Madeline's coat around her body.

Grasping her by the elbow, Jo helped her to her feet. "Let's get you out of here." Then, as if shielding Madeline from flashing cameras instead of from the curious eyes of her staff, she hurried her out the front door and made a beeline for her little red Camaro. She always loved its sleek look, but she suddenly wished there was more room for Madeline to sit in and be comfortable. She opened the passenger door and got Madeline settled before jogging around and getting in herself.

Feeling somewhat safer once she was inside, Jo turned to Madeline and managed a smile. "I'm going to need directions to get you home."

Madeline only shook her head.

"Or," Jo offered, "you can just give me the address and I'll type it into my GPS." She pointed to the device mounted on her dashboard.

"No, I can't go home—not yet anyway. If they're not there already, it's soon going to be surrounded by reporters."

"Well, where do you want to go?"

"I want a drink."

Jo considered this. If she were in Madeline's shoes, she'd want a drink too, but where could she take her in early afternoon hours without drawing any attention?

"Do you have a particular destination in mind?" Jo asked.

"Not a bar."

"I figured as much. Let me think."

In the silence, Jo considered her options, which were few and far between. The desperation she felt fueled her next question. "How does my place sound? You can have a few drinks there and relax. We'll play the rest by ear."

Jo knew she was crossing a line by offering her place as a refuge for her boss, a risky move maybe, given that they barely knew each other—and some of what the mayor thought she knew about Jo was totally false. There was nevertheless some contentment in her heart when Madeline agreed.

"That would be nice." Like a phoenix rising from the ashes, a slight smile emerged from Madeline's grief-stricken face. "Thank you for this, Jo. I appreciate it."

Jo squeezed her hand and nodded. There was nowhere else she could have imagined being, though ironically, considering she was a speechwriter, she knew she would not have been able in that moment to conjure up the words to express that.

There was just something about Madeline Stratton. Every move, every expression, everything she said mesmerized her.

Even when she was in pain, she was captivating. Usually when she brought someone home, she had no more on her mind than getting her into bed.

Not that she couldn't envision doing that with Madeline, but it was different with her. She wanted to know what Madeline was thinking, feeling. Wanted to be there when things were bad as well as good.

She delved deeper into her thoughts as she drove, mentally shaking her head. Wanting to throw Madeline into bed—that was a highly inappropriate thought given the circumstances. And the fact that Madeline was straight, of course. She would have to be content just being Madeline's friend, something she would have once thought impossible.

Friend? Jo rolled the word around in her mind. Was she Madeline's friend? A week ago, she would have considered herself just a staff member, but something had changed between them over breakfast yesterday. Jo hoped the familiarity between them was blossoming into a friendship. Madeline Stratton was one hell of a woman, and Jo would give her left arm to be friends with someone of her caliber, intelligence and wit.

She hoped this visit to her apartment wouldn't ruin those chances. She pictured every nook and cranny in the place. Had she left anything out that would make Madeline view her differently? She didn't think so—she never knew when her mom might pop by, so she was generally careful—but she couldn't be sure. She'd just have to keep her eyes peeled.

The mental inventory did serve to remind her that she was out of beer. Hell, she didn't even know if Madeline drank beer.

"What would you like to drink?" Jo asked, although she would have laid money on the table that Madeline was a whiskey drinker.

Madeline let out a sad laugh. "Red wine, but only when the cameras are on." She hesitated before adding, "I think I'd like to have some Jameson tonight."

Jo had to stifle the sound of approval rising in the back of her throat. The hot ones always drank whiskey.

"Do you want it straight, or should I get something to mix?" Jo asked, again knowing the answer.

"Straight."

The response was hotter than anything Jo could have imagined coming from the mayor's mouth. An intense desire to kiss Madeline rose up within her. Imagining how poorly the ultraconservative woman would react to that, she fought to keep her raging hormones in check.

She stopped at a liquor store and put the car in park. "I'll be right back."

Fumbling with her wallet, Madeline pulled out a credit card. "Here, use this."

"I've got it." Jo smiled. It was the least she could do, and it would be best to keep the liquor store from knowing that the mayor was stocking up on booze in light of her current public relations challenge.

"Well, take it in case you change your mind."

"No," Jo said firmly. "Do you want anything else?"

"A pack of Camel Menthols?"

Jo's smile grew. There was definitely more to Madeline Stratton than met the eye.

"You got it," Jo said and headed inside.

Scanning the shelves for the Jameson gave her the chance to clear her mind. She was going to have Madeline Stratton in her apartment this evening, and chances were she was going to get drunk. That meant that whatever salacious thoughts Jo had about Madeline were going to have to be locked away. Not that Jo would have acted upon them. Even so, they were dangerous thoughts to be having when alcohol was added to the mix.

She grabbed a bottle of Jameson from the shelves and picked up two packs of Camel Menthols at the counter. She paid and made her way back to her car, promising herself that she wouldn't do anything stupid tonight. She had a job to keep, a reputation to uphold, a secret to hide and a friend who needed her support—nothing more.

CHAPTER SIX

"She was a bitch today. That's all I know." Jacquelyn's words were dripping with bitterness as she once again recounted her side of today's events to Gabe, but all Gabe wanted was to know if Jo needed anything.

He'd like to know if Madeline needed anything too, for that matter. He'd been on the mayor's staff for three years now, and he'd never seen her as distraught as she had appeared during the glance he had stolen as Jo ushered her out the office. With an election coming up in just over a year, there was little doubt that her tensions would have been high anyway. But, given this added stress, Madeline was entitled to a breakdown. Jo was simply helping Madeline out. He felt his protective instincts emerge.

"She's not a bitch, and we can't talk about each other that way. You know that, Jacquelyn. Jo was probably freaked out, like the rest of us are. She took the bullet for you, remember, since Ian was out of town? She stepped up, way above her pay grade, because neither of us wanted to be the fall guy."

Gabe had tried time and time again to smooth things over, but Jacquelyn was angry, jealous perhaps that the new girl was in the loop and she was not. Jacquelyn wasn't accustomed to being on the outside. As communications director she was the staff member who spent the most time with Madeline. Unfortunately, she also was the office gossip.

"I know," Jacquelyn conceded. "But she didn't have to yell at me. I mean, can you imagine having a staff member yell at you in front of everyone in the office over an issue that you brought to the forefront of everyone else's attention? I mean, if it weren't for me, no one would have known, and Jo couldn't have rushed in and come to Stratton's rescue. I just think it's unfair, that's all."

"Enough!" Gabe had heard this argument at least ten times already and couldn't take it anymore. "Jacquelyn, listen to yourself. Of course, it's unfair. It's an unfair situation and not just for you. Don't forget that a woman we all respect and admire had her world turned upside down today, okay?"

Even though he knew better than to take the side of one staffer over another, he couldn't help but come to Jo's defense. "Besides, Jo was doing what she felt was right, and I think her actions were admirable. Should she have yelled at you? No, probably not. But she was the one who had the courage to walk into Stratton's office and do what neither you nor I wanted to do. She was also the one who had the insight to take Madeline out of the office and make sure that she was going to be okay. And for the record, when she 'yelled at you in front of everyone,' she did so in your office with the door shut and there was nobody in there but the two of you. Otherwise you wouldn't need to be telling me about it. So maybe you should just get off her case and get back to work or you should just go home."

"Fine, Gabe. Take her side." Jacquelyn glanced around the empty office. They had sent everyone else away in order to frustrate the media, who had started turning things into a circus after hearing an on-air teaser from Channel 15 about a bombshell report that it would be airing on the evening news. It hadn't revealed the nature of the story, but it had featured a picture of the mayor and her husband.

The two of them had handled the media queries, providing reporters with the mayor's "no comment" statement as well as doing what they could in "off the record" conversations to protect Madeline—maybe even build some sympathy for her. Until they heard from Ian, her chief of staff, or Madeline herself with more detail or direction, there was little else they could do.

Now, in the quiet of the office, it was as if they were the only two soldiers standing on the battlefield.

Gabe watched Jacquelyn slam shut her laptop and pack her briefcase. He hoped she would go home soon. He would stay. He wanted to be here in case Jo came back, something which looked increasingly unlikely with each passing hour. He wanted to see if she was okay. She had seemed almost as upset as Madeline when they left, and he couldn't understand why. Before today, there had been times when he wasn't even sure that she liked working for Madeline. Today, though, things had been different—as if Jo felt protective toward Madeline. Whatever had happened during that breakfast over the weekend that Jo had mentioned had caused them to bond. It didn't matter, he supposed. He was just thankful that Jo seemed to have made that connection to her job now, that she wanted to be a part of the team even if it meant babysitting an upset mayor.

Glancing at his BlackBerry for the hundredth time since she and the mayor had left, he sighed.

"She's not going to call you back, you know."

"Who?" He asked the question, knowing Jacquelyn didn't really need to answer.

"You know who. Don't play dumb with me, Gabe. You've had it bad for that girl ever since she came to work for Stratton."

"She's not a girl. She's twenty-seven, and I don't 'have it bad for her,' Jacquelyn. You don't have to always butt into everyone else's business."

"Whatever, man. She isn't interested. I can tell you that much. But if you hear from her with an update on Stratton, let me know."

Gabe wanted badly to protest, but deep down he knew that Jacquelyn's words were the truth. Jo had no interest in him, and that didn't appear likely to change.

"Fine. Have a good night."

"Yeah, you too," Jacquelyn replied and left the office.

Alone with his thoughts, he couldn't help but wonder what Jo's type was. Was it something he could become? Not that he believed in changing for someone, but maybe Jo wanted someone who made her laugh or someone who made romantic gestures or someone with a high-paying job or someone who went to the gym religiously. He made her laugh and he liked romantic gestures. He could focus on making those attributes more apparent and work toward improving the other traits. Whatever Jo needed, he would try to be it. Which is why, after sending another text message saying "Let me know if you need anything," he eyed his watch and sat back on the office couch. He would stay another hour, just in case, and then go home. Wherever he was, though, if Jo called, he would go to her. Just as she was Madeline's shoulder to cry on, he would be hers.

* * *

Jo shook her head as she refilled Madeline's glass with Jameson on the rocks. Never in her wildest dreams would she have imagined having Madeline Stratton sitting on her couch, six drinks in, a lit cigarette in one hand and the other petting Jaws.

She stole a glance at her from the kitchen. Madeline's tears had stopped, but her words had not. Apparently, she was the kind of drunk who told endless stories. Stories of the past and stories that she probably shouldn't be sharing with a staff member.

Jo was thankful that Madeline was a talker, though. Otherwise Jo might have been tempted to share some uncomfortable stories of her own. Luckily she was nowhere near drunk enough for that. Madeline had insisted that Jo drink with her, but she had sipped back only two drinks so far. She was not going to get sloppy tonight. She couldn't afford to slip in front of Madeline—even if there was a chance Madeline would forget everything by morning.

Her BlackBerry dinged. She checked Madeline one more time. Deciding she would be all right alone for a few seconds longer, she checked the message.

It was Gabe—big surprise. He had been texting ever since she and Madeline had left this afternoon. She debated about replying. She didn't want to instigate further conversation, but she felt she should at least give him a sign that he didn't need worry about them.

"We're fine. Thanks!"

She typed the response and sent it before she could allow herself to reconsider the move.

Almost immediately, she received three new text messages.

"You're still with her?"

"Are you okay? Do you need help?"

"Where are you? Can I bring anything?"

"Shit," Jo muttered. This guy was becoming a royal pain. It was clear from this and his earlier messages that this was more than matter of him doing his job. She needed some breathing room. There was no way she would ever go out with anyone that needy—guy or girl.

She decided not to reply. She didn't want to say whether or not she was still with Madeline. Would it look suspicious that she was? Or would it make her look like a loyal employee, someone intent on sticking with her boss through the good and the bad?

She hoped it was the latter, but at this point, she wasn't sure how much it mattered. It wasn't the best of circumstances, but Madeline had proved to be a lot of fun and Jo was thoroughly enjoying spending the evening with her. The best part was that Madeline appeared to be enjoying it too. She was also smiling, laughing and seeming to have a good time.

The way Jo saw it, Madeline really needed a friend right now. Contemplating her own loneliness, she realized that she was in no place to turn one away either. Despite the age difference and the fact that Jo worked for her, Madeline seemed to have decided that Jo was, in fact, a friend. That alone was making Jo's night a great one.

As she rounded the corner back into the living room, she found Madeline leaning over her DVD rack, examining the offerings there. She felt as if the air had been knocked out of her. There was no telling what Madeline might find there. She cleared her throat loudly, hoping to distract her. "I've got your drink."

Madeline glanced up momentarily and then looked back down immediately.

"I've never heard of this show," she said, pointing to a DVD box.

"Oh…um…it's not that great. Did you want to watch a movie?" Jo tried desperately to sit Madeline down. "Have a seat, and I'll put one in for us."

It was too late. Madeline had removed the box from the shelf.

"What exactly is *The L Word*?" Jo saw Madeline's eyes widen as they took in the picture of naked women, covering their breasts with their hands, on the DVD box.

Jo searched for words, as her scariest nightmare played out before her eyes.

"It's…it's…"

"'Explores the lives of a group of lesbians,'" Madeline read aloud from the back of the box before looking up at Jo inquisitively. It was comparable to the look she got from Jaws whenever she opened up a container or package of anything that smelled or sounded like it might be a snack—confused, yet intrigued.

"It belongs to a friend of mine. She recommended I watch it."

"Is that why you have six seasons of it?" Madeline's smile grew.

"Uh, yeah. She wanted me to see all of them." Jo hoped Madeline couldn't hear the tremor in her voice.

"Okay," Madeline replied, putting the box back in the rack, but her eyes sparkled with curiosity.

Jo had left the television off all night, anxious to avoid having Madeline catch sight of footage of John and the little blond he had apparently been seeing. She knew that one glimpse of her husband with another woman and Madeline would revert to the sobbing mess she had been earlier in the day.

It had taken her an hour—and several strong drinks—to calm Madeline down after they reached the apartment and then everything in her power to keep Madeline's mind occupied with something other than the day's revelations.

Turning on the set seemed worth the risk now, though, if it could prevent Madeline from asking more questions about the nice little lesbian DVDs she had just found. She grabbed the remote. "Do you want to watch anything?"

"Sure," Madeline answered, then a dark look passed over her face. "But can we watch a movie instead of TV?"

So Madeline had been avoiding the television too. Using it to change the subject had essentially smacked her in the face again with the fact that her husband had been having an affair, Jo thought regretfully.

"What would you like to watch?" Jo asked.

"What all do you have? I'd prefer something funny tonight, if that's good with you."

Jo considered the options. Madeline must have gone through most of the offerings on the shelf if she had made it to her *L Word* collection, which had been carefully tucked behind her other movies. Having nothing more to hide—as far as movies were concerned anyway—didn't make picking something to watch tonight any easier.

Nothing romantic. Nothing about a breakup. Nothing that will remind her of why she's here—as if she could forget.

"How about a mindless comedy?"

"Sounds great. What do you have in mind?"

Jo held up two movie cases she never thought she would show Mayor Stratton. "*Austin Powers?* Or *Superbad*?"

"*Superbad*, it is," was Madeline's amused response.

Jo popped in the movie and took a seat on the couch, making sure to leave a cushion's worth of space between her and Madeline.

Madeline brushed Jo's hand as she reached for the remote, causing a jolt that Jo felt throughout her body. *Easy, girl.* Jo reminded herself of the perils of the situation, to no avail. She decided the only way to maintain her sanity and keep an already bad situation from becoming explosive was to admit to herself that she had feelings for Mayor Madeline Stratton. To admit it, deal with it and move on. That was easier said than done, of course.

Madeline fumbled with the buttons on the remote before finally locating the pause button. She held up her glass. "I'm going to get one more," she said.

"Allow me," Jo offered, wondering how the last drink had disappeared so quickly but standing to take the glass.

"Thank you," Madeline's response came out sounding slightly slurred, enough so that Jo decided to make this Madeline's last drink and to water it down to keep her from getting sick.

She hurried to the kitchen and diluted the drink, stopping only long enough to send one short message from her BlackBerry, addressed to Gabe and to Jacquelyn. Madeline, she knew, had been due for a media visit the following day. And that was before this bombshell. "Cancel all of M's appointments tomorrow. Thanks!" It was better to be safe than sorry, Jo had been taught when dealing with volatile situations in politics, and judging from how much alcohol Madeline had consumed tonight and how distraught she had been, it was a safe bet that she would not be feeling up to performing her mayoral duties in the morning.

Jo's heart caught at the sight that greeted her as she returned to the living room. Madeline had curled up on the couch and was sleeping. Jo wanted to hold her, to tell her everything would be all right, but more than anything, she wanted to do everything in her power to make sure that everything was, in fact, all right.

She set the drink on her coffee table and found a quilt in her coat closet. Covering Madeline with it, she brushed the hair out of her face. Earlier in the evening, Jo had intended to take Madeline home or to a hotel when she was ready. Now, it just felt right for her to stay here.

"Sweet dreams," she whispered, hoping that Madeline's dreams would, indeed, be good ones and that she might have a few hours of peace before hell broke loose. She turned out the light, promising herself as she made her way to her bed that no matter what Madeline needed, she would be by her side.

CHAPTER SEVEN

Jo left a note on the end table by the couch and snuck out of the apartment the next morning, leaving Madeline peacefully sleeping.

"Help yourself to anything in the fridge or cabinets. I canceled your appointments today. Call if you need ANYTHING," she had written, hoping that Madeline would phone if she wanted something from the store, a ride somewhere or someone to talk to.

Now that she was at the office she questioned her decision to come in. What if Madeline woke up and wanted to go somewhere? She didn't have a car at the house, and she probably wouldn't want to take a taxi when all eyes in the city would be on her today.

She would go home for lunch, Jo decided. There were a few things on her desk she should care of, but as soon as she got the chance, she would go back home and check on Madeline.

She braced herself before she opened the office door, taking a deep breath. She had no doubt that she'd be hit with a million questions. No one had seen or heard from Madeline since yesterday afternoon—no one but her. And even though she was early to the office as usual, the parking lot had been full already.

She had received text messages and emails from almost everyone on the staff asking about Madeline, but she had not answered unless they had come from people who seemed to genuinely care about the mayor. And Ian, of course, who had said he wanted to see her first thing in the morning. Everyone was trying to be helpful, Jo knew, but much of their interest had seemed superficial and gossipy. Even here at the office, where the atmosphere should have been that of a family, there were those who seemed only to care about the latest rumors and whether or not Madeline would be publicly harmed by the incident.

Jo swung open the office door and walked to her cubicle to put down her things. In less than twenty seconds, the entire staff was standing around her desk, hovering like news reporters. She felt much as she had as a child, surrounded by church pews full of thousands whose judging eyes made it clear they were eager to bite into a juicy morsel of gossip about the pastor's picture-perfect family. She once again understood what celebrities felt like when they wanted to go buy a carton of milk or walk through the park with their kids but were instead swarmed by people hoping to catch the latest scoop.

"How is she?"

"Is she coming into work today?"

"How'd she take the news?"

"Did she watch the television reports?"

"Are they going to get a divorce?"

Jo stared blankly ahead, allowing the questions to swirl around her for a moment. Finally, she raised her hands.

"Stop, please, and let me speak." The command was stern, but Jo hoped it was not severe. Miraculously, the chatter stilled. She took a deep breath.

"Some of the things that are happening are Mayor Stratton's personal business—like whether or not they'll divorce. I understand that we all share the same concerns about her, but we've got to give her some space right now. I was with her yesterday, and she is doing fine. It's a rough situation, though, and it's likely to get worse before it gets better. I'm sure she'd appreciate us being respectful of her privacy."

What about me? Jo wondered. *Should I be being more respectful of her privacy? No, she asked me for help. She fell asleep last night and stayed at my apartment.*

She steadied her nerves and gripped the edge of her desk. "She won't be coming in today," Jo continued. "She needs some time to sort things out."

Jo surveyed the crowd in front of her desk. No one had moved. "That's all," she said, frustration rising in her tone. Like bewildered puppies, they turned and tried to find their ways back to their respective desks. Clearly, this situation had shaken the entire office.

Finally Gabe was the only one remaining. "Meet me in Ian's office in two minutes," she whispered before he could speak. "And bring Jacquelyn." He nodded and left to find the communications director.

Jo was unsure of what she was doing or how she had gotten involved in this whole mess in the first place. She was not a senior staffer, not by any means at the top of the pecking order, but somehow she was in this up to her neck and she knew she needed to confer with the top staffers. Standing, she walked past Madeline's office to the office where Ian Thompson, the mayor's chief of staff, who had flown back into town late last night, was waiting, along with Gabe and Jacquelyn.

She entered and closed the door. Normally, she'd wait to be greeted and exchange pleasantries, but there was really no point in doing that this morning. They needed to know what was happening. As soon as she saw Ian nod, then, she started filling him in.

"I don't know if I overstepped yesterday," Jo began. "If so, I apologize. I just knew that Mayor Stratton needed someone to make sure that she was okay."

"No need, Jo, none at all. I actually wanted to thank you for what you did." Ian waved his hand, dismissing her concern. "A lot has happened while I've been gone, and I appreciate all three of you taking the initiative. Under any other circumstances, I would have been here running this show so you didn't have to pick up the slack."

The three of them stood silent, unsure how to respond since the death of one of Ian's family members was involved.

Without waiting for a reply, he took a seat and continued. "The fact of the matter is that I'm here now, and I think that we can proceed without too much of a media circus. How is she doing now?"

"Well, she's not coming in today. I had Gabe cancel her meetings, because she looked like she needed some rest."

"That's probably best. Good call, Jo. Where is she? Did you take her home last night or to a hotel? Does she need a car to go pick her up?"

Jo had hoped not to get into this. "Actually, she's at my place. She didn't want to go home last night, and she fell asleep before I could take her to a hotel."

If Ian felt awkward about the situation, he didn't let on at all. "Well, I guess that works," he said. "But what's her long-term plan? She'll have to face it all eventually. I'll cover things on the political front, but she'll need to figure out what she's comfortable with as far as a long-term solution for her living situation."

"Yes, I know, but I think we should give her some time. She can crash with me for a couple more nights if it helps her keep things together right now."

"What the hell? Are you two roommates now or something?" Jacquelyn's voice was just short of a shriek.

"No," Jo tried to explain calmly. "She simply didn't want to go home."

"I just think it's weird, that's all. You know, the new girl sweeps in and decides to play superhero, leaving the rest of us out of the loop. Don't you think, Ian?"

Jealousy was written all over Jacquelyn's face.

"It's not weird, Jacquelyn," Ian said. "It's nice and actually strategic. Jo's stepping up to the plate and taking care of the boss, all the while keeping the mayor out of the public eye. I think it's a good solution for the time being."

"Me too," Gabe offered.

"Well, I think it's odd," Jacquelyn scoffed. "You know, some of us have been with her for years." She turned and looked pointedly at Jo. "*Years*, Jo. You don't just get to come in, save the day and keep her from the rest of us." With that, she stormed out of the office, leaving Jo speechless and the men confused.

* * *

Jacquelyn was sure of one thing—Jo wouldn't last much longer around here. She'd make certain of that. Before yesterday, Jacquelyn had been the one Madeline turned to if she needed anything. From wardrobe malfunctions —"I left my suit jacket at home, Jacquelyn. Will you run over there and grab it?"—to developing complex strategic grassroots operations for her initiatives, she had depended on Jacquelyn. Other than Ian, she had been on staff the longest, even through the campaign. And now, in the course of one day—one unfortunate turn of events—she seemed to have lost her seniority. She couldn't put her finger on why it bothered her so much, but she hated being out of the loop, in the dark.

Who was this Jo Carson anyway? She hadn't even been here a full year, and other than the few times she had gone out for drinks with the rest of the office, no one seemed to know much about her. That didn't seem to stop them from falling all over themselves any time she entered a room, though. Everywhere she went men's eyes seemed to follow. Hell, even some of the women stared. They were jealous, no doubt, wishing they looked that much like a supermodel. Jacquelyn sighed, looking down at the extra pounds her midsection was carrying. As for the men, it wasn't hard to guess what they were wishing.

Jo's charms, it seemed, had worked even on the toughest of them in the office—Madeline. Jacquelyn was not about to stand idly by, however, and watch the hard work of the last few years go down the drain. Madeline was her ticket to the political career she wanted. As Madeline's right-hand man, so to speak, Jacquelyn was positioned to move up the political ladder. Soon she'd be able to run for office on her own.

Unless Jo got in the way, of course. To prevent that, Jacquelyn was going to find out whatever she could about her and make sure that she didn't disrupt the natural flow of the office—or of Jacquelyn's career.

* * *

The place smelled like a frat house. That was Madeline's first waking thought.

"Where the hell am I?" she whimpered, praying there would be no reply. Cautiously she opened her eyes—slamming them shut immediately afterward when she felt the pounding in her head increase.

Something licked her in the face. She jumped, knocking a dog onto the floor. It took a moment before she recognized him.

"Oh, sorry, Jaws," she said, rubbing her eyes. It was all coming back to her now.

Shame swept over her as she remembered how much she had drunk last night in front of Jo. And, even worse, why she was here.

John had cheated. As if hearing it for the first time, she let the news wash over her again, staining her body and her mind. She let herself sink into the feelings of failure and betrayal it generated.

Tears fell from her eyes, and Jaws climbed back into her lap.

"Thank you, little one," she said, ruffling the hair on his head. She took a deep breath, steadying her emotions. Looking around, she wondered again what she was doing here. Refusing to go home—that had been the correct decision. But she should have asked Jo to take her to a hotel instead of barging into her apartment and crashing on her couch.

Jo *had* invited her, though. Madeline remembered the compassion in Jo's eyes, the way she listened intently and saw to it that she had everything she needed last night. The tender way she had wiped away her tears and held her close when she broke into tears in her office.

Taking her time, she assessed the situation. There was no need to feel ashamed for staying here last night. She had been drunk, and Jo had offered her friendship. Although she normally wouldn't have liked to have been such a mess in front of a staff member, under the circumstances it was understandable.

Tonight she would stay in a hotel and regroup. Right now, though, she was stuck. Her car was at the office. As was Jo's probably. She had no way of going anywhere.

Dizzily, she stood and saw the note Jo had left her. Her meetings had been canceled for the day, and she could take some time to delve into her feelings and consider how to move forward. Jo's kindness made her smile.

Madeline made her way to the kitchen for a glass of water. Perhaps she would watch some television or read a book. She never took the time for those kinds of leisure activities anymore, and she needed something to occupy her mind. She perused Jo's shelves of DVDs, spotting the case for *The L Word*, Season One, again, complete with its provocative cover.

She laughed. That brought back a few memories. "Why not? Right, Jaws?" she asked and then laughed again. She was losing her mind, talking to a dog and getting ready to watch a show about out and proud lesbians.

* * *

Jo had had every intention of sitting down to plan Madeline's week with Ian, Gabe and Jacquelyn, but after Jacquelyn stormed out of the office, everything had seemed off-kilter somehow. She knew it shouldn't bother her, but the way Jacquelyn had stared at her when she left had unnerved her. "You'll be sorry," Jacquelyn's icy glare had seemed to say.

Once she was gone, though, they managed to sort things out for the most part. Ian, in his usual brilliant way, had developed an all-encompassing plan for differing scenarios. Informed by as much information as he could grab from quiet sources—and without causing a bigger flurry in the media—he had covered almost every possible angle. Per Ian's instruction, unless Madeline specifically wanted to keep any of her previously scheduled appointments, they were canceling the rest of the week. Gabe and Jacquelyn would attend events in her place and read a letter from the mayor.

Media calls would be handled as always, except those related to John's infidelity. To those calls, the answer was still "no comment." If the media sharks persisted—as they had been doing relentlessly—calls would be directed straight to Ian.

Their strategy was to move ahead full force, just without the boss. Since Ian also served as her campaign manager in his "off" hours, he would handle all campaign communications—should any arise. Anything that needed her signature would simply have to wait until next week. Everything else they would tackle as a team, taking one day at a time. Ian would handle everything the mayor usually called the shots on, and Jo would draft the letters or statements that needed to be sent out. In addition to appearing in the mayor's stead, Jacquelyn would handle all media queries and Gabe would figure out how to deal with important meetings that needed to be rescheduled in the midst of Madeline's personal tragedy.

Jo returned to her desk and quickly crafted templates for all contingencies she could envision cropping up. When she was done, Ian and Gabe told her to spend the rest of the day tending to Madeline and helping her get settled in wherever she chose to stay. They suggested a hotel near City Hall. Jo decided she would present Madeline with options—Jo would take her to a hotel, she could continue to stay at Jo's or she could go home.

All the options were fine with Jo, although if she were being honest with herself, she had to admit she wanted Madeline to stay. There was something invigorating about having another person in the apartment, even if it was close quarters and even though it meant having to keep a secret from her.

There was a warmth about Madeline, even when she was upset, that made the thought of going home more enticing to Jo. That transformed a lifeless space into something like the sanctuary she wanted it to be.

On the drive across town, Jo figured it was as good a time as any to pick up her phone and call her father. He had been calling all day, but she simply had not had the time or the energy to deal with him.

Her hands shook slightly as she hit the speed dial button that would connect her with him, wishing that she could avoid it, but also knowing that his persistence wouldn't fade. Unlike the media, this was a call she couldn't ignore.

The phone hadn't even completed its first ring when she heard him pick up.

"Hey." His voice was rushed with anticipation. "How is it going? Is everything okay?"

"It's all going to be fine, Dad," she said, unable to stifle a sigh.

"Is it? We need her in that office. We can't let the liberals and progressives take it back."

"It's Oklahoma, Dad. It's the reddest state in the country, and her reelection is going to be a cakewalk. And in case you were wondering, she's also a human being who has emotions. This is about a little more than poll numbers."

"Of course it is," he quickly responded. "But, the fact of the matter remains that there's a lot at stake here. Are you working hard to make sure that it's handled correctly?"

"That's not exactly my job alone, but we're all working very hard."

"Good. I'm glad to hear that. A couple of the guys likely to be running against each other in the Democrat primary have publicly stated their support for both abortion and gay marriage. We can't have that kind of influence leading our capital city."

Every word was like a blow to her gut, but she hung on. She fought the urge to tell her dad that it didn't even matter. The mayor's office was a city post; it would have no real bearing on those issues anyway. They were largely peripheral for anything but a state or federal seat. She didn't want to debate.

"Thanks for checking in, Dad. Have a good night."

"Keep me posted," he squeezed in before she hung up.

She knew deep down that he meant well, but every conversation with him seemed to reinforce the fact that she was never going to be able to please her parents. Her heart pounded, each beat angrier than the last, as she tried to focus on the issue at hand. The mayor was the most important thing to worry about right now.

As she thought of Madeline, her smile returned. Jo hoped that she had slept well and that she would ultimately choose to stay, even if for only one more night. She didn't care if Madeline slept on the couch or if they only made small talk while Jo cooked her dinner. She just wanted her nearby. Wanted to hear the sweet sound of Madeline's laugh again, wanted to relive the closeness of last night.

It was selfish, she knew, considering all that Madeline had been through in the past twenty-four hours, but still, she had enjoyed being there for someone else—enjoyed being someone's rock.

That kind of intimacy was something she had all but forgotten. These days, she was lucky to have a conversation outside of work with a convenience store clerk or a one-night stand. The notion of having friends had pretty much died when she took this job. For one thing, the hours did not really allow for maintaining friendships. For another, it was hard to be close to someone and not divulge the deep secrets she was keeping.

Regardless, she was determined to find a way to win Madeline's friendship and keep her secrets in the process. There was no sense in letting a golden opportunity like this slip through her grasp simply because she was too weak-willed to hold on to it. There was also no point in jeopardizing her job.

She pulled into the Starbucks drive-through a few blocks from her apartment and ordered two coffees. After Madeline's drinking binge last night, coffee would likely be appreciated. Minutes later, she was getting out of her car and walking to her front door. She unlocked it and swung it open—a difficult task while carrying two cups of coffee—and her smile instantly faded.

Madeline was sprawled out on her couch…and well into Season One of *The L Word*.

Jo's jaw dropped open, while Madeline fumbled for the remote—acting very much like a clumsy teen who had been caught watching porn.

To make matters worse, at the moment an intense sex scene was filling the screen, complete with moans of pleasure. Jo's surprise was compounded when Madeline turned her gaze back to the screen, seemingly unable to tear her eyes away from the sight of the two women who were enjoying each other's bodies. She shivered and finally found the off button when the two women on screen began to get dressed.

The silence in the room was almost palpable. Jo wished she could think of something to say. Instead, she walked awkwardly into the kitchen, set down the coffees, removed the messenger bag holding her laptop and briefcase and busied herself refilling Jaws's food dish and water bowl.

It was Madeline who finally broke the silence, calling to her from the next room. "I'm sorry."

Despite the tension, Jo laughed. "You don't have to apologize to me." She moved back into the room, though she took care not to meet Madeline's gaze directly. She watched as Madeline followed suit, diverting her eyes and shifting uncomfortably in her seat. Jo stood awkwardly in the corner, hoping Madeline couldn't hear her heart beating uncontrollably.

"That show is...um...very interesting, actually," Madeline admitted, her cheeks flushing.

"It's not bad."

"Have you watched it all the way through? I mean, through Season Six?"

Jo nodded. She had watched it time and again when it first came out on DVD. It had made her feel as though she wasn't the only lesbian in the world. She knew she wasn't, of course, but in her family, her circle of friends, her world—she was.

"I may have to rent it and watch it through sometime. It was entertaining me." Madeline paused and appeared to be thinking through what that meant.

"Guess those gays aren't so bad after all, right?" Jo laughed.

"I don't have a problem with gay people," Madeline said quietly. "But you can't exactly embrace everyone when you run for office."

"I understand. It's how our donors think, how this area of the world works," Jo conceded. "I doubt that you would have received many votes if you supported the gays, even though you were running strictly on the issues of government accountability and limited spending."

"You sound like a campaign commercial." Madeline attempted a laugh, but the sound fell awkwardly in the space between them. "But what about you, Jo? How supportive are you of the gay lifestyle?"

"I have many friends..." Jo trailed off as Madeline's brow arched in curiosity. Jo could tell where this was headed.

"So are you...?"

"Do you need clothes or anything else from your house?" Jo interrupted. It was better to avoid anything that personal for right now.

Jo could see that Madeline wanted to pursue the subject. She had to find a way to cut her off at the pass.

"I can go get them for you if you'd like," she continued, determinedly steering the conversation down a different path.

"I'll go with you." Madeline finally gave into the subject change. "And then you can drop me off at a hotel. That way, I can be out of your hair and your life can return to normal."

"You are more than welcome to stay here."

"Oh no." Madeline waved her hand in the air, dismissing the thought. Jo's heart fell a little as she continued, "I'll give you your space back."

CHAPTER EIGHT

Madeline hadn't expected Jo to come home so early. She needed to have a talk with Jaws.

"A warning bark wouldn't have killed you, you know?" she imagined telling him.

At least Jo hadn't walked in an hour earlier when the heat on the television screen had become too much for Madeline to take. She had given into temptation and pleasured herself on Jo's couch as she watched two women make love, long-forgotten lust reawakened by the images.

It had been electrifying, and she hadn't been lying when she told Jo she'd check out the show sometime. In fact, it was nearly all she could think about as they drove to her house to pick up her clothes.

At the same time, she couldn't help but wonder about Jo. Why did she own all the DVDs of a lesbian television series if she didn't enjoy watching two women together? Was this why the DOMA speech had been a little soft at first?

Was Jo Carson a lesbian? She let the thought circle around in her head. She secretly hoped the answer was yes. It wouldn't play well in the press if anyone learned that one of Mayor Stratton's staff members was a lesbian, but Madeline hoped that one day—if Jo were, in fact, a lesbian—she could come out of the closet and embrace who she was.

Madeline knew she was dreaming. Times were changing, but no one in the world of politics was that lucky or that free. Everyone was restricted. Everyone had the full attention of the media on them at all times. Everyone was under a microscope. So those who had such desires had to keep them under lock and key.

Everyone, Madeline reminded herself again, had secrets they needed to keep. For her, that meant spouting angry words in speeches on the subject of same-sex relationships, words that she could hide behind. It was a necessary evil if she wanted to continue her political career, her "normal" life. It was for the greater good if she wanted to keep trying to accomplish positive changes for the city. In a perfect world, it wouldn't even be an issue. But the world wasn't perfect. All of which meant those feelings of the past had to stay that way.

As Jo pulled into the driveway outside of the house, Madeline was thankful to see that John's car was not there. This, at least, would be quick and easy. She would grab her things and leave. Later on, after the dust had settled and the paperwork was drawn up and signed, she would return to take whatever she needed and never again come back to this place...*The House of Broken Dreams*, she decided to call it.

Jo helped her from the passenger side of the vehicle, her hand steadying her. She was thankful for the support, even though she was overly aware of the tenderness of Jo's touch. A strong, independent woman, Madeline rarely admitted, even to herself, that she needed help, but she was honestly not sure that she could have survived the events of the past day without Jo's help.

There was kindness and compassion in everything Jo did. Madeline had come to rely upon it, actually. If she were being honest with herself, she didn't want to spend the night at a hotel. In fact, there was nothing she wanted less than to be utterly and completely alone. But it didn't seem right to continue to hole up in Jo's apartment, intruding on her privacy.

Jo didn't speak, didn't push, as they went through the house, packing clothes and toiletries, and for that Madeline was thankful. Jo's intuition was strong enough to sense when words weren't necessary. It was a trait Madeline valued greatly.

Madeline tried, as she and Jo went through the house, to remember the good times she and John had shared there, however long ago that might have been. Over and over, though, the truth came spewing forth like a gusher in the oil field, reminding her that life wasn't fair. Not every story had a happy ending. A love that seemed good—great even—could fall apart in front of your eyes, leaving you with nothing but a packed suitcase and the memory of silent glances, separate bedrooms, looks that said, "I don't love you anymore." She and John had become roommates who hated each other. There was no more passion, not even kindness. Whatever spark of friendship they had once shared had burned out and grown cold.

Madeline let out a long sigh. "That should do it for now," she said. She heard a car door shut outside. "Dammit, let's go." They gathered her suitcase and cosmetics bag and went out the back door.

Madeline couldn't get over the fact that she was fleeing her own house. It was all so ridiculous, but she did not want to see John again, not under any circumstances.

When they rounded the corner of the house, though, instead of seeing John's car she saw three unfamiliar vehicles. She craned her neck to make out the faces of the people standing at her front door. As soon as she saw their cameras, she pulled back, prepared to run back into the house and hide out until they left. But she had stared a moment too long and was spotted.

Apparently, reporters could move at the speed of light. Before she could get even a few steps away, they were at her side. One was snapping pictures, while another was thrusting a microphone in her face and signaling to her cameraman to start filming.

"Mayor Stratton, did you know that your husband was having an affair?"

Madeline stared at her, dumbfounded, recognizing the co-anchor of the evening news at KWWG, the largest station in the city. This story clearly was a much bigger one than she had hoped it would be.

The reporter, an experienced interviewer, tried again. "Let me rephrase that. Do you know this woman?" She held up the picture of a gorgeous blond.

Once again, Madeline didn't speak, but the shock she felt was most likely evident on her face. She hoped they would interpret it as dismay at being confronted with the reality of her husband's cheating, but yes, she knew the woman in the picture. All too well, unfortunately.

"If you're not staying here, where are you staying? In a hotel?"

A reporter clutching a pen and pad chimed in. "Yes, which one? We've checked for you at each of them."

"You haven't been seen out and about since we broke the story yesterday about your husband's affair. Are you still fulfilling your duties as mayor? Do you plan to seek reelection next year?"

Madeline had seen this trick many times, reporters firing so many questions at you at once that you felt compelled to answer at least one to shut them up. Even if she wanted to, though, she found she couldn't speak.

"Do you plan to file for divorce?" the sweaty man with the pen and pad asked.

Before another question could be fired her way, Jo positioned herself between the reporters and Madeline.

"That'll be all for the questions today," Jo spoke with ease despite the stressful situation. "Mayor Stratton is saddened by the news of her husband's infidelity. Betrayal in a relationship is never an easy thing to deal with, but the mayor is a strong woman, with a strong faith, and her office has issued a statement on this issue. If you have further questions, please direct them to Jacquelyn Smalledge, the mayor's communications director."

Jo forced a tightlipped smile and practically marched Madeline to the car.

Madeline was amazed by Jo's poise and strength. "Thank you," she offered. "You didn't have to do that, but thank you."

Jo just smiled and nodded, putting the car in gear and quickly driving away from Madeline's house. Followed by a caravan of relentless reporters, unfortunately.

"Who the hell do they think they are, paparazzi chasing Brangelina or Kimye?" Jo asked.

"You'd be amazed at how often this happens." Madeline's reply sounded sad and tired, even to her own ears.

"Well, I know two things for certain," Jo replied. "First, you should hold on, because I'm going to lose them. And secondly, I'm not taking you to a hotel for those vultures to rip you to shreds the first time you come out of your room."

Madeline didn't reply, but she was touched by the gesture and by how much Jo seemed to genuinely care.

"You're coming back home with me, and you can stay as long as you'd like." Jo's voice was defiant, as though nothing could change her mind at this point. Madeline wasn't about to try. Even though there was no doubt that the media was now on to the fact that Jo was accompanying the mayor wherever she went. Madeline watched as Jo flipped the car into overdrive. As if she were a professional stunt driver, Jo began to whip the Camaro into back alleys and side streets. In a matter of minutes, they were alone, parked in the underground parking garage of an office complex.

Madeline hadn't felt that kind of a rush in a long time. "You are incredible." She smiled at Jo. Jo beamed as if she had just been crowned as Miss America.

As Madeline's heart rate slowed to normal, she glanced down. It was only then that she realized she was holding Jo's hand. At some point during the excitement, she must have grabbed it. Jo seemed to realize at the same moment. Quietly, each pulled her hand away from the other's.

Madeline couldn't explain it, but she still felt the warmth of Jo's hand in hers. *I wonder what it would be like to kiss her.* She immediately looked out the side window, embarrassed, as if Jo could read her thoughts.

Jo cleared her throat. "We should probably wait in here for a good twenty minutes or so before we venture back out, just in case they're lurking around somewhere."

"I just want to make sure you have your privacy," Jo added.

"Thank you, Jo—for everything. You really are too kind." To Madeline's ears, her words seemed laced with embarrassment. She hoped that Jo heard only her sincere appreciation.

* * *

Jo couldn't stop remembering how it had felt to have her fingers intertwined with Madeline's, something that had happened shortly after Jo had slipped their pursuers and turned into the garage. The minute Madeline's hand had grazed hers, Jo had felt electricity shoot through her body, warming and tensing every part of her. This woman was driving her crazy.

As soon as Madeline had noticed she was holding and gently massaging Jo's hand, though, a look of embarrassment and terror had clouded her face. Jo looked away to downplay the moment and ease Madeline's embarrassment. The truth was, she had been enjoying every moment of being physically—if totally innocently—connected to Madeline.

Hating how the moment had turned so quickly awkward, she decided to change the subject. She turned in her seat to face Madeline.

"Is there anything you want me to tell the press or write in a statement?"

Madeline stared back at Jo, but it was obvious she hadn't heard a word coming out of Jo's mouth. Jo shivered at the intensity in Madeline's blue eyes and shivered again as Madeline cupped her face with shaking hands, very gently pulled her closer and kissed her. The shock Jo felt was overpowered by her deep need to have Madeline's mouth on hers. Madeline didn't pull away, so Jo deepened the kiss. Madeline's hands were tangled in Jo's hair, pulling Jo even closer.

The intensity of the moment was broken when the car next to them rumbled to a start.

"Shit," Madeline said, pulling away and putting her head down. Jo turned and looked at the car pulling out of the adjacent space.

The man in the driver's seat wasn't paying any attention to them. He didn't even cast them a sidelong glance.

"It's okay," Jo said, putting her hand on Madeline's shoulder. "He didn't see anything."

"I'm sorry." Madeline looked away from Jo. "I shouldn't have done that."

Jo didn't regret the kiss. The only regret she had was the sudden hesitation and the disappointment displayed on Madeline's face. "Don't apologize," Jo said, shaking her head. "It was as much me as it was you."

The hot and cold nature of Madeline's signs of affection had had Jo wondering if she was imagining that things were changing between them. There was no way she could have imagined a kiss that powerful, however.

She started the car. "I'm sure the press is off the trail now. We might as well go home."

On the drive back, Jo wanted to revel in the fact that Madeline had kissed her, wanted to relive every moment of those soft lips pressed against hers with Madeline's tongue sweetly caressing Jo's bottom lip. But she couldn't help but recognize that Madeline was not reveling in anything that had happened. The look on her face signaled that she was mortified and needed her space. Jo vowed to try to give it to her.

CHAPTER NINE

Just because Jo looked like an angel didn't mean she was one. That's what Jacquelyn kept reminding herself as she once again typed "Jo Carson" into the Google toolbar of her computer screen.

Since it had become apparent that Madeline wanted nothing to do with any of her staff except for her new little pet, Jacquelyn had made it her mission to discover more about Jo. She wanted to know something she could use against her if she needed to do so.

It wasn't so much that she wanted to get Jo fired, but if she did, she wouldn't have to worry about Madeline replacing her. That wasn't all that farfetched, unfortunately. When she was Madeline's go-to person, the times she'd screwed up at work had been overlooked. Now, though, it would only take a couple of wrong moves, and Jo could easily slide into the position of communications director, leaving Jacquelyn out in the cold. Without this job and without Madeline's recommendation, Jacquelyn would have to start all over. She hadn't put in years of hard work to start back at the bottom of the ladder.

For the second time today, she scrolled through the list of websites, looking to see if she'd missed something. There wasn't anything really helpful—nothing out of the ordinary. All the information online was stuff she already knew. Jo was the daughter of Michael Carson, the pastor of a mega-church in Tulsa and a former resident of Oklahoma City. She had been a bridesmaid in several weddings. There were freelance columns written by Jo, her Facebook page, media from various awards she had won during college. Everything there was squeaky clean.

"I'm screwed," she said to herself.

Perhaps she should stop by Jo's house to check in on her and see how she was doing. Jo might find it suspicious, but if Madeline were there, she might think it was a nice gesture. It would give her the chance to see how Jo lived too. Maybe she wasn't as squeaky clean as everyone thought. She'd do some asking around to see if any of the local bartenders knew her as a regular. If so, did she leave with strange men all the time? Was she perhaps an alcoholic? There had to be some area of Jacquelyn's life that she could say was superior to Jo Carson's.

Jacquelyn mulled these ideas over for a bit, then decided she would have a beer and make more important decisions later.

* * *

Back at her apartment, Jo fixed Madeline a cup of vanilla chai, then went to work making her favorite comfort food, double chocolate brownies. She hummed while she cooked, glancing over occasionally at Madeline, who was sitting at the kitchen table. She appeared deep in thought. She tried to smile anytime she met Jo's gaze but she couldn't mask the turmoil she was feeling.

"What can I do?" Jo asked.

"You've done more than anyone," Madeline said, her voice sad.

"But is there anything else you need? Do you want to talk about it? Do you want me to shut the hell up?" Jo felt as though she were trying to cheer up one of her nieces or nephews. Which was stupid. A trip to the ice cream store wasn't going to make everything all better.

Madeline took a deep breath. "I'm just so hurt and confused," she finally offered.

Jo nodded. "Confused about what?"

"Well, it's just...I'm not sure that I'm supposed to feel how I feel right now."

"Okay?"

"I mean, I'm not stupid. I saw the signs that my marriage was in trouble a long time ago. And don't get me wrong, I'm very hurt that John was seeing someone else. But my feelings get a little more complex after that."

Jo waited in silence.

"I feel somewhat relieved, I guess." Madeline sighed. "It sounds awful, I know, but I just feel as though I can now move on with my life."

"That's not awful." Jo waited for Madeline to continue.

"It means that there will be no more hate-filled looks over breakfast and no more coexisting before heading off to separate bedrooms for the night."

Jo's heart broke. She had no idea that Madeline had been suffering through anything that severe.

"It also means there won't be anyone around. It'll be lonely. There was some comfort in having John there, even if we were unhappy." A single tear trickled down Madeline's cheek.

"You won't be all alone, you know?" Jo offered. "I know I'm one of your staff and that you may not see me as a friend right now, but I'll be here if you need anything—even after you move past this step."

The tears fell harder. "Of course you're my friend, Jo. In fact, it feels like you're the only friend I have right now." Madeline stood and excused herself to the bathroom. Minutes later, she returned, composed again and having scrubbed the mascara streaks off of her face.

"I'm sorry, Jo. I didn't mean to fall apart like that. You're just such a good listener."

Jo had made a special effort to keep distance between the two of them since the hand-holding incident and the kiss, but now she crossed the room and hugged Madeline.

"Don't apologize. If you need to cry, cry. If you need to laugh, laugh. There are no rules here right now. It's just about you feeling better."

The timer for the oven dinged. "Let me get the pan out of the oven, and then we'll have brownies with our chai," Jo told her. As she turned back to the oven, she began to hum again.

"What is that you're humming?" Madeline asked.

"Just a song stuck in my head." Jo grabbed a potholder and removed the brownies from the oven. "It's by Sugarland," Jo added.

"Will you sing it for me?" Madeline asked.

"I'm not sure you want that," Jo replied with a wink.

"Actually, I do. I've been wanting to hear your voice again since I caught you singing in the office. You truly are talented, Jo."

Jo smiled at the compliment. She didn't sing in front of just anyone, not since her church choir days had passed.

"Please," Madeline pressed.

Jo began to sing.

"'I've been beaten up and bruised, yeah, and I've been kicked right off my shoes…'"

Jo paused, realizing why the song had been stuck in her head all day. It very accurately portrayed the situation Madeline was going through right now.

As she continued through the chorus, she watched as Madeline fought back tears. Finishing up, Jo looked deeply into her eyes. "'…tears may fill my eyes, but I'll stand back up.'"

Jo let her voice trail off, as she dished up two warm brownies and covered them with a scoop of ice cream.

"That was beautiful." Madeline's voice was sincere. "It was a pretty good fit on the song too. Thank you."

"Thanks. Here you go." She smiled at Madeline, handing her the dish. "Therapy in a bowl."

They settled into their chairs, and the mood was lighter than it had been before. Jo silently attributed the peacefulness to the brownies. Chocolate had healing powers, she was certain.

Madeline's mood had eased noticeably as well.

"So let's get back to our 'getting to know Jo' conversation," Madeline said.

"Sounds a little boring to me, but okay. What do you want to know?" It was a dangerous question, and Jo knew it. But after the kiss they had shared, she had decided Madeline deserved to know the truth. Only if she asked, though. Jo wouldn't volunteer the information.

"Let's see," Madeline teased. "How many questions do I get?"

Jo thought this over in her head. "Seven," she answered.

"Why seven?"

"It's a lucky number." Jo took a bite of her brownie. "And now you're down to six questions."

"Damn, I guess I'll have to be more careful."

Jo nodded.

"So when you were a kid, what did you want to be? Was it always a political speechwriter?" Madeline asked and they each laughed.

"Honestly, I wanted to be a kangaroo," Jo said, sending them both into a fit of laughter.

"Seriously?" Madeline asked.

"Yes, seriously, but when my mother told me that wasn't possible, I told her I'd settle for being a ninja. Over time, I grew up and wanted to be an author."

"You could have been a ninja kangaroo who wrote books," Madeline offered.

"That would be the definition of living the dream, now wouldn't it?"

Jo loved these moments. She loved sharing her life with Madeline.

Madeline's face turned serious as she began to ponder her next question. Jo mentally prepared herself to explain everything, but the difficult question didn't come.

"What's your favorite color?"

"Red," Jo answered.

"Why do you want to be an author?"

Jo considered the answer. "I wanted to be an author. Now I'm not so sure."

"Why not?"

"You're down to two more questions, but I'll answer anyway. I'm not sure what I want to do anymore. I've spent a lot of time being the dreamer, the optimist, the one who believes it'll all work out in the end. But I've seen enough of life now to know that it doesn't always. So I don't know how realistic it is to think that I could write books and make a living. It's much more practical to have a steady job and use whatever talent I possess at that."

"It sounds like reality took the dream away from you." Madeline's tone suggested she knew what that was like.

"I guess so," Jo replied.

"Okay, so question number six is..." Madeline trailed off, obviously wanting to make the last two questions count. "Well, you don't have to answer it if you don't want to, because it's a little more personal."

Jo nodded. She knew what was coming.

"Jo, are you...are you...? Never mind, I'll think of another question."

"Go ahead and ask it, on one condition," Jo said, knowing the extent of the risk she was taking.

"Okay. What's the condition?" Madeline asked.

"Whatever is said here, stays here. We don't tell anyone else, and we don't let it affect work."

"Deal," Madeline said. "I mean, after all you've seen, I hope the same applies to everything I've said." She glanced away, with a bit of shame coloring her cheeks. "And everything I've done," she added.

"Of course," Jo reassured her.

"Okay, well, then, my question is...are you a lesbian?"

Answering this question wasn't easy for Jo. In fact, admitting it to herself had been enough of a challenge. The first time she admitted it to someone else—her college roommate, the only person she'd ever told aside from girls she slept with—it had been excruciatingly painful. Nonetheless, she owed Madeline this much. She took a deep breath and forced herself to exhale, closing her eyes for a moment of stability as her heart hammered in her chest. She meant to answer audibly but couldn't find the strength to open her mouth. Her entire career—her whole life potentially—was on the line. It came down to trust, and she trusted Madeline. She took another breath and…nodded.

Madeline smiled, much to Jo's relief. "Why do you work so hard to hide it?"

The question was gentle, but it cut Jo to the core. Why did she hide who she was like she had the plague? She *had* to, damn it! Oklahoma City might have a policy that prohibited discrimination in employment for sexual orientation, but elsewhere in the state discriminating on the basis of orientation was perfectly legal. Hell, the governor had gone so far as to try to institute a local version of "Don't ask, don't tell" in the Oklahoma National Guard. And don't get her started on what she'd heard in local pulpits from childhood until she'd finally stopped attending church several years, pleading the press of her work.

"It's not that easy, I guess. My parents, friends, co-workers—they wouldn't understand." Jo gave a rueful laugh. "Hell, I never thought you would understand, especially after that DOMA stuff."

"Sometimes we feel like we have to keep secrets. I get that, but I think you should know that who you are is beautiful. In fact, I think you should embrace it and be who you are."

Jo felt relief flow through her body.

"Also, I'm sorry about the whole DOMA thing. I must have come across as a royal bitch," Madeline said. "It's just…You have to do that stuff to get elected on our side of the ticket nowadays. And I have to get reelected. There are still so many issues to tackle, like our continuing problem with corruption. If I can get in for one more term, I can keep working for the greater good of the city. It's a necessary evil."

"It doesn't make it any easier to deal with," Jo said with a shrug. "But I get it. After all, I was raised in that environment. You say what you have to say to keep people off your trail, to keep people happy."

"You probably get it a little too well," Madeline said, a mixture of sympathy and embarrassment over her simplistic political stances playing on her face. "I really am sorry."

Jo nodded, taking the apology to heart. Coming out to Madeline was much easier than Jo could have ever imagined. Madeline still had one question left, though. Jo wasn't sure she wanted to remind her. Before she could decide, Madeline shocked her again, blurting out, "I've slept with a woman."

Jo's jaw fell open. This wasn't the kind of thing one simply said and then moved on to discuss the weather or the prospects of the local pro basketball team. It caught her totally off guard.

"Really?" was the only reply she could manage.

"Yes, really." Madeline closed her eyes as if trying to relive every detail. "Her name was Natalie. We were roommates our freshman year of college. She was beautiful, and I felt so comfortable sharing my life with her. We would stay up late talking every night, well into the morning hours. We would go to lunch every day in the cafeteria. We were pretty much inseparable." Madeline paused, smiling at the memory.

"One night, at a party, some guys dared us to make out with each other. We had been drinking heavily, so we did. I don't remember much about it, but we can blame that on the Wild Turkey. All I remember is feeling incomplete when she pulled her lips from mine. When we got back to our room that night, she shut the door behind us and threw me up against the wall. She kissed me passionately, and when she pulled back, she told me that she had wanted to do that all night."

Madeline opened her eyes and came back to present day.

"It was what I had wanted too. The rest is history. We dated quietly for two years, and then we went our separate ways. A while later, I met John and decided that being with Natalie was just a phase."

"Was it?" Jo's question was daring, but she needed to know.

"I don't know. It had to have been, I guess. In any case, a Republican who wants to hold elective office in a conservative state doesn't get to bat for the other team."

Jo had to wonder at the yearning she heard in Madeline's voice. Was it because she still wanted to be with a woman? Or was it simply remembering college days?

CHAPTER TEN

Two miles into it, Gabe decided his evening run was doing nothing to clear his head. Then again, he'd spent most of it replaying everything in his head.

A week ago, Jo had cringed at the sound of Madeline's name. Now she was willing to drop everything in her personal life to make sure that she was taken care of around the clock.

At least, that's what he figured she was doing. He had tried to call, text and email. Jo hadn't responded, so he had been patient. But he couldn't wait around forever. He needed to know that everything was okay with her, not to mention being kept apprised of his boss's decisions.

It was Wednesday, and they didn't know if Madeline would be returning tomorrow, next week or ever. He didn't even know if Jo planned to come back to work any time soon. No one else did either. Earlier in the evening, he had made the mistake of calling Jacquelyn to ask if she had heard anything. Of course she hadn't, she had snapped. He should have known. Jacquelyn and Jo appeared to be engaged in a fierce battle for Madeline's favor, and Jo was clearly winning. That hadn't stopped Jacquelyn from entering the pissing contest, of course.

He jogged the remaining few yards into the parking lot of his apartment complex. Checking his BlackBerry, he pulled up the calendar function. Okay, so it had only been slightly more than a day—but that was an eternity in political terms. Jo owed him—okay, them—an explanation. She wasn't allowed to fall off the face of the earth with their boss with never a backward look back or update. They had a city to run. They needed information!

Maybe he would drive over to her apartment, stop in to see how things were going. After all, she had said she would get Madeline to a hotel this afternoon. Now, no doubt, she was recovering and possibly in need of a friend with whom to decompress. He knew where she lived, having driven her home from the bar one of the few times she had gone out with the staff after work.

It was a solid plan as far as he was concerned. Jo would view his visit as a thoughtful gesture, and he would get some answers, find out how everything had gone with Madeline so he could put Jacquelyn's mind at ease. He showered and got dressed, feeling like a teenager again. Jo had him so wrapped around her little finger; he hoped she'd like whatever shirt he picked.

He tried on three before finally settling on a professional—and slightly pretentious—black and gray pinstripe one. Of course, Jo saw him every day at the office, but this was different. He wanted to show her that he was handsome and charming outside of work too.

After browsing his wine rack for a while, he settled on a nice bottle of pinot noir. He didn't want to show up empty-handed, and he hoped that Jo might invite him in for a glass. If she didn't, he would give her the wine and leave, but it was worth a shot.

He was almost out the door when his BlackBerry rang. Jacquelyn's name showed on the screen, and for a moment he thought about ignoring the call. He really didn't want to sit and listen to Jacquelyn bitch about the woman he cared so deeply about. As a senior staff member, though, he had to be accessible to his co-workers.

"Hello?" Gabe answered.

"Gabe, you'll never believe it. Turn on the fucking news."

"Calm down. Whatever it is, it'll be okay. I'm actually heading out the door."

"This can't wait. There's footage of the mayor and Jo all over the news. Your little girlfriend didn't even bother to pick up the damn phone and give me a call. I thought we had a rule about informing the media person when the media picked up a story—especially when they got an on-camera interview."

Gabe sighed. He wasn't going to win this argument unless he actually turned on the news. "Okay, Jacquelyn. I'll check it out. What channel?"

"Fifteen," she replied curtly.

Madeline's face appeared on-screen, but she wasn't saying a word as questions were being hurled at her by reporters who appeared soulless on-screen. Then, suddenly, Jo stepped in between Madeline and the cameras and gave an off-the-cuff, but very professional statement.

Gabe could see why Jacquelyn was upset, but he had to admit, Jo had handled herself nicely. And it was hot.

"It'll all be okay. Talk with Ian and have him handle it. He can take her into his office and remind her to go through you with all media stuff—and to let you know immediately if there is a camera incident like this one."

"It'll all be okay, huh? Is that what you think? Gabe, put your personal feelings for this girl aside. She screwed up today. It is not her job to give statements to the media. She should be fired." Jacquelyn's voice was laced with so much hatred, it took Gabe by surprise.

"You want her fired over this?"

"That's right. She broke protocol. We can't just have staffers going to the media. She totally went rogue, and if that were anyone else in their first year, they'd be out on their ass right now. But because she's the mayor's new buddy, it'll all be forgiven. It's bullshit, Gabe. Bullshit!"

Gabe cleared his throat. "We'll talk to Ian about it, okay? But she didn't go to the media; they came at her, at Madeline actually. She was acting on instinct. Who's to say that you or I wouldn't have reacted in exactly the same way given the circumstances? You saw how vicious the reporters were being. She didn't really say anything, Jacquelyn. Also, if you watch the end of her statement, she instructs them to contact you."

"Screw you," Jacquelyn yelled before hanging up the phone.

"Wow," Gabe said to himself, scratching his head.

He had no idea how to handle this situation. Even if he weren't infatuated with Jo, he thought she was damn good at her job, and he had no problem with how she had handled those reporters today.

Even so, he shot Ian an email. It was always best to give the chief a little warning when it came to such situations. After all, he had to deal with twenty-plus employees every single day. If a storm was coming, he deserved to know about it.

Gabe regrouped. He was distracted now and a little less prepared for seeing Jo, but he still wanted to go. He grabbed the bottle of wine and headed to her apartment.

* * *

Madeline and Jo had settled in the living room and were playing a game of *Taboo*. They had amended the rules so that even with only two players, it was a fun game.

It was so easy spending time with Jo. Madeline felt as though she could empty out her heart right here, and Jo would be the only one who cared enough to listen and help her heal.

She could not remember the last time she had had a friend like Jo. They had not really talked much or even spent time together prior to last weekend, but it felt as if she had known her forever. They shared an instant connection—an easy friendship.

Madeline was enjoying it, and given the circumstances, that was totally unexpected. She was thankful that the hotel thing had not worked out tonight. Being here with Jo in her cozy little apartment with long talks, brownies and laughter was much better than being all alone in a stuffy hotel room.

The past day and a half had been an emotional roller coaster. It was far from over, Madeline knew, but she was content at the moment. She was sure she would have times when she needed to cry it out in the future, and she was sure that her life would become increasingly more difficult the next time she had to face John. Still she had made a friend, and she had not had a true friend in years.

It was amazing how something as simple as friendship could turn on a light switch in someone's life. It was as if Madeline had been stumbling along in the dark for years and now suddenly could see again. She could see that the future was going to be okay—even if she had no idea when that might happen or how.

Glancing up, she realized Jo was waiting on her to give clues.

"I just realized something," Madeline said, setting down the card in her hand.

"What's that?" Jo asked.

"We never did get around to question seven."

"No, I guess we didn't. We got too busy going over the details of your hot, lesbian affair." Jo laughed.

"I guess you could call it that."

They laughed again, and then Madeline added, "I actually have two questions left."

"Hmm." Jo gave Madeline a serious face that fell short of actually disguising her amusement. "I might go for that, but ask the first one and we shall see."

"Okay, do you have a girlfriend?"

"I sure don't," Jo answered. "That would be a little hard to hide from Daddy and his mega-church, let alone from all the snoops who want to get a glimpse of the inner workings of the mayor's staff." She winked.

"That's true."

Madeline took a long drink of water. "So what do you think? How does one more question sound?"

"I guess I kind of cheated you out of your first one, so shoot."

"How many women have you...well, you know...been with?"

Jo winced. Madeline had taken it a little too far with that question.

"You don't have to answer, if you don't want to," she added.

Jo's forehead wrinkled as she conducted an internal count. Suddenly Madeline was not one hundred percent positive she wanted to hear the answer. Her curiosity had gotten the best of her, though. Someone as attractive as Jo could have had her choice of women—even if only in secret.

"This is not something I typically do," Jo began, drawing her words out longer than necessary. "I feel like I can trust you, though, and you have already shared so much with me…so I will tell you."

"Okay," Madeline urged.

"Twenty-three," Jo said, letting out a long breath.

"I don't doubt it," Madeline said, looking Jo up and down. "You are drop-dead gorgeous, not to mention witty, funny and one hell of a cook."

"Well, thank you." Jo giggled, and a slow blush came to her cheeks.

Damn, she was sexy. Madeline remembered how she had felt when she was kissing Jo in the garage. It had been wild and reckless, sure, but it was more than that—so much more. It had been invigorating, had ignited for the first time in years a passion that was almost too hot to be ignored. She might have ripped Jo's clothes from her body that instant had it not been for the sound of the car starting next to them.

"Did any of them mean anything? I mean, have you been in love?" Madeline couldn't resist the urge to know more.

Jo shrugged. "I don't really have much of the chance for something that lasts longer than a night or two. I try to keep a low profile."

Madeline could see the sadness in Jo's eyes and wanted to make it go away. Jo spoke before she could try to make it better.

"You know, this might be an overshare, but…" Jo said.

Madeline cut her off. "Oh, honey, we passed overshare a while ago."

"True."

"So what is it you were saying?" Madeline winked at Jo. She loved the way Jo returned her gaze, loved the fire she could see in Jo's eyes. Even if she would not admit it for fear of being rejected, Madeline could tell what Jo wanted.

"I was saying that you're…"

The doorbell rang, interrupting a thought that Madeline desperately wanted to hear.

"Are you expecting anyone?" Madeline pointed toward the door.

"Just the strippers." Jo laughed.

Madeline shook her head. As Jo went to answer the door, she entertained herself with the thought of watching Jo strip. That would be one hell of a show. Silently she scolded herself. This was wrong on so many levels. Jo wasn't only off limits because she was a woman; she was also an employee…

Jo peered through the peephole. "It's Gabe," she said to Madeline.

"Jo?" Gabe called through the door. "Who are you talking to?"

She unlocked the door and opened it.

"Hi, Gabe," she said. "Is everything okay?"

"May I come inside?" He held out a bottle of wine, as if paying a cover charge to get inside a club.

"Oh, of course, I'm sorry. Come on in."

He stepped inside, then noticed Madeline on the couch. "Oh, hello, Mayor Stratton."

Madeline had to smile. Gabe looked like an uncomfortable schoolboy going through that awkward pubescent phase. "Hello, Gabriel. How are you doing tonight?"

"I'm doing well, and yourself?"

"I'm just fine, thank you." She enjoyed Gabe's company most days at the office, and he was a nice young man. Most importantly, he was very good at his job. Unlike with Jo, though, she did not feel as if she could simply let loose in front of Gabe. Having him here made her acutely aware that she was wearing sweatpants and a T-shirt from some beach in Florida. Which belonged to Jo. They had somehow forgotten to grab anything for Madeline to wear to bed in their earlier rush at the house.

The silence had grown past awkward when Jo spoke. "So what brings you out this way tonight, Gabe?"

"I was just…uh…checking to see how you were doing. I knew you had been with Mayor Stratton today, and I wanted to see how she was doing as well, so I guess I was checking on both of you."

Madeline had never seen him act so nervous. He clearly was not himself around Jo. She had watched them interact in the office and thought that they would make a cute couple, but now she knew otherwise. It would be just like it was with her and John.

"Thank you, Gabe. That is awfully sweet of you," Jo said, giving him a hug. "I really do appreciate it. I'm doing well, and Mad—Mayor Stratton is doing well too."

Jo had almost slipped and called her by her first name, which had somehow become taboo among the staff. They all called her Madeline when she wasn't around, she knew, so she had no idea why it was such a big deal when she was in the room.

"Well, that's good. I'm glad to hear it. Anyway, I just wanted to bring you a bottle of wine to say thank you for all of your hard work. Will I be seeing you tomorrow?"

"Yes, I'll be coming into the office tomorrow," Jo said.

"Me too," Madeline chimed in.

"That's great," Gabe said. "I've canceled all of your meetings for tomorrow, but we can figure something out if you want."

"No," she said, waving her hand in the air. "I'm not sure I'll stay all day, but it will be good to get back into the swing of things."

"I'm glad to hear it," Gabe replied. "I'll let you two get back to your night. I just wanted to stop by and make sure you were doing all right."

"Don't you want to stay for a glass of wine?" Jo extended the invitation, even though Madeline could tell she would rather go back to the couch and finish their discussion.

"No. Thank you, though. I'm going to go home and get some sleep."

"Oh, okay. Well, thank you," Jo said. She showed him to the door.

"You two have a good night, and I'll see you tomorrow."

After he left, Madeline smiled at Jo. "You know he is interested in you, right?"

Jo nodded. “He is pretty hard to ignore. He gets me coffee, compliments anything I wear and has almost asked me out about seventy different times.”

“It must be awful,” Madeline joked.

“No, of course it’s not awful,” Jo said, laughing. “It is flattering, and Gabe is a sweetheart. He’s just not my type.” Her smile grew. “He is a little on the masculine side for my tastes.”

“Poor Gabe,” Madeline teased. “He doesn’t have a clue that you prefer sex with women.”

Madeline enjoyed seeing the flicker of arousal that danced in Jo’s eyes after hearing Madeline use the word “sex.”

She was wet and tense, and she had a feeling Jo was too.

CHAPTER ELEVEN

The sheets were rumpled when he woke, but it was still dark outside. John Stratton glanced at the bedside clock, trying to get his bearings. It was only eleven p.m.

He shook his head, as if to clear the fuzziness there. Memories began to trickle back in as he lit a cigarette. He used the flame from the lighter to survey his dumpy hotel room, then snapped it shut. He could have found a classier place to stay, but he hadn't wanted to alert the media. In fact, all he wanted for the next little while was to lay low.

The day the news cameras had captured him leading that little blond up to a fancy hotel had been the day that his life fell apart. Publicly at least. The day that his life actually fell apart had been years ago, but no one else had been privy to that—no one except for Maddie, and he knew she would not have told a single soul.

Here he was, hiding out from anyone who might delve deeper into the story, who might ask too many questions.

John knew the reality. If all his sins were publicly displayed, he would lose out on the one thing that had kept him by Maddie's side, playing second fiddle to the woman in the spotlight, all those years. He took a drag of his cigarette. Unfortunately, it did nothing to alleviate the pain in his head. Apparently, when you got drunk during the day and passed out before six in the evening, hangovers did not fade quickly. It was a lesson he had learned over the past couple of days.

Exhaling the smoke, John decided to see if a shower would clear his head. He had a lot to figure out, and he was not about to sit idly by while his future went up in flames.

In the shower, he began to replay his current predicament in his head.

Maddie's maiden name was Carmichael, meaning that she was loaded. The very first time he laid eyes on her, he knew that she was a rich girl. It was evident in everything she did, the ski trips, the European vacations, the summer home she mentioned down on the beach. It was also all too evident in how she carried herself, how she dressed, and the elegant ease with which she spoke.

From day one, it was apparent that underneath the wild party girl front she put on for all to see, Madeline Carmichael was all class. Her wealth was not what had drawn John to her in the beginning, however. She was smart and witty and a bombshell to boot.

During his senior year of college, they had met at a frat party. He had drank most of a keg by himself. Maddie was clearly drunk as well. Even half in the bag, she was stunning.

Her blue eyes shimmered underneath the lights, and her perfect figure tantalized his senses. That deep laugh kept him guessing, and when she slid one of those soft hands down his arm, he was hooked. She hadn't needed to say anything or do anything more. He was already hers. At that point, he would have done anything she asked.

When she said she was going to call it a night and go home, John had offered to walk her. It was dark and almost a mile back to her dorm room; he thought he would impress her with a display of chivalry.

"A pretty little thing like you shouldn't be out walking alone," he told her with a smile.

Maddie gave him a once-over. "So does that make you my bodyguard?" she had said with a laugh.

"That's me," John said, flexing his muscles, thankful that he had been hitting the weight room as hard as he had been for football.

"Okay," she agreed. "Let's go. I'm getting tired."

On the way out, some of his frat buddies tried to give him high fives. Under normal circumstances, he would have played along. But that night was different. He shook his head at them, signaling that this girl was different; she deserved respect.

The night was brisk, but not too cold. Even so, Madeline shivered with the chill of the wind. So he offered her his jacket. John couldn't help but think how great she looked in it.

"So tell me a little about yourself," he said.

"I don't just spill my information to anyone," Madeline teased. "I'm not that easy."

"No..." John stammered. "I...I didn't say you were easy."

"Oh yeah? Isn't that what your friends think?" She changed her voice to impersonate a college boy. "There goes John out the door with that hot little blond. You know he is going to get laid tonight."

She had smiled as she said the words, but her self-doubt was evident.

"It's not like that," John insisted. "I genuinely want to get to know you, Madeline."

"Call me Maddie," she said.

"Okay, well, Maddie, it's not like that. I'm not out here looking to get laid, as you put it. I offered to walk you home, because...well...I'd like to take you out sometime. Maybe we could grab dinner or a movie or just take another walk sometime?"

Madeline took off his jacket then, much to John's dismay. She handed it to him. "Here, I don't need this right now."

"Aren't you still cold?"

"Maybe." Madeline's sassy nature was showing through more and more with each minute. "But I don't need it right now."

With the ease of a seasoned stripper, Madeline had begun to unbutton her shirt and dance around him. She pushed him back in the grass.

"What are you doing?" he asked, knowing he sounded like an idiot, but, after all, they were in public.

A drunken group of kids passed by, not noticing John and Maddie on the grass in front of the school library.

"Just sit there, and shut up," she whispered.

She continued her striptease, further captivating him.

Before he could say anything else, she was completely naked, reaching into his pants and mounting him. "I thought you said you weren't looking to get laid tonight. It sure looks like you want to." Her voice was velvet.

John couldn't resist. He flipped her over in the grass, and they had sex right there on the front lawn of the library. When they were finished, John was sure of one thing—he was falling in love with Maddie Carmichael. She dressed quickly and began to walk away.

"Wait," he called, fumbling with the buckle of his belt.

She turned halfway. Even then, he could tell, it was as noncommittal a move for her as the sex had been. "It was nice to meet you, John," she called. Waving, she turned and left him sitting there.

From that day on, he had been obsessed. He called, brought her flowers and asked her out several times. Each time she told him she wasn't ready for anything serious. She was unattainable, and that made him want her more.

They met up at a few parties and each time found their way to a bathroom, a closet or a secluded area and fucked. After which she again would leave him. The routine left John heartsick. He wanted to be more than Maddie's hookup. He wanted to be the only one she was seeing.

Finally she had relented. He asked her to dinner, and she agreed to go. In time, they began dating seriously. John was in love. Maddie, on the other hand, seemed to enjoy his friendship but appeared disinterested in anything more.

After a year John decided to take the leap. He asked Maddie to marry him. He could sense that she wasn't ready, but she said yes. Looking back, he saw that she had been following some sort of path. It seemed like the right thing to do, marrying John, so she had done it.

Had he always been a move made out of some sense of obligation? He wasn't sure, but he did know Maddie had never truly been attracted to him.

He had had his pick of girls in college. He was on the football team, had the looks of a model. Even now, he could score with most women. That's why he was in this mess.

No, he reminded himself, the reason he was in this mess was because of Maddie. Because even though she loved him, she didn't want him.

They had just finished having sex. Once again, Maddie had faked an orgasm and rolled over to go to sleep. He could tell when they were fake, which was most of the time. She never seemed to be actually enjoying sex with him. Maybe she never had.

"Was it good for you?" he finally worked up the courage to ask.

"Baby, of course it was good," she said reassuringly, patting him on the shoulder. "Good night," she added.

"Maddie, wait. Do you enjoy having sex with me or don't you?"

Maddie sighed. "Yes, I do. It was good. It's always good." Her voice revealed her lack of interest.

"Then why do you fake orgasms? Why don't you let me keep going until I can get you off?"

She sat up in bed, realizing he was not going to let her get away with the lies tonight. "Fine, sometimes I fake it."

"How many times?" he asked, emboldened by her confession.

"I don't know, baby." Her voice was little more than a whine now, begging him to drop the subject.

"Fine. Maybe this will be an easier question to answer. How many times have I actually made you orgasm?"

She opened her mouth but didn't reply. "I want to go to sleep," she finally said.

"Shit! Not once?" He felt like he had been slapped across the face.

She sighed again. "It's not you, John. I swear it's not."

"What is it then? Is it some kind of condition where you just can't enjoy sex?"

"No," she began carefully. "If I admit something to you, you promise not to tell anyone else?"

"We're grown-ups. Husband and wife. We don't have to pinkie swear. What we say is kept between us."

"Right," she said. "Okay, well, I'm still adjusting to the whole sex thing again."

"We've been having sex for almost two years now. What more is there to adjust to?"

"Well, it's just that before you..."

He didn't let her finish. "I know you weren't a virgin that night, Maddie. So what the hell are you trying to say?"

"Let me finish, dammit! Before you, I hadn't been with a man in a couple of years."

"I find that hard to believe," he shot back. "You weren't much of a prude when you spread your legs for me on the front lawn the first night we met."

The accusation should have infuriated her, but she didn't show any sign that the insult had struck a chord.

"I wasn't," she had explained. "I just said I hadn't been with a *man*."

This time he heard the special emphasis she placed on the word "man," but he still had to ask. "What are you saying?"

"I'm saying I slept with a woman for a while and that with you I was trying to adjust to being with a man for the first time. It's not the easiest transition in the world, and even though we've been together all this time, sometimes it's still strange to me. So would you please drop it? I enjoy the intimacy of having sex with you, just like I enjoy knowing that I arouse you. I make sure you get off whenever you want to. Back off and give me some time to sort through everything I'm feeling—everything I've felt—and it'll all be okay."

With that, she had rolled over to go to sleep. He had never brought up the subject again. Not with her, anyway. Behind the scenes, he had done his own detective work. Old college friends of hers were hesitant to share any details, out of a surprisingly fierce loyalty to Maddie, but he finally got enough liquor in one during an outing and got her to give him a name. That was all he had needed. From there, it hadn't been hard to find out more—to find out that the fling Maddie spoke of had been a loving and committed—albeit hush-hush—affair for quite some time.

For years, it had haunted him. There was always something else on Maddie's mind or perhaps someone else. She never did seem to snap out of it. During their entire marriage, she had only a few orgasms, and they always occurred under similar circumstances—when he was licking her and she had her eyes closed.

As the years passed, she didn't even try to fake orgasms anymore. If they had sex, she'd lay there until he finished and then roll over to go to sleep. It was too much for a guy to take, honestly.

So, even though he knew it was wrong, he had started seeing other women. At first, he had gone to prostitutes—that was just about the sex. Then he had dated a string of women secretly. He bought them nice gifts with Maddie's money and kept them quiet.

He knew he should just leave, but over time, the money had become reason enough to stick around. He would stay until Maddie was done with her gig as mayor, ask her for a divorce and demand half of everything simply because he had stayed to help her win an election or two. She *owed* him, dammit.

Now, all that was being threatened. If anyone found out about the other women—found out that this hadn't been a one-time thing—his plan was ruined. He could see it play out in his head. More women would be found or come out of the woodwork to say that they had slept with the mayor's husband—all for fifteen minutes of fame. There was no way Maddie would let him leave with any money then. He would be penniless and alone, with no real career. He'd had one once—working for Maddie's father and angling to take over his multimillion dollar oil and gas production company—but then he'd a falling out with the old man.

When that gig ended, he and Maddie invested most of their money and got by just fine. Maddie, of course, was still a part owner of the company and received large percentages of profits, which meant he had continued to enjoy the finer things like traveling, golfing and not being a slave to a job he hated.

Without the cushion of Carmichael money, though, John wasn't sure what he would do. He had to find a way to keep everything quiet. By the time he finished his shower, the solution was clear. No, it was not ethical, but then neither was screwing a hooker behind your wife's back, and he hadn't had a problem with that. There was an election coming up next year, and Maddie had a lot to lose. She would lose her biggest donors, her voters and the election if anyone found out that the real reason her husband cheated was because she was not interested in sex with men. If she tried to screw him out of a settlement, he would make sure that the world knew exactly what Maddie preferred in bed—a woman's tongue between her legs.

Now he only had to figure out how to get that message to her without getting caught by the media in the process.

CHAPTER TWELVE

Jo divided the last bit of wine from the bottle into two glasses. She and Madeline had decided to enjoy the bottle after Gabe had left.

There was no doubt that Madeline's presence in her apartment had thrown Gabe for a loop. She had received three text messages after he left.

The first simply read, "I thought you were taking her to a hotel???"

Next came, "Well, anyway I look forward to seeing you at work tomorrow."

The last said, "Hope you two enjoy your night."

Finally she had given in and replied, "Thank you. It was very thoughtful of you to stop by. She stayed because of the press situation. I'll see you tomorrow."

Her phone had continued to beep off and on throughout the evening, alerting her that she had new messages. Gabe wasn't going to give up easily. She had known as much, but his persistence tonight was especially annoying. It was interfering with her time with Madeline.

Another beep sounded.

"Oh, answer that poor boy," Madeline said with a smile.

"I don't have anything to say to him."

"He's a nice man."

"Are you suggesting I forget everything I know about myself and give him a whirl?"

"No, I'm not saying you should date him, sleep with him and marry him. That never turns out the way you think it will." Madeline took the glass of wine from Jo. "I'm simply saying that you should answer him and when the time is right tell him you're not interested in him."

"Fine," Jo said, grabbing her phone.

As Jo read the most recent text message he'd sent, she tried to cover the look of concern on her face. She knew she had failed when Madeline asked, "Well, what did he have to say?"

"He wants to know why I'm so interested in spending time with you lately," Jo said meekly. "I've explained to all of them that I just want to make sure that you are doing okay, but it seems like none of them—even Gabe—are buying it anymore."

Madeline shifted her body on the couch to sit a little straighter. "So, why *are* you so interested in spending time with me lately?"

"I'm enjoying it," Jo answered.

Madeline laughed. "They won't buy that answer either, honey. I think you're the only one on staff who doesn't find me severe and intimidating."

"They just haven't given you a chance then, I guess." Jo smiled back at her.

"I'm not sure you've given me a full chance either."

Jo couldn't figure out what Madeline meant. She had opened her home to Madeline, offered her friendship, given her everything she needed.

"What are you talking about?"

"I'm talking about…this," Madeline replied. She took Jo's phone out of her hands and set it on the table, set their glasses of wine beside the couch and ran her fingers up and down Jo's sculpted arms.

Jo tried to keep her breathing even, but she wasn't sure she could resist Madeline's temptations.

"Could you...um...define *this*?" Jo's reply was breathy and deep, and for the first time in years she felt unsure. She was entranced, a high school girl completely captivated by a crush.

Without another word, Madeline leaned in and kissed Jo passionately. Lips intertwined as Jo's shock morphed into pure arousal. She deepened the kiss, massaging Madeline's tongue with her own. Reaching up to cup Madeline's face, she felt Madeline jerk back, saw the passion in her eyes shift into terror.

Madeline jumped up from the couch, shaking. "I can't do this. I mean, we can't do this," she said in a rushed breath.

Jo fought to regain control of her emotions. Even though her hormones were telling her otherwise, Madeline was right.

"I'm sorry," was all she could manage as her mind whirled. She let out a strained breath. "I'm so sorry, Madeline. You're right. It can't and it won't happen again."

Even as she said them, the words made her cringe. How many times had she denied herself true happiness for her career? For the protection of others? For the safer choice? In any case, Madeline's face was hard as stone. Jo was sure that even if she tried to continue the make-out session, it was never going to happen.

"I need to go," Madeline blurted. She rushed to the door, threw it open and slammed it behind her. Outside the door, Jo heard her clearly shout, "Shit!"

Hating having to do the mature thing, Jo stood, smoothed her rumpled clothes and reopened the door.

"What's wrong?" she asked, staring into the distance. She couldn't look Madeline in the eye yet. It was too unsettling.

"I don't have a fucking car." Madeline sighed.

Jo pressed her palms to her eyes, hoping that she could somehow relieve the stress of the situation. "I'll drive you," she answered. "Besides, you need to get your things. Come back inside and get them."

When Madeline didn't reply, Jo stepped away from the doorway, putting distance between the two of them. "I'm not going to maul you, I swear. Come back."

Madeline's eyes narrowed, and Jo wasn't sure whether what she was feeling was attraction or anger. After all, she hadn't started this. Mumbling under her breath, she returned to the apartment herself and started gathering up Madeline's belongings. Taking no special care, she shoved clothes and toiletry items alike into a bag and walked back to the door.

"Here," Jo said, handing her the bag. "You don't have to act like I'm going to grope you. Besides, if memory serves me correctly, you have kissed me twice. I didn't initiate any of this."

When Madeline still didn't speak, Jo threw her hands in the air in frustration. "Seriously, nothing has to happen," she pressed. "Nothing will happen," she corrected. "You don't have to be afraid to be in the same room as me."

"Yes, I do," Madeline said weakly.

"Excuse me?"

"I am terrified of being in the same room as you," Madeline clarified. "You don't get it, Jo. I'm afraid of what I want when I'm with you."

"Because I'm a woman?" Jo asked.

"Because I'm your boss, and because you're a woman."

The sincerity in Madeline's eyes cut to Jo's core. She swallowed hard and nodded. "Okay, then, I guess I better take you home."

"No. I'll walk."

Before Jo could protest, Madeline added, "I'm not afraid of you. I'm afraid of me. So, please, Jo, don't call me, text me or contact me except at work."

Jo felt anger flood her body. She knew it was wrong to pursue her boss, but to be thrown out of the friendship they had been building stung. She gritted her teeth to keep herself from saying things she shouldn't. Instead she simply said, "It doesn't have to be like this."

Madeline's lips tightened into a straight line before she answered, as though she too was carefully choosing her words.

"Yes, it does. And if you break my rules, I will fire you. This is wrong, and we need to keep our distance."

Without another word, she turned and disappeared into the darkness of the night.

Jo had watched many women walk away from her doorstep, but this time was different. This time her heart truly ached—as if it was magnetized, and Madeline was its matching half.

CHAPTER THIRTEEN

Controlled chaos normally filled the mayor's office. Today, though, it was filled with a slew of confused staff members who were milling around in slow motion. The junior staff members looked bored out of their minds for the most part, not knowing any better, and the senior staff members were taut with tension.

Jacquelyn was sick of it. Gabe was pacing again, and even though he had been taking Jo's side over hers, she felt badly for him.

"Let's grab some coffee," she said, reaching out to grab his arm.

"What?" He looked up at Jacquelyn, clearly not having heard a word she said.

"Coffee. Let's go. You are scaring the children." She jerked her thumb in the direction of one of the office's newest interns, who looked like she might cry.

"Okay," Gabe conceded, glancing at the intern. "It's not my fault she picked a crappy week to start working here," he mumbled.

They walked over to the break room, where Jacquelyn poured them both a cup of coffee.

"Drink up. And tell me why you're so upset."

"It's just…they said they would be here this morning and they're not."

"They?" Jacquelyn asked.

"Yes, both Jo and Madeline said that they were coming to work today."

"Did Madeline email you? Or were you finally able to get her on the phone?"

"She was at Jo's apartment last night," Gabe admitted, avoiding eye contact. "I stopped by to check and make sure everything was okay. I wanted to find out how Madeline had been earlier in the day. But apparently, she is still staying with Jo."

Jacquelyn lifted her coffee mug to her lips, masking her reaction. Inside, she was reeling, but she had made a decision not to show her anger to her co-workers anymore—especially Jo. A covert attack would be much better than one Jo could see coming.

Gabe was rambling, "I just want things to go back to normal, you know? I'm tired of sitting at my desk with nothing to do. I'm sick of rescheduling events, wondering when Madeline will come back to work. I'm tired of staying up late at night, trying to rethink my career path if for some reason she does not win the election next November. You realize that's just a year away, don't you? If she doesn't snap out of it, this thing could ruin her career."

"I'm well aware of that, thank you, Gabriel." Madeline's voice was amused.

Gabe jumped, spilling coffee down the front of his shirt. "Shit!" he yelled. The curse was followed quickly by a mumbled, "Sorry for my language, ma'am."

Jo was nowhere to be seen, but the mayor stood confidently before them. Jacquelyn beamed from ear to ear at seeing Madeline without her new friend. "Good morning, Mayor Stratton. Gabe and I were just talking about how we hoped you would show up this morning. We have sure missed you around here."

"It's good to be back, even if only for a little bit," Madeline said.

"Excuse me," Jacquelyn said, scurrying to pour another cup of coffee. She added a cream and two sugars to it before extending the cup to Madeline.

"Thank you." Madeline smiled and turned to survey the front office. "It looks dead in here," she commented.

"It has been," Jacquelyn admitted, then, her curiosity getting the best of her, "Where's Jo this morning?"

Madeline shrugged as she turned back to face them, but the gaze she leveled upon Jacquelyn was piercing. "I'll be in my office talking to Ian, but if you need anything let me know." She turned toward her office, but stopped to add, "I don't think I want to take any calls today, so if you can hold those, that would be great. I'm only staying an hour or so."

"Yes, ma'am," Jacquelyn replied.

From the break room, Jacquelyn could hear the front office door swing open and closed, just as she could hear the familiar clacking of high heels on the floor.

"Speak of the devil," she said snidely to Gabe, who shot her a puzzled look. Jacquelyn couldn't help but notice the way Madeline's hands shook at Jo's entrance. After all, there could be little doubt who it was. Everyone else was in the office, working as they should have been.

All eyes turned to the entrance of the small room, as the footsteps approached. Jo rounded the corner, and Madeline moved to the side to let her enter.

"Good morning, Jo," Madeline said, nodding in her direction before leaving for her office.

Gabe chimed in, "When did she stop calling you Josephine? I've been here for years and she still won't call me Gabe."

"Have you ever asked her to call you Gabe?" Jo asked, lifting an eyebrow.

He considered for a moment. "No, I guess I haven't. Is that what you did?"

Jo nodded, taking another sip of her coffee.

"Okay, whatever," Gabe replied. "So how is she doing? And why is she staying at your place still?"

Jo opened her mouth to respond, but Jacquelyn didn't want to sit around and listen to Jo talk about being Madeline's new best buddy.

"I would love to sit around and chat about the latest gossip with you two, but I think I will get back to work." Jacquelyn could hear the bitchiness infusing her voice, but she didn't care.

"Gabe?" Ian's voice boomed down the hallway.

"Looks like you won't have time for your idle chitchat anyway," she said, tossing the words in Gabe's direction and watching his face fall as he realized that he wasn't going to have a chance to be alone with Jo.

An unwilling but well-trained puppy, he headed to Ian's office. She followed close behind him, stopping at her office, which was beside Ian's. She let out a sigh.

"So what's on the agenda today?" her intern asked, looking up from the files he'd been sorting.

"Survival," Jacquelyn said dryly.

* * *

Jo busied herself at her desk. Like other staffers, she was accustomed to the air of chaos that usually engulfed the mayor's office. With the press frenzy being largely handled by Ian and Madeline's appointments all canceled, there was little for her to do aside from write letters for staff members to read on the mayor's behalf. Days that seemed trivial were unsettling. Once she had finished prepping all necessary letters, she hammered away on her computer, outlining some of the speeches that would be needed in the coming months. She needed the distraction.

If she let down her guard for even a few seconds, her thoughts shifted straight back to Madeline. The past few days, she had been riding a roller coaster of emotions. Was it the thought of a forbidden love that had enticed her so completely? Or did she really feel this strongly about her? One way or another, everything that had happened had left her feeling confused and hurt, like a leper or a loser who had made a pass at someone and been rejected.

Cursing herself under her breath for her stupidity, she tapped her fingers anxiously on the desk. She wanted to see her—to talk to her and smooth things over.

She glanced at the clock on her computer screen. Only forty-five minutes had passed since she had arrived. She felt like she was in a cage. Scanning the office, she confirmed what she already knew—everyone was staring at her, trying to figure out the change in her demeanor or how to get a juicy piece of gossip.

"Did you hear that she's staying with Jo?" an intern who had yet to learn how to whisper asked his neighbor in the corner cubicle.

Jo stiffened and, after a deep breath, stood. On her way to Madeline's office, she rehearsed what she had to say. When she stood at the door, though, words escaped her. Forcing herself to be strong, she knocked gently on the door.

"It's unlocked," came Madeline's voice from the other side.

Jo opened the door and stepped inside, closing it behind her. "We need to talk," Jo said quietly enough to thwart curious ears—but with enough assertiveness to let Madeline know that she meant business.

"We have nothing to talk about," Madeline said. "Besides, Ian will be in to meet with me shortly."

"You can't shut me out."

"I have to," Madeline said, the defeat evident in her tone. "Now if you'll excuse me, I have work to do."

"If that's how you want it," Jo replied and left the office.

Stopping in the hallway, she tried to steady her breath. There was no logical explanation for how her heart raced when she saw Madeline or how her entire body tingled when she smelled her perfume.

One day she would be strong, not give all this another thought. Jo Carson was not the type of woman to throw herself at the feet of someone who did not want her nor the kind to get involved in an inappropriate work affair. Now, however, she could not be here.

She approached Ian's door, knocked and stood in his doorway until he glanced up from his computer.

"Good morning, Jo." Even though he smiled, the stress and worry remained evident in his eyes.

"Good morning, Ian." Jo attempted to return his smile.

"What can I do for you?" he asked.

"I think I need to work from home today," she said, knowing she shouldn't press her luck, but also knowing if she spent one more second here, she would go crazy.

"Is everything okay?" The genuine concern in his voice reminded Jo that she wasn't entirely alone in this world, even if it felt like it.

"I'm fine," she managed. "I'm just exhausted and need to catch up on a few things. Now that the mayor is staying at a hotel, I can put my life back in order. I'll be back in tomorrow."

"Take the time you need," he reassured her. "I appreciate all you've done. Go take care of whatever you need to do."

Jo nodded her head and, with a last fleeting glance toward Madeline's closed door, she forced herself to walk away.

Gabe was waiting for her at the end of the hallway. He obviously wanted to know what was wrong, but she wasn't ready to talk about it yet—or ever. Even so, she valued his friendship.

"What's up, Gabe?" she asked, walking toward him.

"Want to get out of here for a little while? I thought maybe we could grab something at the coffee shop and talk about everything."

Without thinking, Jo glanced back toward Madeline's office. "Actually, I was just…um…going to go home for a bit," she stammered.

"Come on, it'll be good for you to clear your head with conversation over a bagel. Then you can go home."

"You might just be right," Jo agreed.

As they walked to the coffee shop across from the office, Gabe began asking his questions.

"Are you and the mayor still getting along?"

"Of course," Jo answered, a little too quickly perhaps. "I mean, she's a great person, a great mayor. I was just trying to be there for my boss when she needed someone."

"Was?" Gabe asked, noting her use of past tense.

"Yes. She's staying at a hotel now."

"Well, that's good," Gabe commented, nodding his head as if in thought. "How'd you make it work while she was there, though? Isn't your place pretty small?"

His tone was neutral, but that didn't stop Jo from feeling like she was on trial for some crime.

"It's small, but we made it work." Jo added, a slight edge to her voice, "I had my own space, and so did she."

Gabe took a step back and stared at her. "Why are you acting so defensive?"

"I'm not," Jo retorted before realizing that he had pegged her attitude correctly. She turned to face him. "I'm sorry. It's just that it's all been so stressful lately. I need a break—from the millions of questions and the scrutiny."

"You took the mayor home with you, Jo." Gabe's voice was gentle but matter-of-fact. "Of course there's scrutiny. What did you expect?"

"Friendship and a little privacy would have been nice," Jo shot back.

Gabe sighed and shook his head. "We work for the mayor. Privacy is out the window when you work in politics. You should know that."

Jo shook her head. She was sick of the questions and the curious glances she was getting over and over. Nobody could accept the fact that she had been the one there when Madeline fell apart and that, up until last night, she had been the glue holding Madeline together.

"You know, I don't think I want anything from the coffee shop. I think our little talk is done." Jo spun around to walk back to her car.

"Jo, come on. Let me explain." Gabe grabbed her arm, pleading.

"Don't touch me," she responded, quietly but with enough intensity to stop him in his tracks. She was halfway down the block when she heard him start to follow her.

"Jo, stop," he called out, chasing her down the street.

Fine, Jo thought. She would stop. She would hear him try to defend his asinine remarks, and then he would hear her out, loud and clear.

She stopped and turned around, throwing her hands in the air. "What, Gabe? What is it you have to say?"

"I was just asking why you two have become inseparable. Why she no longer engages with the rest of her staff. I wanted to know why it has been that way since we got the news. Or was, until today. Today you and Madeline have been acting strange, and your 'save the day' mission is complete. I want to know what the hell is going on, and why everything is suddenly better. That's all."

"Really? Because it seemed like you were jumping on the bandwagon with everyone else." She changed her voice to imitate her colleagues. "Why Jo? Jo isn't even one of us yet. She's new and young and doesn't know what's going on here. Why doesn't Madeline turn to someone who has been around for a while? I think Jo's just sucking up. Don't you think it's suspicious how the mayor needs someone like Jo to help her out?"

Gabe had stepped back, but Jo continued to unleash her pent-up fury on him. "What the hell was I supposed to do, Gabe? Huh? The woman was in *pain*. Did you have any suggestions then? Do you have any *now*? No, you didn't and you don't. And neither do any of the other nosy staffers. You don't care about Madeline. All you care about is who gets the most of her attention, who is on the inside track to follow in her footsteps. Well, fuck you all!"

She wanted to rein in the anger in her voice, but she was past the point of no return. "By the way, I think the spot for her go-to person is now vacant. So good luck. Go in there and fight for her attention like the rest of the vultures. I'm done with this bullshit. All I want to do is get back to my own life and my career."

Jo stopped to take a breath.

"Besides which, maybe you should take a minute to realize that this is a woman's life—a woman who doesn't have real friends as a necessity. She keeps everyone at an arm's length. I haven't figured out if it's because of the job or because she just doesn't want to get stabbed in the back, but she doesn't have a support group. Her father is too old, too distant, too wrapped up in his own world to get it. He hasn't even called her. Neither has her sister, who's off on some world cruise or something. She's alone, Gabe. Realize, when you're in there battling over who gets her attention, that it's not about you or your career."

Jo waited for a response. If Gabe had anything more to say, she was willing to hear it. He didn't even budge, though. He just stared at his wingtips, a chagrined look on his face.

There's nothing quite as unsexy as a weak man, Jo thought. Not that she regularly thought of men as sexy in the first place—but weak ones were the worst.

"Lay off of her and lay off of me," she said sternly. "Stop worrying about your precious egos and back the fuck off."

With that last barb, Jo turned to walk back to her car. She caught sight of his face as she did so. He looked like the words had delivered the final knockout blow. Great, he'd gotten the message finally. Maybe now he would leave her the hell alone.

CHAPTER FOURTEEN

John paced back and forth in his hotel room. He needed to get in touch with Madeline—needed to let her know that her secrets wouldn't stay that way if she tried to screw him out of his share of their money.

He had tried both of her phones, and both had gone straight to voice mail. Apparently she was in no mood to talk to him and was ignoring his calls. She carried those damn things everywhere, so he knew she must have received his voice mails. He had avoided being forceful or threatening in them, but he had gotten his point across, he thought. He hadn't heard a word from her, though—not so much as a peep.

A bulb lit up above his head as the solution came to him. He went to the front desk. In a place as shady as this one, he knew he could get the front desk clerk to do anything for an extra buck. Moments later, after a little coaching on his part, he waited while Elena, the front desk clerk dialed the phone, with a masked number.

"Hello?" she finally said. "I'd like to speak to Madeline please." There was a pause. "Yes, this is her sister, Cynthia."

John's palms were sweaty. This would work. Cynthia rarely called, but whenever she did, Madeline took the time to talk. Madeline desperately wanted a closer relationship with her sister, but Cynthia had always been the free-spirited type, flitting off to wherever the wind blew her and forgetting about her family completely.

Elena handed him the receiver and walked away from the counter. He had asked her to give him a moment of privacy once the call was made. Just as he thought, a crisp fifty-dollar bill in her pocket had made anything attainable.

The hold music on the other end of the line made his blood boil. She HAD to answer this call. Finally, he heard her voice, "Cynthia?" The words were laced with disbelief.

"Hello, Maddie," John replied, grinning.

There was silence on the other end of the line.

"You don't have to speak, but I need to say some things," he instructed, doing his best to keep his voice even.

"You have thirty seconds, you bastard."

"That will work. I've got a little proposition for you. I know that since I was caught, you think you get to take all the money and run, isn't that right?"

"This is about money, John? Are you fucking kidding? You slept with another woman—and not just *any* woman—and you want to talk about money?" Her voice was quiet, but she couldn't hide her contempt.

"Yes, I do want to talk about money, darling. Here's the deal—I cheated. And yes, with you-know-who, but you checked out a long time ago, and we both know why. I wasn't what you wanted, now was I?"

"What?" Madeline's breathing increased, and John knew he had gotten his point across.

"You wouldn't want me going to the press about how Mayor Stratton likes the ladies, would you?"

"You wouldn't."

"Oh, Maddie, I believe you know I would. And I will, unless you promise me half of everything."

"That's blackmail."

"I suppose it is." John laughed. "You let me know if you want to take your chances and call my bluff."

"I can't split everything down the middle and go on like nothing happened, John. You slept with someone else."

"This isn't a negotiation. You can hand over half of what you're worth or you can try to explain to everyone that you were blackmailed—*after* you're labeled a lesbian by the media and all your constituents. You know, the ones who elected you. If you're even thinking about a second term, this should be of importance to you."

Madeline didn't respond. John knew she had only run for mayor to stop the corruption in local government. While she had higher aspirations, this was her current, most pressing goal. She had worked hard to do that this term and accomplished a great deal. Earlier this year, she had hinted that maybe one term was enough. That said, he knew that this was not a story she wanted to share with anyone—let alone the media.

"You have until tomorrow to decide. I'll be expecting a call around five p.m. If I don't get one, the media gets a juicy story."

He hung up the phone, feeling very pleased with himself. He would be set up after the divorce settlement, and he could move wherever he wanted.

* * *

Madeline let the receiver fall from her hand. This was exactly what she had hoped to avoid by having the staff hold her calls and by ignoring every one of John's attempts to contact her. When she heard that Cynthia was on the line, though, she had decided to speak with her. Now what? How could John be so insensitive? How was she going to deal with this?

It wasn't about the money. She would still have enough to live comfortably for the rest of her life. It was about her pride. If he walked away with half of everything she had, it would feel like he had won. She wanted that cheating bastard to suffer just a little bit—especially when the face of his mistress continued to cut into her heart.

Then again, what he had already done was going to mar upcoming campaign efforts. If he made good on this threat, it would threaten everything.

She could resort to his games, she knew. She knew plenty of his secrets and could beat him to the punch by secretly spreading those to the media. She wasn't sure she wanted to resort to those tactics, though. In politics, she had learned early to be careful how quickly you pull the trigger.

She sighed. She would pay him off. The thought made her angry, but it would get her one step closer to having him out of her life for good. Maybe then she could move forward.

She wanted to talk to someone who would understand. But the truth was she had no one. Not any longer. She glanced at the staff chart beside her phone, letting her eyes linger on Jo's name. She couldn't disguise what she felt. She was hopelessly drawn to her, wanting to be her friend—and so much more.

She picked up the phone, placed the receiver to her ear and let her fingers hover above the number keys. Never before had she been so at war with herself. She tightened her grip on the receiver and slammed it down.

"I won't do it," she said with a sigh. This was something she was going to have to do on her own—completely alone.

* * *

An apartment that until recently had seemed perfectly normal was now hauntingly quiet with walls that seemed to be closing in on her. Jo had done anything and everything to occupy herself. She had taken Jaws out for a walk, but when the temperature had turned colder, she opted for cleaning the apartment top to bottom. With nothing left to do, she had to get out of the house.

Jo made her way through her neighborhood to a place she knew all too well. As she stood on the sidewalk and stared at the sign above the door, she felt the sadness settle in her heart. She had never expected to care—but she did.

"Kay's Pub," the sign read. Jo let out a depressed laugh, thinking that it would be better if it simply said, "Welcome back."

She opened the door and stepped inside, allowing her eyes to adjust to the darkness around her.

"We're not open until five," a woman's voice called out of the darkened room.

"Not even for a regular?" Jo questioned, knowing the answer.

"Is that you, Jo?" Kay appeared from behind the bar.

Jo smiled and walked over to hug the woman.

"Back from the dead? On hiatus? Sabbatical?" Kay asked, laughing. "Where the hell have you been, girl? We've missed you around here."

"I've only been gone for a few nights," Jo said with a laugh.

"A few nights around here is like a lifetime," Kay said, returning to stocking the fridge. "I know we don't see you every night, but you come around every little bit to have a drink, play a new role and leave with some poor unsuspecting girl."

Jo shook her head and smiled. "You know me too well, Miss Kay."

This was one of the few places that she had never had to hide who she was. It was Jo's safe haven. Kay was one of the only people who knew that Jo was a lesbian, and thankfully she never asked questions or probed too deeply about what Jo did for a living, even though there was little doubt she already knew. And right now, it was the only place Jo wanted to be—the only place that she *could* be without causing more trouble.

"So what have you been up to and why do you look so down?" Kay asked as she poured Jo a beer.

"Troubles of the heart," Jo said with a shrug, taking a seat on a barstool.

Kay stopped wiping down the bar to look Jo in the eye. "Someone finally got to you?"

Jo took a long swig of her beer. "Something like that."

"Damn," Kay said, shaking her head. "Never thought I'd see the day. Who is she?"

"Let's not talk about it, okay?" She had never made a practice of spilling her feelings out for others, and she was certainly not going to start now.

"Okay," Kay replied. "But I will say one thing. She must be some girl to have caught your heart. Don't let her go without a fight."

The words stung, though Jo knew Kay meant well. She gulped the rest of the beer down and set the empty glass on the bar. "Thank you, Kay," Jo managed before slipping off the stool and dropping a ten-dollar bill on the bar.

"You leaving already?"

"I may be back tonight," Jo said. "I need to go now."

She had no clue where to go or what to do—only that she could not sit around and talk to Kay about "the girl" who had her head so messed up. Kay had said she should fight for her, but Madeline obviously did not want that, and she certainly wasn't a "girl." She was a woman and a brilliant one at that.

She leaned against the cool side of the brick building to compose herself. "I'm Jo Carson. I'm strong, and I'm going to get through this," she whispered to herself. Taking a steadying breath, she straightened her shoulders and began her walk home.

Of one thing Jo was certain—she was not going to change from the strong person she was to some broken soul because of Madeline Stratton.

CHAPTER FIFTEEN

Knowing exactly what she needed in order to deal with her stress and feelings of isolation, Madeline picked up her office phone and called Jo.

After a ring, Jo's sweet voice filled the line. "This is Jo. Can I help you?"

"I sure hope so," Madeline said with a laugh.

"Yes, ma'am. I'll be right in." The amusement in Jo's voice was evident.

Madeline heard the click and was grateful to see Jo approaching her doorway. There was a look of concern on her face. Without saying a word, she seemed to be asking if everything was okay.

"Please shut the door."

Jo nodded and did as she was told.

"Lock it," Madeline whispered.

Jo silently slid the lock into place.

"What's going on?"

"I need you to do something for me," Madeline said.

"Okay, whatever you need, just let me know."

Always one to comply and provide help, Madeline thought with anticipation. She took a deep breath. Simply being in Jo's presence alleviated her stress.

"Come closer," she whispered, thankful there were no windows in her office.

Jo smiled. "Right here, right now?" Her eyes sparkled with interest.

Madeline nodded. As Jo moved closer, Madeline whispered in her ear, "I need you to help me deal with the stress and confusion."

Jo leaned in to kiss Madeline's neck. "I think I can help with that."

Without wasting a second, Jo slipped her hand up Madeline's skirt and began to relieve all the worries and erase any thought other than the pleasure she was receiving.

She came quickly and had to bite her lip to keep from making any sound.

"You're incredible," she whispered as she shivered from the excitement of it all.

"Glad I could help," Jo said with a wink.

Madeline woke with a start. What the hell had she been thinking? She sat up, rubbing her forehead in frustration. The last thing she needed was to be having sex dreams about Jo Carson. She had been stupid to get a hotel room so close to Jo's place, though she hadn't had a lot of choices since she had been walking and hadn't wanted to attract attention by calling a cab. Doing that had been almost as idiotic as taking the afternoon off to nap and letting her mind wander. Recalling the dream and the defeated look on Jo's face this morning, Madeline was strongly tempted to pop over to her place and talk about all of this. She decided that a trip to the hotel bar would have to suffice.

* * *

Jacquelyn was tired of the games. Both Madeline and Jo had disappeared from the office today, and she wanted to know why. She pulled Gabe into the hallway, knowing that she should show more professionalism, but she was unable to stop herself.

"What did she say this morning while you were getting coffee?" Jacquelyn demanded. "Why are the rest of us banished from Madeline's presence while she gets to be the golden girl?"

Gabe shook his head, looking tired. "Enough, Jacquelyn."

"No, it's not enough. I need to know. We all deserve to know. Madeline can't drop out of sight and shack up with Jo Carson. The media will start questioning where she is."

"She was in the office today," Gabe replied. "Besides, they're not 'shacking up' anymore. Madeline got a hotel room yesterday."

The news came as a surprise to Jacquelyn, and she was not fond of surprises when they related to her boss. "Why didn't they say anything? And how long should we expect this to last? When is she going to slip off again and not tell anyone but Jo?"

"I don't know, and I probably won't get to know. Let's drop it, okay?"

"What do you mean?"

"Jo blew me off this morning, like she's been doing to everyone else. I don't have any answers because now I've pissed her off too." Gabe looked defeated. "I think we need to back off for a while."

"You can back off if you want to, Gabe, but I can't. If we don't get it together around here, we are all on a sinking ship. Do you really want to go through job interviews again and the starting-over process? Are you prepared for that? Because, I'm not. In the event Madeline ends up doing some kind of public face plant, I don't want the stain of it on my résumé. Even if we don't have to worry about Jo messing things up, we can't sit around and pretend everything is just peachy."

"I want to be informed and kept up to date as much as you do, but we're not going to get anywhere by hammering either of them with questions. Trust me, I tried."

"Did you? How hard did you try? You're so afraid of pissing Jo off that you walk on eggshells around her. She's single-handedly hijacking this operation. You get that, don't you? She's been the one calling the shots, saying where Madeline goes, what she does—and what she doesn't do. Suddenly she outranks me, you and Ian. How do you feel about that?"

"I think you're overreacting. In any case, I'm pretty sure she's relinquished that responsibility," Gabe replied, his voice shaking from frustration.

"What do you mean?" Jacquelyn's curiosity was piqued. "Did something happen between them? Are they fighting?"

"I don't know, Jacquelyn. Drop it."

"What exactly did she say? Is she going to lose her job?" Jacquelyn tried to breathe through her rapid-fire questions, but this was too good.

Gabe sighed. "I don't have details. If you want to know so bad, you ask one of them."

They stood in silence for a few moments. Jacquelyn was determined to get to the bottom of this. Jo Carson had done things she considered unforgiveable, not only practically destroying the relationship between Madeline and Jacquelyn that Jacquelyn had worked so hard to develop but also standing in the way of keeping Madeline in the spotlight, something that was essential leading up to an election. Ian eventually would serve as volunteer campaign manager with a separate campaign staff—and she wouldn't be in the mix of campaign messaging—but she needed to make sure that Madeline didn't mess up. If she was not reelected, they would all be out of jobs. She needed to know what Jo's agenda was and exactly what had caused her fall from grace.

Good, bad or ugly, they needed to get Madeline's face back in the news, needed her to start doing on-camera interviews and answering the questions that people had been asking. Questions that Jacquelyn could not address, because Madeline hadn't told her anything. Questions that she was sure Jo knew the answers to but wasn't sharing with anyone.

She had received about twenty press questions a day since the news of John's affair broke—to all of which she had simply said, "No comment." She needed time with Madeline. She needed to know: Did Madeline know John was cheating? Had she suspected? Was she planning to file for divorce? What would happen to their property?

"I want answers, and I want Madeline back," Jacquelyn said, leveling her gaze at Gabe.

"That's what I want too," Gabe finally admitted.

* * *

When had life come to this? Looking at the crumpled muffin wrappers and empty Red Bull cans scattered around the van, Isaac Williams had to ask. When the need to pay child support got critical, he supposed. He put his head in his hands, wishing desperately that he could take a nap. To say he was a man down on his luck would have been putting it mildly.

The pamphlet he had been handed during college about the exciting life of a cameraman for a news station had lied. There was no glamour or excitement. There was just a van that he felt like he had been pretty much living in for days.

Something had to give soon. It had to, he thought, recalling his last conversation with his boss.

"They're not commenting," Isaac had told him after several unsuccessful attempts to get a statement out of Mayor Stratton's staff.

"That's just great, Isaac. Our competition stormed her house and got live coverage, and you can't even get a damn written statement."

"I've been by her house. She's not staying there, apparently," Isaac had argued.

"I'm not paying you to tell me where she is or isn't staying. If you want to keep this job, get me something new. Get me something that other stations haven't run. Hell, do some more digging on the husband. Get the other woman to talk. I don't care, but produce something—and fast. News doesn't sleep, and neither should you until you have something for me."

"Yes, sir," Isaac had said softly before heading out again. What he had really wanted to tell his boss was that he could shove the news up his ass. The truth was, as much as he loathed his job, he was going to do whatever it took to be able to spend one weekend a month with his son—even stalk the mayor.

He was staked outside of her house for the second day in a row, waiting, watching. There had to be activity around the place at some point. He had tried all of his phone options, but everything had come up flat.

Badly in need of a nap, he called the mayor's office again. After three rings, someone answered—an intern, he guessed.

"Mayor Stratton's office, this is Chris. May I help you?"

"Hi, Chris. It's Isaac from Channel 4 News. Can I talk to Jacquelyn?"

He knew the drill. The intern would check and see if she was available while he sat and listened to on-hold music that made him want to slit his wrists.

"This is Jacquelyn." Stress and frustration filled her voice.

Good, he thought, maybe he'd actually get her to break this time.

"Jacquelyn, it's Isaac with Channel 4. How are you today?" He tried his best to sound cheerful.

"Good." Judging from the tone of her voice, she was probably forcing a smile. "How are you?"

"I'm good. I was just checking to see if you all had issued a statement or were planning to at some point in the near future?"

"Not at this point, but I have your contact information and will send you anything in the event that we issue a statement."

He wanted to scream. This meant he would be getting the statement at the same time as everyone else. There would be no breaking news, and Channel 4 would not come out on top.

"Thanks, Jacquelyn. If you have anything else you would like us to run, be sure and let me know that too."

"I will, for sure," she replied.

"When will the mayor be back at the office?" He tried another approach, getting a tired sigh from the other end of the phone in response.

"The public wants to know," he urged. "Remember—these are the people who put her in office. They deserve to know what she's doing."

"At this point, I am unable to comment on the mayor's schedule," she said curtly.

"That'll be all then, but do consider issuing something soon. Thank you."

As he hung up, he decided this wasn't going to cut it much longer. Obviously, the mayor wasn't coming home anytime soon, and the husband was obviously laying low. He wasn't staying with the little blond he had been caught with, though. Isaac had checked that out.

He needed someone at that office to talk. He would find them, find out what he needed to knew. But first he was going to get some sleep.

CHAPTER SIXTEEN

Chicken simmered in vodka sauce, and Tracy Chapman played softly on the stereo.

Jo stirred the chicken, attempting to get her mind off the situation at hand. Alcohol had not been the answer. She knew that much. It had only made her head swim with more questions and thoughts of Madeline.

Every time she successfully diverted her attention from her—even if for a few seconds—something pulled her back instantly. It didn't matter if it was as simple as a song, or as complex and stressful as the conversation she had with her mother this afternoon, peppered with questions about whether Jo's job was in jeopardy.

She pushed the thoughts away, focusing on the meal in front of her. Cooking in an empty kitchen—another meal alone—had not made anything better. "Looks like it's back to eating alone, buddy," she said, reaching down to pat Jaws on the head. "I guess it's not going to get much better than this."

The doorbell rang, both startling her and filling her with hope. Maybe Madeline had decided to come back and talk things over.

She made her way to the door and glanced through the peephole. In an instant, hope turned to dread.

"Jacquelyn, hi," Jo said, opening the door.

How the hell do all these people know where I live? she wanted to scream. Never before had she had to worry about someone from work popping in randomly.

Jacquelyn walked in, without having been invited. *Rude, but expected*, Jo thought.

Jo glanced into the kitchen, then hurried to turn off the stove. "I'm making dinner. Do you want to join me?" she asked, hoping Jacquelyn would have the good sense to politely decline.

"That would be lovely. There's just a couple of things I would like to discuss with you, so I thought I would drop by tonight. We can work through them and then I'll be out of your hair tomorrow."

The smile on Jacquelyn's face was forced, but Jo knew hers was as well.

"Sounds good. Let me finish up really quickly," she replied.

As she set the food on the table, Jo glanced around the kitchen. Thankfully, there was nothing out of the ordinary, except for a few everyday items that Madeline had left behind in her abrupt exit.

To her credit, if Jacquelyn noticed anything out of the ordinary, she covered it well. They settled into a somewhat normal pattern, as they ate.

Jacquelyn swallowed. "This is wonderful."

Jo offered her a smile. "So what did you want to talk about tonight?"

She did not want Jacquelyn in her apartment any longer than necessary, so she figured she might as well get the ball rolling.

"We need to formulate a plan of response," Jacquelyn said, taking a sip of wine. "Basically, the press won't wait forever. They've been calling nonstop, and given the election next year, we can't just disappear."

Jo agreed, but she did not want to push Madeline too far, too fast. Besides, at this point, she didn't even know where Madeline was.

"Why are you asking me?" Jo asked.

"Because you're the one she let in, I suppose. You seem to know what is going on with her, where she is and maybe what she wants me to tell everyone."

Jo resisted the urge to scream and hoped that her face was masked. "Sorry. I don't know. As you can see, she's not here anymore," Jo said, gesturing around the small apartment.

Jacquelyn's brow furrowed. "Did the two of you have a falling out?"

Jo took a sip of wine. *God, why is this suddenly such a popular topic of discussion? First Gabe, now Jacquelyn.*

"No, it was always a temporary thing, just until she got her feet under her, which didn't take long, thank goodness," Jo replied with a forced smile. "As you can see, this is a small place."

"Right," Jacquelyn said, obviously not buying the excuse. "How did you make it work for as long as you did?"

"It was a day and a half, not an eternity, though it may have felt like it to Madeline. My couch isn't the world's most comfortable." Jo was getting sick of this. "She needed someone, and I was there for her. End of story. Now, if you want me to help formulate strategy, I'd be more than happy to do so—but I'm tired of being interrogated."

Jacquelyn straightened in her chair, looking taken aback.

Jo softened her tone. "I'm sorry. It's just I've heard them all before, and I'm tired of being verbally assaulted and targeted with a million rapid-fire questions—all because I was acting with human decency and helping out someone in need. "

Jacquelyn's eyes narrowed, but she let it go. "Fair enough. Now, what do you think I should tell the press?"

"Well," Jo began, "I think you need to talk to Ian and Madeline directly on that one."

"I've already talked to Ian. We have his statement that we can give once Madeline approves it, but the people don't want to hear from him. They want her words."

"I don't think we can overstep our boundaries on this one."

"I'm not going to," Jacquelyn said, a wicked twinkle in her eye. "She still has to approve his statement, and it's my job to get her to approve what's said publicly. But I also want to know what she has to say. Let's speakerphone her in right now and get her input."

Jo's heartbeat quickened, and she hoped that Jacquelyn couldn't tell how agitated the suggestion made her. She didn't want to step on Ian's toes, and she certainly didn't want to hear Madeline's voice right here, right now, with an audience. She tried to keep her breathing even, reminding herself that she had to work with Jacquelyn, and this was about work.

Jacquelyn placed her cell on the kitchen table and started tapping the buttons to call Madeline. Jo wanted to protest but resisted. The questions she wanted to ask, of course, were ones she couldn't ask with Jacquelyn in the room—and ones Madeline likely would not answer at this point anyway.

"Hello? This is Madeline." The voice she'd been longing to hear came in over the speaker on the phone, breaking through the jumbled thoughts in Jo's head.

"Hi, Mayor Stratton. It's Jacquelyn and Jo. We wanted to talk to you about media strategies. Do you have time to talk?"

The mayor cleared her throat. "Sure."

Was Madeline drinking again? Jo thought she detected a slight slur to her words. Maybe she was just tired. She shot a glance at Jacquelyn. It was good to know Madeline was having a difficult time tonight too. As much as she wished Madeline was doing well, her breakdown might mean that she cared, even a little bit. Jo considered the thought, and her guard went up. If Madeline had been drinking and wasn't in full control of what she said, it could be dangerous. Jo would have to make sure Jacquelyn didn't get wind of what had happened between them.

She wanted to invite her back over, wanted to tell her that she was sorry. But none of that was appropriate—and she knew it. Madeline was her boss, and anything romantic between them would be dishonorable, not to mention grounds for her dismissal, Madeline's impeachment or both. She had to get a grip.

She heard Jacquelyn ask Madeline what she wanted to say to the press.

"Well, I'm sure I can guess most of them," Madeline said. "But can you give me an example of the questions you've been getting?"

"Sure," Jacquelyn said. "Did you know about John's affair before the news broke? Do you plan to file for divorce? Do you know the woman he was caught with?"

"Okay, I can answer these," Madeline said, although her pain was evident in her voice. "No, I didn't know John was cheating and with whom. I plan to file for divorce."

The words sounded rehearsed and rolled off the tongue too easily, obviously a practiced lie—at least in part. There was more to that story, Jo was sure.

"Okay," Jacquelyn answered. "There are a few more things."

She turned to Jo. "Did you have anything to add, Jo, before we move on?"

Jo stiffened. She had a million things she'd like to say, but only one came out. "We would like to give you all of the time in the world to deal with this, but the media has been persistent. I think that at some point in the near future we should hold a press conference."

Madeline didn't speak.

"I think that's a great idea," Jacquelyn said. She sounded as though she was finally happy to have someone on her side in the matter.

"I'll consider it," Madeline said. "But it'll be on my terms, and it won't be right away."

"Okay. I just think it would be best," Jo added.

"Thank you for that, Josephine," Madeline said.

The use of her full name cut Jo deeper than she had expected. It seemed that even their friendship had disappeared.

"Now, what else was there, Jacquelyn?" Madeline asked, cutting off any further response from Jo.

Madeline's dismissal of Jo's idea, instead of relieving Jacquelyn's curiosity, seemed to have added fuel to the fire of her interest. She had a hungry, even predatory look in her eyes as she continued. "Who will get the house? Will you continue your reelection efforts? And when do you plan to fully return to work?"

"The house and possessions will be decided at a later date. I will continue my reelection efforts." Madeline paused. "Be sure to add something about how my top priority is to serve the people despite the difficulties of my personal life. As for returning to work, I came back today, didn't I? I intend to continue to fulfill my duties as mayor to the fullest. Is that all?"

Jacquelyn pursed her lips, obviously wanting to delve deeper. But she knew when to stop. "That's all for one night. We can deal with the rest as we move forward. Will you be in the office tomorrow?"

"At some point. I'll talk to you more then. Have a good night," Madeline said before ending the call.

Little was said as they finished dinner, although it was obvious Jacquelyn had a million more questions. It was an uncomfortable environment to say the least. Finally, Jacquelyn finished her pasta.

"That was wonderful," she said, rising to leave. "I'll call Ian on my way home and fill him in on everything. I think we can finally move forward. Thank you for having me."

"You're very welcome. Have a good evening."

As Jo walked her to the door, her heart stopped in her chest. *The L Word* case was still on the coffee table from the other day. If Jacquelyn's eyes drifted that way, she didn't say anything—but that didn't put Jo at ease by any means. If Jacquelyn had questions about that, she was smart enough not to ask them. Which only meant that she was going to do the digging herself. And that, to Jo, was much scarier than actually fielding her queries.

At the door, Jacquelyn asked, "Will I see you at work tomorrow?" Her tone was more than a little condescending.

"Of course. Will I see *you*?" Jo couldn't resist spicing up the conversation with a little snarkiness of her own.

Jacquelyn forced a tight smile. "Always."

She turned to leave and then turned back for just a moment. "You know," she said quickly, "looking at this couch and seeing the cozy layout of your place, it's hard to imagine Madeline sleeping out here. I would have thought you might have offered the mayor your bed." She let the words linger, and Jo's heart hammered in her chest. She couldn't formulate a response, trapped in her own fear of being found out. "I just thought you might have camped out on the couch yourself. Either way I guess it's probably good for you to have your space back."

Jacquelyn waltzed out of the apartment, leaving Jo in a whirl of crazed panic. She leaned against the closed door and sank to the floor, feeling dizzy. Jacquelyn's words had achieved exactly what she had wanted them to.

* * *

The minute she ended the call with Jacquelyn and Jo, Madeline had to fight to keep the nausea at bay. Of course, she knew the "other woman." John knew how to wound and he had done so by sleeping with Natalie—of all people.

Since she had been confronted with the picture of the woman John had been caught with, her mind had been plagued with concerns over who knew what—who remembered Natalie as Madeline's lover and friend and might come forth with a million-dollar revelation to the media. Far more pressing, though, had been the unbearable sadness that came along with the discovery that the only person she had ever truly loved and been intimate with had stooped to such a low. The fact that Natalie was capable of inflicting so much pain on her had cut the legs right out from under her, turning a seasoned and skilled political mind into that of a weak and damaged woman.

The loneliness she felt glued her to the floor. Before she had been lonely—but she had not been alone. She had been surrounded by people at all times. Now, the silence seemed to echo around her, reminding her that she had no one.

There was no one she could call. No one she could share her pain with. No one she could reach out to for stability. Her sister was flighty and checked out long ago, her father was too busy, too absent. Aside from her circle of political friends—all of whom she kept at arm's length, fearful of them digging too deep into her past and her sham of a marriage—she had no one. She wished she had been able to meld her professional life with her college life, keeping those friends who had meant the world to her in her life, but it had been impossible. The minute she had started climbing the ladder, lobbying on behalf of her father's company, she had been forced to shed her party girl image and the people associated with it. Besides, those people knew too much, and it had been smarter to steer clear of them.

There was no one she *would* reach out to either. With power came responsibility. She would not let an inappropriate relationship with a staff member mar her service to the city she cared about nor would she allow her feelings to compromise Jo's career. She cared about her too much to allow something like this to mark her and ruin her future.

She would find a way to deal with it all on her own—the loss of her husband and the loss and betrayal of her first love.

* * *

Back in her vehicle, Jacquelyn tried to process what she had seen. Jo was clearly on edge tonight, reeling from whatever had happened between her and Madeline. Jacquelyn was thankful to have some answers, but she was still curious. Why had Madeline abruptly cut Jo out of her life, after so quickly ushering her in? And why was there a lesbian DVD on Jo Carson's coffee table?

She recalled how Jo repeatedly had come to Madeline's defense, how tenderly she'd looked at the mayor. She thought at the time that there was something odd about that, but she had decided her suspicions were ridiculous. Now, however, Madeline was speaking to her with a chill in her voice and avoiding her. Jo had to have done something that repulsed Madeline. Jacquelyn considered the possibilities. Had Jo made the living environment uncomfortable? Had she perhaps made some kind of pass at Madeline? Jo seemed to have a world of secrets, and soon, Jacquelyn swore, she would uncover them all.

She smiled to herself; she might have finally figured out a way to torpedo Jo's career. Much as she wanted to rebuke herself for the malicious thought, she couldn't find the will to do so. She could not escape the person she was becoming, even if she had wanted to do so. And the truth was, she didn't want to. Jo could destroy everything she had worked so hard to build; it was time for her to go. First, though, she had work to do.

She pulled out her cell phone. After a quick call to Ian to get the green light, she sprang into action. She had promised to alert the media when Madeline had more to say than "No comment." She would issue a written statement to everyone when she returned to the office, but she thought she'd give a slight jump to the reporter who had been the nicest. It never hurt to help those who had shown tenderness and compassion, she thought.

She dialed the phone. "Isaac," she said as he answered.

CHAPTER SEVENTEEN

Getting back into the flow of a normal work week had not been easy. For the first time in two weeks, the morning's headlines had said nothing about her or her philandering husband, but staff emotions still were running high, with early November winds reminding them that an election was less than a year away and the pace would soon pick up. It would pick up for her most of all, Madeline knew, but for the moment things were oddly calm. The buzz about "Who gets the house? And who loses their dignity?" had finally ceased—at least for the time being, as if the media seemed to have reconciled itself to the fact that there were other stories to be covered.

She was rarely followed by news cameras now. It could have been the inconspicuous gray sedan she had rented in place of her Suburban in hopes of throwing the press off her trail. Someone had tipped off the media that she was staying in the hotel, but after a day of frenzied camera-clicking and microphone-thrusting they had backed off, thanks to some stern words from the hotel's management about pursuing trespassing charges and the statement Jacquelyn had issued. That, the fact that divorces took time and marking the reopening of a major business that had been destroyed by a tornado the previous year seemed to be keeping the bloodsuckers at bay, at least for now.

Madeline cricked her neck to the left to alleviate the tension building in her shoulders. Her lawyer had been in the office for thirty minutes now, going over all the possibilities of the divorce. She just wanted it over. She was going to give John half of everything, as he had demanded. It was better this way. Despite media revelations about his repeated infidelities, she was ready for it to come to an end.

She had yet to decide if she wanted to pursue another term, though. Publicly, she had stated that she would definitely run, but she was tired and ready for all of this to be over. If she could accomplish in the next few months the goals she had set when she ran, she could announce that she wasn't running, finish her term as mayor and go back to a quiet, private life. She had the money to take some time off for traveling and clearing her head, and then she could return to the work that had landed her into office the first time. Not the family company perhaps—it was time for a fresh start, something other than hiding behind her family's name and money in the place she'd always called home—but there was no shortage of other oil and gas companies that needed someone to work on communications, marketing, strategy or even behind the scenes.

With her experience, going back to the private sector would be easy. What would happen to Jo, though? It was stupid to be concerned about that, she knew, but if she decided not to run for another term the other staff members would simply move on. They'd continue to climb the political ladder, taking jobs in new offices or on new campaigns. But what about Jo? She had never heard her express an interest in staying in politics long term, nor should she. Jo was unequivocally creative with a slew of varied talents, and her time would be best spent writing a novel, singing to entertain or sharing her talents with the world outside of Oklahoma City. Whatever she chose to do, Madeline hoped she would go somewhere where she could live a life of authenticity without having to worry about what everyone thought.

She was only twenty-seven, after all. Madeline felt a pang of jealousy. She had settled down too early, had settled for a marriage devoid of true intimacy, all for the sake of being who she thought she was supposed to be. The oil and gas industry was something she cared about, but not the only thing. If she could do it all over again, there were so many things she would change. Maybe she, too, would have a chance at a more authentic life as a result of all of this—one where she didn't have to run from her pent-up desires.

Madeline brought herself back to the present. She couldn't keep letting her mind dwell on the very person who was responsible for her near moral downfall. She sighed. This had to end—just like residing at the hotel had to end.

Yesterday Ian had pulled her aside. "We need to start looking for a place for you, something permanent, stable. A place you can put down new roots," he had told her. It was easy to read between the lines. What he was really saying was, "Get your shit together, Madeline, and show the voters you're going to be sticking around." She told him to go ahead and contact a realtor. She would start looking at houses this weekend.

Last night, she had looked through materials the realtor had brought to the office, including a flyer for a four-bedroom house with a wrap-around deck. It was beautiful, but she honestly didn't need that much space. At this point, it was hard to say what she did need.

Her lawyer snapped his briefcase closed, bringing her back to reality again. "Call me if you have any questions, but we'll get you through this."

"Sounds good, thank you." As he walked out, she couldn't recall a word he had said, but it didn't matter. The divorce proceedings could go on without her, as far as she was concerned. John could take everything, and she would still find a way to be happy.

Alone in her office, she stretched her arms above her head. The cycle she had been living lately was exhausting. When she had announced to the staff that she was coming back full-time and that she wanted the appointments she had missed the previous week rescheduled, they had wasted no time in putting together a grueling schedule for her.

She had been in meetings all day every day since—albeit mostly ribbon cuttings and speeches where she could do her business as mayor and then escape—with early retirement to her hotel room for sanctuary every night. There'd been a short press conference too, in which she had addressed basic media concerns without delving deeply into the issues at hand. Even though she was the mayor, she reminded them, she was entitled to privacy and respect when it came to her personal life.

Luckily, she had managed to do that—even more so since the divorce than ever before. She knew the respect for her personal time had largely been because they viewed her as the victim, and it would soon fade. Nonetheless, it had been a welcome reprieve.

She glanced into the hallway and out toward the cubicles. Jo was not among the staff working there for a change, she was glad to see, though her absence also roused her curiosity. Knowing that she could always count on Gabe for a smile and having not yet conferred with him today, she walked toward his desk, intent on clarifying her day's schedule.

"Good morning, Mayor," he said, looking up from his computer.

"Is it still morning?" Madeline managed a laugh.

"For a few minutes, anyway." Gabe returned her smile. "How was the meeting?"

"It was fine, Gabriel, thank you," she said, hoping to deter further questions. She wanted a nap, a drink or someone to rub the tension out of her shoulders. Her thoughts drifted to Jo's soft hands—but she jerked them back quickly.

"So what's on my agenda for the rest of the day?" she asked him, trying to rein in her thoughts.

"Let's see here," Gabe said, turning to his computer screen. "It looks like we've got you pretty well booked up." He pivoted the monitor to allow her to see the calendar.

"Good. Let's get all caught up. Thanks for the hard work," Madeline said before turning down the hallway to return to her office.

It was best to keep busy these days.

* * *

Antonio's had been her mother's choice for their lunch date. The whole thing had been her mother's idea actually. The atmosphere at the overly elegant, overpriced Italian restaurant reminded her too much of her childhood. The Carson family was all for show. Her mother's black dress, pearls, intricately manicured nails, and newest Dooeny and Bourke bag all assured Jo that nothing had changed.

She looked down again at the pencil skirt she had chosen for the day to appease her. It wasn't going to be enough. It never was. But she was not her mother, although the two of them looked almost identical. Staring across the table at her, she could clearly see what she would look like in a few years. The same hair, same green eyes, same smile. Her mother had hardly aged, it seemed.

There was a difference in their expressions, though. At least she hoped so. Her mother's was more stern, more focused, more ruled by expectation. The expectations had never changed nor had the commands that came with them. *Sit up straight. Smile. You can't wear that. Don't say that. What will people think?* Jo had heard those and other admonitions a million times. As she sat stiffly across from her mother, they were the only things she could think of.

"So, are you seeing anyone?" her mother asked, raising an eyebrow while directing upon her the soul-piercing gaze that Jo had known her entire life, her mother's way of nonverbally heaping on pressure.

Jo had been waiting for the deeper issues to surface. "Not at the moment, Mom." She took a bite of a breadstick, hoping that having her mouth full would excuse her from making further comments at the moment.

"Jo, you know you can't just work your life away, right?"

Instead of replying, Jo simply waited, knowing her mother would soon continue her speech.

She didn't disappoint. Martha Carson was nothing, if not predictable. "I mean, there's still a chance, even at your age, that you will find someone. You have to put yourself out there, though. Be approachable."

Jo fought the urge to snap back that she *was* approachable and wasn't sitting at home pining for someone to sweep her off her feet. Her mother wouldn't appreciate hearing the truth, though: that most of the time she was the approacher—always on the lookout for a cute girl with a pretty smile to take home. That's where Madeline had been different—dangerously so. She wasn't some unfocused girl with no expectations other than one night. She was refined, intelligent, driven and complex.

She focused on eating the Caesar salad in front of her. One bite at a time, she'd dutifully consume it and the sermons being served up by her well-meaning mother. And then she'd go on with her life.

"Maybe you could meet him at work," her mother mused.

Are we still on this? And why did I take off of work for it? Jo silently wondered how her mother could go on and on about finding the love of your life when she herself was so unhappily married.

"Are there any nice, handsome, eligible men at work, honey?"

"No." Jo quickly dismissed her mother's fantasy.

"Oh, well, what about at church? Are you still attending regularly?"

"I go when I can, Mom, and, no, there are not any men I'm interested in at the church."

Not at the church—not anywhere.

"How are you and Dad? What's new with you all?" Maybe if she could change the subject, things would move more quickly.

"We're doing well. He has been up at the church working late every night to prepare for the big revival we are having in a few weeks, and I've been working on our latest remodel. When are you coming home next? You'll have to see what we've done with the place. You will hardly recognize it."

"I'll have to come check it out sometime," Jo agreed, trying her best to sound enthusiastic.

"Tulsa *is* only two hours away. We're close enough to visit you, and your father is always visiting churches here, speaking at events and helping organize community events. This is his hometown, after all. The road goes both ways, you know. Remember—he is the one who helped you secure your job. His connections with the churches here, his acquaintance with Madeline and his deep pockets helped pave the way. That—and the fact that we're your parents—should warrant an occasional day trip, at least. Sometimes I think you forget that."

Always pressing, pushing and prodding. "I don't forget. I just work close to twice the hours a normal person does in a week."

Her mother's eyes widened. "Oh," she said, drawing the sound out longer than necessary. "Speaking of work, what is happening with your boss?"

"She's going through a rough time." Jo didn't want to discuss Madeline. She tapped her foot under the table nervously, wishing she were back at the office.

"Well, the media was all over the story for a while. You probably saw…They interviewed that lady a while back—the one her husband was caught with. Pretty woman, but not too bright, if you ask me. She sat there and admitted nothing. It was like interviewing someone who can't speak."

"Maybe she had nothing to say," Jo said. "What would you say if you were caught fooling around with the husband of someone famous?"

"I would never," her mother replied, obviously offended.

"Mom, that's not what I meant. I meant if you put yourself in her shoes, you probably wouldn't want to talk about it anyway. But, having said that, I think she's an adulterous whore."

"Jo Carson, watch how you speak in public," Martha scolded.

"Sorry," Jo muttered. Nothing had changed between the two of them since Jo was a toddler, it seemed.

"I can't believe how working for politics has turned you into such a crass person."

"I'm not crass. I'm just tired. I said I was sorry." Jo went back to eating her salad.

"Very well, we'll forget about all of that. But back to your boss. Is this all going to blow over? She wasn't in the news today, but there are bound to be things that people still want to know. Is she going to stay at that hotel they caught her in the other day? Is she going to get a new house? Is she going to run for another term?" The questions poured out of Martha's mouth like a faucet running at full blast.

"All that is being made public is what you have seen on the news."

Martha looked like she was going to pry for more details, but Jo wanted off the subject. "So, tell me about the new Bible study you're leading."

And, just like that, they were onto another subject. Jo breathed a sigh of relief. Her mother continued talking as Jo ate, laying down her fork only when she heard the familiar ding of her BlackBerry.

"Excuse me, Mom," she said, holding up her finger to halt her mother's story—not that she was paying any attention.

It was a text message from Gabe. "Will you bring back some lunch for M? I have her working straight through a break."

Jo pictured walking into Madeline's office with a peace offering of lunch and having Madeline actually speak to her—instead of brushing her off as she had been doing. The thought of having a conversation with her made Jo smile. Too late she remembered that her mother was watching her like a hawk. She tried to recover.

"Oh," once again Martha drug out the sound too long. It was starting to get on Jo's nerves. "Who is that from?"

"It's just work. One of my co-workers," she said.

"Why the big smile then?"

"Oh, it's nothing." Jo glanced back down at her phone and began typing a reply. "Sure thing." She clicked the send button and set it down on the table.

"Jo, don't leave that phone on the table," Martha reprimanded.

"Sorry," she said, putting it in her lap. "They are having some trouble locating one of the files they need to reference, and I have it. They're looking for it but are going to call if they need me to come back in to find it for them."

"You work too hard and spend too much time on that thing," Martha said. "Shouldn't a girl like you be less worried about running back into the office and more worried about sitting here, having lunch with your mother?"

"What do you mean 'a girl like me'?" Jo questioned, hating the fact her mother still regarded as her a child—and one of a certain type, no less.

"I just mean a girl who has so little in her personal life. You should be focused on finding a suitable husband or at least seeing your family from time to time."

"I don't want a husband," Jo shot back.

Martha Carson looked as if she had been slapped across the face.

"And why not?" she asked incredulously.

Jo reached into her purse under the table and pulled out her personal phone. Using a trick she had learned a long time ago, she used it to speed-dial her BlackBerry number. When that rang, she grabbed it with the other hand and hung up the phone so that it didn't echo. *Saved by the bell*, she thought, breathing a sigh of relief.

She glanced down at the screen immediately. "It's my boss, Mom. Hold that thought," she added, even though she wanted Martha to think about anything else than why she might not want a husband.

"Hello?" Jo answered.

She paused a moment, pretending to listen.

"Uh, yes. I have it on my computer. Were you not able to find it?" she asked, improvising her end of the conversation.

With one more believable pause, she added, "I understand. I'll be there as soon as possible."

She hung up the phone. "I'm sorry, Mom. I've got to go. I'll visit soon." It was a lie, but hopefully it would get her mother off her back.

Quickly, she stood, dropped cash on the table for her half of the check and hugged her mother. She ignored her mother's urging her to pick up the money and let her treat her to lunch. "I do love you, Mom, even if we don't always agree." She kissed her on the top of the head and left. For a moment, she felt guilty, but her fight-or-flight instincts were too strong to allow her to stick around Martha any longer than she had to.

On the drive back to the office, she put on some angry rock music, letting the sounds of Five Finger Death Punch take her into another dimension, where she could think more quickly, sort through what she was feeling and bang her head to the music a bit. Her thoughts raced to the beat of the music. What was she doing in this situation? Was staying in this job worth continually being thrown onto an emotional roller coaster every time Madeline glanced in her direction? She had never fallen for anyone the way she had for Madeline. Was it simply because it was all too taboo to be real?

She prided herself on being independent, on steering clear of tied-down relationships of the sort that tended to choke the life out of people. Growing up, she had witnessed the way her father controlled her mother, the ways he held his job, his money, his power over her head. Had seen how, out of duty and out of overwhelming love for the man, her mother had stayed.

The way Jo saw it, her mother was trapped. Trapped by love and, given the tenets of her faith, trapped forever. It was one of the reasons Jo had so carefully avoided commitment herself.

That was not the real issue now, of course. The issue was that she wanted—more than anything—to give into love. For as long as she had been running from commitment, she had known—or hoped, at least—that someday someone would come along and stop her in her tracks. Someone who would make doing so worth it.

Madeline could not—would not—be that one. Jo steeled herself, gripping the steering wheel tighter. It was wrong, and she admired Madeline for putting a stop to it. At the same time, she hated herself for wanting it so badly, for spending so many nights fantasizing about Madeline's touch.

Her BlackBerry rang.

"Hello?" Jo answered.

"Hey. Where are you at?" Gabe asked.

"Shit," Jo answered. "Sorry. I forgot about lunch. I'll stop and grab her something and be back in just a few."

"No worries," he added. "I have to hustle off to a meeting off site, but she should be free in about twenty minutes if you want to run it into her office for me."

Jo swallowed and let out a sigh. "Sounds good. Thanks, Gabe."

"No, thank you, Jo. I appreciate it," he said before hanging up.

The last thing she wanted to do at this point, fantasies aside, was to waltz into Madeline's office and put herself through more torture. Still, if she was going to continue working there, she would have to face the music at some point.

She pulled into a Wendy's drive-through and ordered Madeline a chicken wrap. Not the most dignified lunch for the mayor, but it would have to suffice.

All the way back to the office, she reminded herself that she was simply an employee, doing her job and making sure that her boss's needs were met. Unfortunately, that's what had gotten her into this mess. As she approached Madeline's door, she felt like a nervous schoolgirl having to confront someone who had rejected her invitation to the school dance. She took a steadying breath and knocked on the door.

"Come in," Madeline replied.

Jo opened the door with a newfound confidence. She would drop off lunch and return to her cubicle. The surprise on Madeline's face when she saw her was evident, and Jo's confidence drained away as quickly as it had arisen. It was one of their unspoken rules. Jo had not passed the threshold of Madeline's door since she had been asked to keep her distance. But now, here she stood, chicken wrap in hand.

The fire in Madeline's eyes was hard to disguise. Jo stood wrapped in it, unable to move, chills running up and down her spine.

"What can I do for you, Josephine?" Madeline asked finally.

"Uh...sorry," Jo said, pulling herself together. "Gabe said you needed lunch."

Madeline's mouth curved into a half smile, but it did little to curb the intensity that still showed in her eyes. "Thank you."

Jo nodded and set the wrap on Madeline's desk. "Enjoy," she said, awkwardly, wanting to stay. Wanting to do so many things that were not permissible.

"I will," Madeline answered, her eyes never wavering from Jo's.

Jo decided to take a chance. "Can we talk sometime?" she asked quietly.

"I don't think that's a good idea," Madeline replied.

Why does her voice have to be so damn sultry? Jo wondered. "Okay, then," she said with a sigh and turned from the office.

Back at her cubicle, she found it impossible to focus. It was ridiculous how Madeline unnerved her. She couldn't take this anymore. There was a reason she was nobody's girl; she refused to act like some damn lost puppy, begging to be let into a house.

The passion she had felt minutes before turned to a burning anger. She hadn't been the one to kiss Madeline. She hadn't done anything wrong, but she was the one being punished. Without second-guessing her newly discovered bitterness, she opened up the word processing software on her office computer and began typing furiously.

It was time to take a stand.

CHAPTER EIGHTEEN

Natalie Longworth took a drag of her cigarette. Glancing down at her bright red nails, she shuddered. When had she become this person? She was all dolled up, hoping to meet a nice, rich man to take her home for the night. "Sugar daddy bait," she called it.

That was what it had been with John. Of course, she had known who he was. Anyone with a fucking television knew who he was, knew who his wife was.

Natalie knew a little bit more about his little wifey than most, though—at least she thought she did. Maddie hadn't broadcast the shit she had done in college. If she had, she'd have never been elected mayor, for one thing, and for another the media already would have caught wind of the connection between Maddie and her.

As it was, John would be paying her to keep their secrets. She'd told him if he didn't pay up, she'd go to the press with the fact that she used to share a bed with the high and mighty mayor. She meant Maddie no harm, but she needed the money. And John had been more than willing to pay up.

"That's my secret to tell," he had said. She didn't know what the hell he had meant by that, but it had put a few thousand bucks in her pocket, so she wasn't complaining.

Part of her had felt guilty when she had seen Maddie on the news. She just appeared frazzled—until they thrust the picture of Natalie into her face.

"Do you know this woman?" the TV reporter had asked, desperate for a story.

Maddie had said nothing, but the look on her face spoke volumes. It was a mix of fresh heartache and bitterness.

Good, conservative Maddie had never been big on threesomes, so Natalie was pretty sure it was the first time she had to deal with the fact that someone she had fucked had been fucked by her husband. Maybe that's why she had done it, Natalie thought. Because after everything they had together, Maddie had turned ultraconservative and thrown the book at the gay community. Sure, Natalie had cheated back in the day. It had only happened once, at a drunken party, but Natalie's apologies were met with nothing but an inability to forgive. As she remembered it, they had broken each other's hearts. Her fleeting infidelity had apparently turned Maddie cold and bitter.

Natalie, on the other hand, had continued to live it up every chance she got. She smiled, thinking about the women she had dated, the men she had dated, all the fun she had enjoyed in the past twenty years. She wasn't getting any younger, and her insatiable appetite for thrills seemed to increase with every passing year.

Maddie had needed out of that marriage, of that there was no doubt. And Natalie had needed the money, so she let John Stratton fuck her brains out. It was as simple as that.

Still she couldn't help the emptiness that nagged at her heart as she thought about the questions Maddie would have to answer at some point. Sooner or later, the truth was bound to surface, and when it did, when people learned that Maddie knew her and how, all hell would break loose.

Behind her, she heard a loud whistle. "Hey there, gorgeous."

She turned, feigning disinterest, all the while wondering if this was going to be tonight's payout. She wasn't a prostitute, she told herself time and time again, but sometimes it felt like it. After all, men never actually paid to have sex with her. They paid later—to keep her from going to their wives, to keep her around because she was one hell of a lay or to keep their secrets for themselves, as John Stratton had.

The man who had let out the catcall approached her. "Oh, hey, you're that girl."

Dammit. John Stratton might not have been worth it, after all.

"What are you talking about?" Natalie asked innocently.

"The one that Mayor Stratton's husband was seen with. It's you, isn't it?"

She sighed and turned away. Although part of her wanted to tell this jackass he was wrong, she decided it wasn't worth the fight.

As she walked the five blocks back to her rundown apartment complex, she tried to remember the last time life had seemed worth the fight. As if she were watching them on a television screen, memories played back in her mind. She loved to party, but she always ended up with the same old empty feelings inside the next morning. So it couldn't have been her party days. She went further back in time, until she saw a genuine smile on her face. She had been an artist with promise back in the day. She had genuine talent. Her art professors had said so, and she had won awards.

But none of that had mattered as much as the praise she received from Maddie. "I believe in you. You're going to take the world by storm, babe," Maddie had said, planting a sweet kiss on Natalie's lips.

She recalled the night she had drawn Maddie, sketching every inch of that amazing body. The result had been a masterpiece—not because of her talent, but because of Maddie's sheer perfection.

"Oh, Maddie," she whispered, as tears streaked her face. What had she done?

* * *

Reality did not become less real in dim light. That was unfortunate, John thought, as he scratched the stubble on his face. He stumbled around the big, empty house, wishing the divorce proceedings would hurry themselves along so they could sell it and he'd get his half. At least when he had returned to it, he'd found that the news cameras no longer gave a damn about him. That was happy news.

When the news first had come out, for a few days anyway, he had felt like a stud—like Tiger Woods had to have felt when the whole world knew that he could get laid any day he wanted. Now he felt more like a leper. Women around the state seemed to be making him the target of their anger—at least that's how it felt when they shot him go-to-hell looks and scurried by him on the streets as if he were a piece of garbage. As soon as the divorce came through, he was going get the hell out of town—out of the state even. Then when he walked down the street, women wouldn't point and stare as though he had the plague.

In the meantime, clearly, he wasn't going to be getting laid any time soon, not unless he was willing to shell out some money. In the shape he was in, that might not be a bad idea, he thought. As he stretched out in his recliner to mull the possibility over, his phone rang.

Natalie calling, the screen read.

Maybe he wouldn't have to hire a professional, since he was already paying one. Sure, she was a blood-sucking scoundrel, but since he had already paid her off, he wouldn't mind fucking her again. He laughed and answered.

"Miss me already?"

"Fuck you, John." Her tone told him two things—she was drunk, and she didn't want to deal with any bullshit.

He cleared his throat. "What's going on, Natalie?"

"I need to get in touch with Maddie."

"You should have tried that before you slept with her husband. I doubt she wants anything to do with you now." John knew it was the truth. More importantly, he couldn't let her get in the way of his plans.

"John, I'll go to the press with this if you don't give me her number," Natalie threatened.

"No, you won't. I paid you, remember that, you lying whore?" John's blood boiled as he spoke the words.

"It's about more than the money." Natalie's voice trembled, but John could tell she wasn't backing down any time soon.

"What do you want? You want more money?"

"No," Natalie paused as if thinking the question over and then continued. "No. I don't want more money. I want to talk to Maddie."

John resisted the urge to hang up the phone. He needed to have Natalie's word that she wouldn't spill the beans. If Madeline wasn't trying to cover up a secret, she had no reason to pay him off. "What's it going to take for me to get you to drop this whole thing?" John finally asked.

"I want her phone number. That's all."

"No deal. What else?"

There was an angry sigh on the other end of the line. "I've got in my hand the number of the guy who interviewed me from Channel 4."

John's heart rate quickened as she read the number aloud.

"You tell me what it's going to be, John. I can call this number, or you can give me Maddie's."

He had no choice, and if there was anything John hated, it was being trapped.

"Fine. Don't expect her to answer," he said, reluctantly reciting from memory the number of Madeline's work Blackberry.

"That'll be all," Natalie said.

He wanted to tell her that she was damn right that would be all. He never wanted to hear from her again, but she had already hung up. A dial tone buzzed in his ear, and he threw his phone across the room, watching it as it collided with the wall and shattered.

CHAPTER NINETEEN

Jacquelyn felt the effects of the wine flow through her like tiny fingers running up and down her body. At one point in her life, she would have insisted she was merely "tipsy," but she was woman enough to admit that tonight she was drunk.

She rose from her seat at the bar. Every night since the news of the affair broke, this little place called Larry's had been her escape from the hellish time she was having.

Sure, Madeline had returned to work—but did it really matter? She no longer interacted much with any of the staff—including Jo. She dismissed the importance of on-camera interviews unless they were in the form of ten-second sound bites.

In fact, she had lost her edge. Her fire was almost totally gone when she gave speeches. Much as Jacquelyn would like to blame that on Jo, the speeches themselves were still good ones. It was the speaker who was at fault. The passion that had helped Madeline pull in piles of campaign donations three years ago had all but disappeared.

At the same time, in a strange way, she appeared to be happier than anyone had ever seen her. She just didn't appear to want to be mayor—or a mayoral candidate—anymore. She was slacking off, shirking her public duties, and people were beginning to notice.

In light of her apparent apathy, Ian had questioned her about her intentions to run for reelection. He had recounted the event to Jacquelyn later with obvious confusion.

"She says she wants to run, but she didn't seem convinced," he had told her, scratching his head. "She sounded like a parrot, repeating things she had said a thousand times before, and she wouldn't look me in the eye. When I pressed, she told me that she couldn't handle another major shift in her life right now and that she still has things she wants to accomplish in office."

The fact of the matter was that Madeline was being irresponsible, and Jacqueline had decided to follow suit. If Madeline didn't care, why should the staff? Each night, she drank until she felt a little out of control, and then she took a cab home. Tonight, though, she was feeling a little more adventuresome. She wanted to take it a step further.

"What would Madeline do?" she asked aloud to no one in particular, laughing at her own joke. Actually, Madeline would probably duck out of here and go hide out somewhere. Jacquelyn laughed at this thought too, hiccupping from the alcohol.

She stumbled and fell into a man sitting at the bar.

"Are you okay?" he asked, helping her back onto her feet.

"Thanks. I'm good." She smiled at him. He was pretty attractive, at least to her drunken brain, she thought. "Are you okay?"

He smiled. "I'm fine, thanks. By the way, I think we have actually met before. I'm Isaac Williams. Do you remember me?"

"Oh shit," she said, covering her face. The TV guy was here. Was he going to run a story on what a drunken mess the mayor's communications director was becoming? "I'm going home," she managed to blurt out before turning to walk away.

"Hey, wait," Isaac called, slapping some money down on the bar to pay for his drinks.

She continued walking until she was right outside the door. She would wait fifteen seconds to see if he followed, but if he didn't, she would continue home. She started counting aloud. She was only at two when he burst through the door.

"Jacquelyn," he said as he reached her. "I just wanted to tell you not to worry. I'm not filming right now, and besides, I wouldn't do that to you. You saved my job for me by calling me first that night."

His smile grew and she relaxed some. He wasn't going to blow her cover. The last thing she needed right now was a public fall from grace. Even with Madeline's apparent aloofness, it probably wouldn't be long before Jo would get a promotion of some sort. The natural progression for speechwriters was to move on to becoming communications directors. For Jo to reap the reward of all of her ass kissing, someone had to get the boot. That someone was probably Jacquelyn, so she had been making sure to walk the line.

"Thanks for not saying anything."

"Oh, of course," Isaac said. "That's the last thing you all need right now. I imagine life is hell for all of you."

"You have no idea," Jacquelyn answered.

"I'm living in the back of a news van," Isaac said, pointing across the parking lot. "I think I probably have a pretty good idea of what hell looks like."

They laughed, and she leaned in close, drawing in his scent. It had been a while since she had stood close enough to a man to let the smell of his cologne linger on her senses.

She smiled up at him. "You schmell good," she slurred. "Either that or I'm drunk, but I think you actually schm...smell good."

He laughed and stumbled a bit. He was as drunk as she was—if not more so.

"You smell good too," he said. "And I know it's not because I'm drunk."

"Oh yeah? Look at you, Mr. Sober Man." She imitated his staggering walk.

They both started laughing hysterically, and Jacquelyn leaned against the wall for support. After a moment, she caught her breath and turned to face Isaac.

"Are you going to kiss me?" she asked, suddenly wishing that sober people could just ask the things drunk people did. Life would be easier if you could just say what you wanted.

"Well, we do have a lot in common. I mean, we both smell good, and we both hate our jobs," Isaac said, stepping closer to her so that their faces were only inches apart. "The real question is, do you want me to kiss you?"

Embracing her new risk-taking side, Jacquelyn did not reply. Instead she grabbed the back of his neck and pulled him in to kiss him wildly and drunkenly. It was a sloppy kiss, but he didn't seem to mind. He returned it just as wildly.

A witty comment popped into her head, and she giggled, breaking apart their kiss.

"Did I do something wrong?" Isaac asked, suddenly self-conscious.

"No." She was still laughing. Drunk Jacquelyn was hilarious, she thought. She loved when she made herself laugh. When she was sober, people said she wasn't that funny. That's why she had decided she liked being drunk, because then, at least *she* thought she was funny.

"Well, then what is it?" he asked.

"I was just going to ask if this was off the record."

He laughed, and Jacquelyn decided right then that she liked him. If he laughed at her jokes, that was good enough.

Isaac caressed her right breast. "That wasn't off the record, but this is," he said, rubbing his hand in a circular motion.

She let out a low moan. "Take me home, Isaac."

It was as simple as that. She was going to be dangerous, and she was going to enjoy it.

* * *

Jo had two envelopes sitting on her bedside table. Her brightly illuminated bedroom and an unruffled pillow mocked the fact that it was three a.m. and she had not even laid down. Thoughts of the day's events and her awkward lunch delivery continually played through her head. When her BlackBerry rang, she reached for it automatically.

Answering the phone in the middle of the night had become routine in college—you never knew when someone had made a smart decision to call for a ride home after too many drinks. Jo had had a deal with her friends. If they called—and she wasn't drunk too—she would come and give them a ride. Now, in the line of work she was in, middle of the night calls sometimes meant that there was an emergency.

"Hello?"

A woman's voice filled the line. "I'm sorry to call so late."

"No…it's fine." Jo couldn't place the voice. "I just needed to talk to you," the woman said shakily.

"Who is this?" Jo asked.

"Please don't hang up," the woman asked frantically.

"I'm not hanging up," Jo said. "Who is this?"

There was a moment of silence. Jo was tempted to hang up and put herself to bed, but she remembered the raw emotion with which the woman had begged her not to hang up. Compassion for the unknown caller filled Jo, even as tired as she was.

"Hello?" Jo tried again.

"It's Natalie."

Jo had heard the name Natalie enough in the news throughout the past two weeks to have the name stop her in her tracks. There were a lot of people named Natalie, though, and there would be no way for John's mistress to know who Jo was.

"Natalie who?" Jo said, clearing her throat.

"Maddie, it's me."

"I think you have the wrong number," Jo said, trying to steady her breath. She couldn't imagine how anyone involved in Madeline's personal life would have her work number.

"Please don't hang up," Natalie pleaded. "I need to tell you I'm sorry."

And I need to tell you to fuck off, Jo thought. This woman had the nerve to screw with Madeline's life so badly by sleeping with her husband and then want to say she was sorry. Jo was disgusted.

"Look, I don't know anyone named Natalie, and my name isn't Maddie." Jo's voice had turned into a hiss. "I'm sorry, but you have the wrong number."

Jo clicked the phone off, but as soon as she did, the same number was calling again. She answered and hung up without speaking. The truth seeped in. Madeline did, in fact, know the woman—enough for Natalie to call her "Maddie." Putting the puzzle pieces of possibility together, she gasped. If this was the Natalie from Madeline's college years, the threat of information leaking was much higher. Her heart was pounding, and fear of being outed warred for precedence over sympathy for Madeline's broken heart. She couldn't make sense of why anyone would have her number—or what that might mean about what else had been disclosed.

Quickly, she dialed Madeline's cell phone, not caring that it was the middle of the night, fears about someone finding out her secret beginning to fly through her mind.

"Hello?" Madeline answered groggily, obviously having been woken up by the call.

"It's Jo. Who did you give this number to?" she asked, accusingly.

"What the fuck, Jo? It's three in the morning."

"I know what fucking time it is. But I just got a call on my BlackBerry. A woman asking for you, calling you 'Maddie.' What have you been telling people about us, and why are you giving them my number?" She was angry and trying to figure out what kind of games Madeline was playing at, diverting personal calls to Jo. She shouldn't have to put up with this after everything she had already done.

"I haven't said anything." Madeline sounded drained. "And you promised not to call me. Do I need to fire you right here, right now?"

The threat didn't scare Jo. Hell, it might be easier if she was fired. She glanced at the letters on her bedside table.

"There's no need for that," she said stiffly. "But, seriously, did you say anything to anyone? Why is *Natalie* calling me—of all people?"

There was silence. "You spoke with Natalie?" The question sounded as though it came from a wounded child.

"I sure did." The mix of anger, confusion and fear Jo felt erased all her inhibitions. "She wanted to apologize. Me, on the other hand, I have some questions I want answers to. Let me start with these. Is the Natalie who slept with your husband the same as Natalie, your ex? Because she sure seemed to think of you as a friend. And if that's the case, why the hell is she calling me?"

Madeline's breathing had become uneven, and Jo felt hers match the pace.

"She's the same woman," Madeline finally answered. "And I'm not sure how she got your number. I certainly haven't spoken to her. John knew I was staying with a staff member, but he didn't know who. I don't know what else to say. I'm trying to absorb all of this as well."

"Okay. I think we're done here. Thanks." Jo knew the words were cold, but she was tired of turning the other cheek. If taking a stand meant being brusque and high-handed, so be it. She glanced at the envelopes and nodded, her decisions validated. Before Madeline could say anything in response, Jo hung up.

So, John knew that Madeline was staying with a staff member, though not which one, and he had once had access to staff contact information. That wasn't enough to explain things, though. Especially since the media had reported that the mayor was now living in a local hotel.

She studied her phone, racking her brain for other explanations. As she fiddled with the buttons on it, she realized that her BlackBerry number and Madeline's were identical except for one number and the digits that differed were one above the other, which could lead to misdialing. That would make more sense, especially with an upset caller, but it still left her unnerved.

She was thinking about calling to apologize and asking if Madeline thought the call could have been the result of an accidental dialing of a five instead of a two when the phone rang again, flashing the same number on the screen. This Natalie was nothing if not persistent. Jo reached over and hit the ignore call button. She did it another dozen times before the caller finally gave up and she was able to slip into bed and try to forget the way Madeline's voice still got to her.

CHAPTER TWENTY

The Spanish tile gleamed, and the interior was breathtaking. There was an island in the kitchen where breakfasts could be served or friends could gather during a party. The living area was spacious, and the Jacuzzi tub in the master bath alluring. Yet all Madeline saw was the windows.

There were windows everywhere. In this house, there would be no privacy—no chance of ever giving into the passions she felt. Even with the next house a good distance away, Madeline felt as if she were on display.

It was Saturday, and she had gone to look at houses as she had promised Ian. This was the fifth she had seen, and though it was by far the nicest, it made her very uneasy.

"I think it's time for me to head to the office for a bit," Madeline told the Realtor, trying to let her down easily. The truth was that she wasn't ready to decide on anything yet, not with her whole life so up in the air.

"Okay, well, please let me know if you need anything," the Realtor offered, extending her hand for a handshake.

"I will. Thank you," Madeline offered as kindly as possible.

She headed back to her car, still feeling unsettled. She wasn't sure yet that she wanted to serve a second term as mayor. Or if she wanted to live in Oklahoma City anymore if she didn't. What she would do with a whole house to herself anyway?

To further complicate matters, Jo's call last night was driving her crazy. The fact that Natalie had broken through to not only her personal life, but also to her professional life was as frightening as the way she had reacted to Jo's voice on the phone.

She drove back to the hotel, stopping for a bottle of tequila on the way. At some point, she had stopped caring about buying alcohol in public, though she was careful about where she did it. In the shadier parts of town, no one even knew that she was mayor. They didn't seem to care about anything as long as she had cash.

The fact that she felt the need to take even that much care upset her, though. She was done worrying about all of this. It was time to hang it up, she decided. There would be no second term for her. She wasn't sure how to break the news to her staff, but she was certain now that she was done.

* * *

Tired and frustrated from the previous night's events, Jo stared at the envelopes on her bedside table, trying not to overthink her decision. She had been staring at them for the better part of the day, regretting that she'd have to wait until Monday to deliver them. If she weren't afraid of having a face-to-face conversation in a hotel room with Madeline, she would march them over to her immediately. She needed out, and it needed to happen now.

Working in politics was *not* the place for her any longer. She didn't know what was, though, or where she'd go from here. She couldn't keep living a lie, pretending to be someone she wasn't. Leading a double life was exhausting. She needed out of the spotlight and out of the line of Madeline's confusing stares.

The rain beating against her windows echoed the call in her heart. The day's weather had gone from sunny and cool to rainy, dark and cold in an instant, a reflection of how she felt. It was time for a clean slate—time for everything to be washed away.

She watched the rain stream down the window and, having come to a decision, felt the storm within her heart begin to ease. She could now freely admit to herself that she had fallen for Madeline Stratton, just as she could admit that it was a stupid thing to do. It was time to move on to a new job, possibly even a new city. Most importantly, it was time to move on from Madeline.

A knock on the front door interrupted her thoughts. She got out of her chair, no longer surprised by the arrival of guests at odd hours. Her apartment had become the go-to spot for confused or curious co-workers, it seemed. She flung the door open without checking the peephole, resigned to the fact that it would be someone from the office. Her breath caught in her throat at the sight of Madeline, soaked to the skin from the rain.

For a moment, neither of them spoke. Words would have only interrupted the intensity of the stare they shared. Looking deeply into Madeline's eyes, Jo felt her body tense, her every nerve tingle. She wanted this woman more than she had ever wanted anyone.

She cleared her throat. "Do you want to come in?"

"Thanks," Madeline said, stepping into Jo's apartment unsteadily.

She was drunk. Jo checked quickly to see if she had driven over and was relieved not to spot her car in the parking lot. Thank god Madeline's hotel was within walking distance—for her sake and that of everyone else on the road tonight. "Are you okay?"

"I shouldn't be here," Madeline said. "But I needed to see you."

"I'm glad you are," Jo said. "I have something I need to tell you."

"It can wait," Madeline said, throwing her arms around Jo's neck.

Everything inside of her told her to run, but Jo couldn't resist. Like a magnet, she was drawn into Madeline's embrace and easily melted into her arms. Powerless to resist anymore, she kissed her passionately. Madeline tugged at the T-shirt she had been lounging in.

"We shouldn't," Jo replied weakly as Madeline clawed at the material covering Jo's body.

"Fuck what we should and shouldn't do. I want you," Madeline replied hurriedly, running her hands down Jo's arms and then across her breasts. She circled the now-hardened outline of Jo's nipples, causing her to gasp.

As Madeline's thumbs continued to brush her nipples, Jo knew there was no turning back—not for her, at least. The tension that had been building between them for weeks was demanding to be unleashed.

"Are you sure?" Jo didn't know if she could stop now, but she didn't want Madeline jumping into something if she wasn't ready.

"I'm sure," Madeline said in a sultry voice.

"You let me know if you want to stop at any point, okay?" Jo offered, hoping Madeline would never want to stop.

Madeline's only reply was to push Jo to the couch and position her body over Jo's. She slipped her tongue into Jo's mouth and massaged it against Jo's tongue, continuing to tease Jo's nipples with her fingers.

Jo wasn't about to let Madeline have all the fun. She reached up, pulling Madeline's shirt over her head and expertly unhooked her bra, allowing Madeline's beautiful breasts to bounce free.

"You're beautiful," Jo said, savoring the sight of Madeline before grabbing a breast in each hand. "So beautiful."

She leaned up and flicked one of Madeline's hard nipples with her tongue. To her delight, Madeline moaned. Not wasting another second, she wrapped her lips around the nipple and began to suck, laving Madeline's hardness with her tongue.

Madeline had begun to pant. "Oh, Jo," she moaned, twisting her body in pleasure.

Jo paused for a moment to steal a kiss, trying to convey her hunger and her intent to please Madeline as she had never been pleased before.

"Tell me what you want me to do."

"Fuck me, Jo. I want you to fuck me." Madeline's bright blue eyes were on fire, burning with lust.

"I will." Jo teased Madeline's other nipple with a flick of the tongue. "But not just yet. I want to take my time with you."

"Please," Madeline begged, as though she couldn't wait much longer.

Jo responded by sucking one nipple again while she rolled the other around with her fingers. She knelt by the couch, removing Madeline's pants and underwear to reveal what she had been hungry for all this time.

Madeline was hot, and Jo was going to enjoy every second of this. She laid Madeline down on her back and climbed on top. Jo kissed her again and then trailed down to kiss her neck and nibble her ear. With each caress, each kiss, Madeline moaned more loudly and breathed harder.

Gently and tenderly, Jo kissed her way down Madeline's body, caressing each inch with her tongue. Glancing up to look Madeline in the eye, she saw there a hunger every bit as real as her own.

She made her way in between Madeline's legs, though she wasn't ready to give in to Madeline's begging just yet. She licked her thighs, making Madeline moan and lift her hips up, pleading with Jo to release her.

Jo breathed in, mesmerized by the scent of Madeline. Finally, she tasted her. Madeline was wet and tense, and as Jo's tongue went to work, Madeline went off like a rocket.

"Jo!" she screamed as she arched her back, exploding in a release of ecstasy.

As she finished, Jo smiled and moved to lie beside her on the couch. She kissed her gently and wrapped her arm around Madeline's still quivering body.

"That was incredible," Madeline finally managed.

"My pleasure," Jo whispered, kissing the back of Madeline's neck.

"I want to do the same for you."

"I want that too," Jo replied. "But this was about you. We should get some rest."

Jo wanted badly to let Madeline return the favor. She also knew that Madeline was exhausted and drunk. And she had enjoyed making love to Madeline almost as much as she enjoyed having a good orgasm. So, overall, it was a glorious night.

In fact, Jo decided, there was nothing that could ruin this night. The question that had been plaguing her had been answered: Madeline wanted Jo every bit as much as Jo wanted her. And soon there would be nothing to make what they were doing wrong. With a smile, she grabbed Madeline's hand.

"Do you want to stay?"

Concern and confusion clouded Madeline's eyes again. Apparently, she had sobered up enough to remember all the reasons they shouldn't be together.

"You don't have to," Jo said. "But I would like for you to, if you want." She leaned down and kissed her, gently this time. "It's totally up to you."

"I want to stay, very much," Madeline answered. "But is that crossing a line?"

"I think we've already crossed that line," Jo said with a laugh.

"Just one night," Madeline agreed.

"Come on," Jo said, standing and extending her hand to Madeline. "Let's go to bed."

Together, they walked to Jo's bedroom. Jo took off her clothes. "I want to lie with you, skin on skin, if that's okay with you."

Madeline nodded and smiled, drunk on a mixture of tequila and pleasure. She lay down, and Jo lay beside her, draping her arm around Madeline. In seconds, both were asleep.

* * *

Jo leaned down and softly kissed Madeline's neck.

Madeline stirred, having fallen asleep after being pleasured a second time. A sweet smile crossed her face, relieving Jo's fears that she might wake up unhappy about what had happened.

"Are you ready to go again already?" Madeline asked, pulling her in for a kiss.

"I'm always ready to go again," Jo said with a laugh, "but right now, I'm just taking it all in."

Lazily, Madeline reached up and fondled Jo's breasts. "You're pretty damn hot, Jo," she said.

Jo laughed. "So are you." With a soft kiss, Jo broke their contact.

Reaching across to her bedside table, Jo grabbed the envelopes sitting there. Now was the perfect time to tell Madeline what she had been planning.

"These are for you," she said, handing them to Madeline.

"What are they?"

"The last two things I will ever write for you," Jo said. "My letter of resignation and your own resignation speech—should you choose to use it at some point."

Jo couldn't gauge the look on Madeline's face.

"You're quitting?"

"Yes. I can't do it anymore," Jo said.

"Well, that's probably a good thing," Madeline said, a smile growing on her face.

"Why's that?"

"Because otherwise you would be fired," she said, laughing.

"What for?"

"For fucking your boss," Madeline said, pulling Jo back on top of her.

Jo kissed her passionately before pulling back. "What about the speech?"

"We'll talk about that after round three," Madeline said, reaching down to touch Jo.

"Fair enough," Jo said, giving in to the moment of pleasure.

CHAPTER TWENTY-ONE

Like fireflies insisting on maintaining their place in the sky at dawn, nerves kept flitting hither and thither, ruining Jo's anticipation of freedom. She had made up her mind, but she couldn't help but wonder at what she was doing. Was she totally stupid to abandon a steady job? Where would she go from here?

Still, there was no going back. In the end, she had made her decision not based on her feelings about Madeline but because she wanted to stop fighting so damn hard every second of every day. She could stay here and live under a microscope, trying to hide every detail of her personal life, or she could make the bold choice…and run like hell toward freedom.

Choosing to run, she walked boldly up to Ian's open door and knocked on the door frame, causing him to look up with a quizzical expression.

"Good morning, Jo," he said with a bit of surprise. "You're early—even for you."

"I know," Jo said, clearing her throat. "I need to talk to you, if you have a minute."

"Of course," he said, waving her in. "What can I do for you?"

"Well..." Jo took a steadying breath. "To start with, I want to say thank you for everything."

"I'm not sure I'm following."

"Thank you for taking a chance on me, for making me part of your team and for teaching me everything that you have," Jo said.

"Wait a second," Ian interrupted. "This doesn't sound good."

"No, I think it is good. I think it's for the best, actually," Jo continued. "You see, I need to move on—and I think that the whole Stratton team will be happier this way."

Ian looked like he wanted to protest but couldn't find the words.

Before he could say anything, Jo reached into her briefcase. "Here," she said, handing him a sealed envelope. "This is my resignation. Like I said, I thank you for everything—but I just can't continue down this road."

"Things are going to get better, Jo. This scandal will blow over," Ian finally said.

"I hope so, but that's not the issue. I've decided that politics is not the right place for me anymore, at least not these kinds of politics. Leaving will also resolve some workplace relationships that have become awkward."

Jo regretted those final words even as they left her mouth.

"What do you mean—'these kinds of politics' and 'awkward workplace relationships'?" Ian asked.

"I just mean that it's best for me to go," Jo said. Knowing she owed him some kind of explanation, she tried to divert attention from her slip-up. "I'm tired of being in the public eye in any way. I grew up with that lack of privacy, and I don't want my work life to mirror my childhood. I want to try something new." As soon as she said the words, she stood.

"But what about Madeline's upcoming speeches?" Ian asked. "Can you stay on until we find a replacement?"

"I can't—at least not in the office. I'm sorry. I'm resigning immediately. After I clean out my desk, you can email me what needs to be done if you want, and I'll take on what I can on a freelance basis." She knew that staying would only complicate matters, and she couldn't—wouldn't—put herself or Madeline in that position. Madeline had too much to lose. She had tried to resist crossing the line, but given what had happened between them, there was no going back. She clicked the off button on her work BlackBerry and handed it to him, completing her termination.

He nodded tight-lipped and she walked to her cubicle, finally letting out the breath she had been holding. It was done. She put a few personal things in the box she had brought with her and wrote down the computer passwords for whoever would replace her. She was thankful that she had chosen to come in extra early; she didn't want to face anyone. With only Ian and an intern in the office, things had gone smoothly. Nothing could have prepared her, then, for the jolt she felt when she heard Madeline's laugh coming from the direction of the front desk.

"Is Jacquelyn in yet?" Madeline asked the intern sitting there.

"No, ma'am," he stammered. "She called to say she would be working from home today."

"That's perfectly fine." Madeline's laugh filled the office. "God knows I've taken my share of personal days lately."

The sight of Madeline walking toward her in her perfectly tailored red suit made Jo smile. She was breathtaking.

"Good morning, Josephine," Madeline said, stopping in front of her cubicle.

"Good morning, Mayor," Jo said with a smile.

"I would like to speak with you in my office, if you have a moment."

The twinkle in Madeline's eyes gave her away. Although she knew she shouldn't, Jo stood and followed her. Madeline was mesmerizing. There was no doubt about that. She could have asked Jo to do nearly anything, and Jo knew she would do her best to oblige.

Once in her office, Madeline closed the door behind them. "Did you talk to Ian?" she asked.

"Yes, I resigned, effective immediately, but will freelance until he finds a replacement."

"A replacement is going to be hard to find," Madeline said, a smile lighting up her eyes.

"I'm sure there's someone equally good out there and possibly even better. I'll get on the phone and see who we can find," Jo said, forgetting she no longer worked for the mayor and turning to return to her cubicle and begin the hunt.

Madeline grabbed her arm, spinning Jo back to face her. "The problem is, I don't think you'll be able to find someone who will be as good at this," Madeline said, pulling Jo into an embrace and kissing her deeply.

"We shouldn't," Jo said, pulling away. "Not here."

"You're right," Madeline said, straightening her jacket.

A moment passed with neither of them saying anything. The tension in the air was palpable. Jo leaned in this time.

"I can't help myself."

"Neither can I," Madeline replied. Their lips met again in passion. Jo was pressing Madeline gently up against the wall, getting lost in their kiss, when a knock on the door startled her, causing her to jump backward and knock over a pile of papers on Madeline's desk. As they scurried to pick them up, Madeline called, "Come in."

Gabe opened the door slowly, taking in the scene.

"What happened in here?" he asked.

"You know me." Jo laughed nervously. "Talking with my hands again."

"Oh, okay. I've got someone on the phone for the mayor. She says she's a personal friend but wouldn't give a name, so the intern transferred it to me when I walked in."

"Take a message, please," Madeline said. "I'll get back to her as soon as Jo and I have finished here."

"Aren't you a little worried about *her* calling up the office?" Jo asked when Gabe was out of earshot, her own fears crashing in at full force.

"Don't worry about it," Madeline answered, brushing it off, clearly not wanting to entertain thoughts of Natalie. "You know how it is—everyone who wants a special favor claims to be an old friend."

"I guess you're right," Jo said, standing, yet, she could not shake the sense of dread that had overwhelmed her after hearing Gabe's words.

"Come see me after while. I'm going to be working in the hotel suite this afternoon, so you can meet me for lunch if you'd like."

* * *

In the soft light of afternoon fading to evening, Jacquelyn's red curtains made her room appear pink. She knew she should be out of bed and doing something important, but for the fourth time this week, she had known exactly how to let off some steam. It had been all too easy. She sent the text, and fifteen minutes later he'd let himself in.

Was that all this was—letting off steam? She wondered if it was just that for Isaac too. He kissed her wildly, pulling off her clothes, and she shut off the thoughts in her mind and focused on the only goal she had at the moment—pleasure.

When they finished, he rolled off her and lay next to her.

"Thank you," he said, trailing his finger down the side of her face to brush the hair to the side.

She smiled. "No, thank you."

"I've been thinking that we should actually go out sometime." Isaac said the words carefully, as if afraid she would shoot his idea down.

"Is that so?" Even though she had been enjoying the physical side of this relationship, she might be interested in more.

"Mmmhmm," he said, kissing her gently. "I'd like to take you to dinner one night soon, if you want to."

"Don't you think you're being a bit forward?" she joked, stroking him underneath the covers.

His body writhed. "Possibly," he said breathlessly. "But I think we would have a good time."

She smiled and brought both of her hands above the covers. She just wanted to tease him a little and keep him hanging on. Of course, she wanted to go to dinner.

"Sounds good. Are you free tomorrow night?"

"I sure am." He kissed her and then glanced at the clock on her nightstand. "But I've got to go now. I'll be here to pick you up tomorrow at seven."

"All right. I'll be ready." She pulled the sheet around her body and watched as he got dressed. She had no idea what she was thinking, getting involved with a cameraman for the local news station—especially right here in the middle of the workday. After all, she spent most of her days trying to avoid letting the news get a closer look at her, her boss or their jobs. With Isaac, though, she had given him as many close looks as he had wanted. It was the closest thing to sleeping with the enemy she ever planned to do. It had been fun, though, and right now she desperately needed fun. Jacquelyn wasn't going to stress out about how things looked for the next election, since Madeline couldn't be bothered to. She already had begun searching for a new job. In the meantime, she was determined to enjoy the rest of her time here.

Shortly after she heard the front door close behind Isaac her cell phone began to ring. Just as she had every other time it rang this week, she closed her eyes and imagined throwing it at the wall, then dutifully answered it. Working from home had its disadvantages sometimes, like the fact that she couldn't just blissfully enjoy her day "off" the way she'd like to.

"Hello. This is Jacquelyn," she said, offering the greeting she always did when the number on the screen was an unknown.

"Jacquelyn, I didn't know who else to call," a man's voice answered. "I figured since I knew you better than the other staffers, I'd give this a try."

"Excuse me, who is this?" Jacquelyn answered.

There was a second of silence. "It's John Stratton, and I need to talk to Madeline as soon as possible."

"I'm afraid that's not possible, John, but I can pass along the message," Jacquelyn answered.

Even though she was curious to see what he wanted, she decided that she would extend her loyalty to Madeline one last time. Sure, it was a sinking ship, but Madeline had never actually wronged her. And John was a cheating asshole.

"It's highly important," John insisted.

"Let me know what it's regarding and I'll pass along the message to her."

"Jacquelyn," John practically hissed her name. "It cannot wait. It just can't. It is urgent! She messed up with an old friend of ours. If she doesn't get her shit together her skeletons are going to be on display for the world's viewing and soon. She needs to stop screwing around."

"What are you talking about?"

John hesitated. "Well, I might as well, I guess. You're going to find out soon enough when Natalie goes to the media."

"Natalie?" Jacquelyn said, her voice rising. "The Natalie you slept with?"

"That's the one," John answered gruffly. "She knows some of Madeline's old secrets and might be going to the media with them since Madeline blew her off on the phone when she called."

"I'm confused," Jacquelyn said. "She knows the mayor?"

"Let's just say they're old friends. But hey, Jacquelyn, I'm going to get off the phone now. You find a way for Madeline to call me in the next hour or I guess you can hear the story on the news—like the rest of the state."

The line went dead.

"Shit," Jacquelyn said.

What on earth was she going to do? She had to get in touch with Madeline—and fast. John had never called her before. Sure, she had been fairly well acquainted with him from working with the mayor over the years, but he had always been so polite and refined. Today, he was a different man, callous and angry and threatening.

As quickly as possible, she dialed Madeline's number.

It went straight to voice mail.

"It's Jacquelyn. Please call me back as soon as possible. It's urgent."

She sent an email, begging Madeline to call her within the hour. Reverting to communications director mode, she knew that if a story was going to break, she needed to get on top of it.

First and foremost, she needed to know what the story was and who had access to it. Then she could fight back. Draft statements, schedule a press conference if necessary and possibly arrange a video address to the media.

Quickly, she dialed Jo's number. It went straight to voice mail. Frustrated, she resorted to desperate measures and tried Jo's personal cell number. It rang three times, before Jo answered, sounding a bit out of breath.

"Jo, it's Jacquelyn. I need to talk to Madeline. Can you get in touch with her? It's urgent," she said.

"Of course," Jo said. "She's actually right here."

Jacquelyn was surprised they were together, but she wasn't about to question it at this point. She was desperate. She heard the phone changing hands in the background as Jo explained that it was Jacquelyn on the phone and that it was important.

"Hello, Jacquelyn." Madeline sounded winded too. What the hell were they doing?

"I have a message for you," Jacquelyn began, letting out the breath she had been holding. "And I have a couple of questions too."

"Okay. What's going on?"

"John called, and he said some stuff that makes me think we may have a major mess on our hands soon—very soon, actually." Jacquelyn knew she didn't have much time to explain. Still she couldn't just throw John's words at Madeline.

Madeline was silent, so Jacquelyn continued. "He said you knew Natalie—the…well, the other woman…and that she had tried to call you. He said that since you didn't talk to her, there was something she was going to tell the media."

"Shit!" Madeline replied. "Okay. I'll call him. Thanks, Jacquelyn."

"Mayor Stratton?" Jacquelyn needed to get the next part resolved. "Do you have any idea what this is about? I need to have something prepared if whatever it is hits the news."

"I know exactly what it's about, and I'm going to stop it."

With that the line went dead.

What the hell was she supposed to do now? She needed to know what was going on. Before she could think it over too long, she dialed Isaac's number. It rang twice before he picked up.

"Hey there," Isaac answered. "Did you miss me already?"

She cut him off. "Isaac, have you heard anything about my boss? Anything new on the story?"

"No..." his voice trailed off.

"Okay, thanks."

"If there is, you'd tell me right?" he asked.

"Yes," she answered, then reconsidered. Would she really alert one of the media just because she was sleeping with him? She decided to ponder that later.

"Listen," she said. "If you hear anything, please let me know immediately."

"Okay," he agreed. "But the same goes for you. If there's a story, I need to know as soon as possible. My boss is on my ass."

"Sure," she said, ending the call. What next? Should she call Ian or just pray that Madeline could get everything resolved on her own? If she couldn't, things were going to become even more hellish than they had been of late.

She decided to wait a few minutes and give Madeline time to sort things out. If she hadn't heard back from her by 5 P.M., she would call John herself and then Ian, when she knew more and had a plan to propose to him. It sounded like there was no way this was going to miss the nightly news at six, and they needed to be ready.

Jo had to know. Jacquelyn hated her for that. If anyone deserved to be in the loop, it was her, the person who handled all of Madeline's media. And Ian, of course, as chief of staff. At the moment, though, Jo was her only hope. She sent her a quick text, knowing that wherever she and Madeline were Jo was at least checking her personal cell phone.

When this is sorted out, please let me know what's going on. I need to prepare a statement in case whatever this is gets leaked. Please get back to me. Thanks!

Now, she had to wait. Waiting was the hardest when you were on a deadline. That was one of the first lessons she had learned when working with the press.

The wheels in Jacquelyn's mind spun round and round as she tried to figure out what secrets from Madeline's previous life

Natalie might hold. Madeline clearly had been less than truthful earlier. She knew the "other woman," and the "other woman" obviously knew her.

Shit! She couldn't just sit around and wait while there was so much at stake. Going into overdrive, she started calling contacts at rapid pace, trying to make her inquiries as discreet as possible while at the same time playing Nancy Drew. She cringed. She had only forty-five minutes to get to the bottom of things.

CHAPTER TWENTY-TWO

Jo felt as if the ground had collapsed beneath her. Beside her on the bed, Madeline was fumbling with her phone, trying to call John and mumbling to herself. "Natalie never called me. She called *you*. I should have known something was up. Should have called her back. I should have found a way."

"I need to know exactly what she said that night," Madeline said finally, her face completely white. Jo hadn't wanted to rehash the conversation, but they had things to clear up, obviously.

"She kept asking for 'Maddie.' She thought I was you. I told her that I wasn't, but I didn't say who I was. She said she wanted to say she was sorry. I said she had the wrong number." Jo's words were spilling out quickly, and she hoped they were making sense. "After I phoned you, she kept calling. I ignored the calls, because I didn't know what to tell her."

Madeline nodded, then pushed past Jo to go into the hallway.

Jo listened to Madeline's side of the conversation.

"John, it's Maddie."

It was a stupid thing to be concerned about at this time, but Jo wondered why everyone from Madeline's past got the privilege of calling her Maddie. Was it a special club that only a select few got to join? She chided herself for being jealous of the man who had cheated on her precious Madeline and the woman who had helped him.

"Well, she dialed the wrong number. Aside from that, she has some nerve to think she can demand that I take her call." Madeline's voice was nearly hysterical. "She can't make that call to the media." After a brief pause, her voice hit a new octave. "If you want to help so damn badly, give me her number. I'll arrange to meet with her tonight."

Jo watched as Madeline fished a pen out of her purse and wrote something on the palm of her hand.

"Thanks," she said before hanging up the phone.

Jo watched in astonishment as Madeline dialed the number she had just written down. She felt another pang of jealousy as she saw Madeline's eyes brighten at the sound of the voice on the other line.

"Natalie." She spoke the word like a caress, even though the woman had ripped her heart out. Jo felt her heart ache too and wished that she could hear the other end of the conversation.

"No, you didn't speak with me…That was…someone else," Madeline said.

*Someone else…*Jo did not expect a title—or even an acknowledgment—but being referred to as just "someone else"? The words were like a dagger through her heart.

"Sure, we can meet to talk about all of this," Madeline said, agreeing to whatever Natalie had proposed. "Just please don't go to the media."

There was a moment of silence. "Okay, thank you. I appreciate that."

"All right. I'll meet you tonight."

"Seven sounds great."

With each word that came out of Madeline's mouth, Jo felt more and more like she might vomit. Madeline was really going to meet this woman tonight, was going to spend time with her.

"Yes. I agree. Someplace private would be best. Let's meet at my hotel."

As Madeline rattled off the address, Jo turned and grabbed her things. She had come to Madeline's hotel after leaving the office, but she wasn't going to stick around for this. She wanted out of the tangled mess she had gotten herself into, and she wanted out now.

"Jo, wait," Madeline said, stepping in between her and the door. "We need to talk about this."

Jo's anger bubbled up inside her and erupted. "What do we need to talk about? The fact that you're giddy about meeting up with your ex? The fact that you have a smile on your face even though that bitch slept with your husband and ripped your heart to shreds?"

The words were intended to sting and they did. From where she stood, Jo could see they had affected Madeline deeply.

"Not only that, but have you thought about what it could do to you—to everyone involved—if she goes to the press?" More of Jo's anger spilled forth with each word. "You said you didn't know her, and now she's going to spill everything to the media."

"First off, don't try to lecture me on what I should have said to the press. Technically, I think my statement said that I didn't know that John was cheating and with whom, not that I didn't know her. Hair-splitting, I know, but I did the best I could under the circumstances. Also, there's no reason for you to be jealous of her."

"I'm not," Jo lied, hating the fact that she was, indeed, jealous. "But the woman knowingly slept with your husband, disrupting your work as mayor, threatening your reelection and putting you through personal hell. Why would you want to have anything to do with her? I don't trust her. This is a bad idea."

"What else do you want me to do? If she goes to the press, it's going to blow everything wide open, like you said. It'll start with the press delving into my past, but trust me, it'll end with them uncovering the truth about me and you. Are you ready for that? For what your family will say? What it will do to your reputation, your career? I'm inviting her over in hopes of smoothing things out so we can go on with our lives."

Jo wasn't sure Madeline's logic added up. She already had quit her job, after all, and sooner or later, she was going to have to come out to her family and friends. She'd be deprived of her privacy for a while, sure, but at least she'd be able to live a life without lies.

When she tried to put that into words, though, what came out instead was, "What lives are those?"

"Our lives..." Madeline trailed off, before adding, "together. I want us to have a life together, Jo."

The words were what Jo had wanted, but they still shook her to the core. Not only had no one ever said those words to her, but she had never before wanted so desperately to hear them.

Speechless, she leaned down and kissed Madeline. "I'll see you in the morning," she said, pulling away.

"I'd like for you to stay, if you're willing," Madeline said gently. "Please, stay here with me until she leaves. After that we can go back to your place and get some sleep."

"Let me think about it," Jo said, glancing at her watch, noting that she had several hours to figure things out. "I think I'll take Jaws for a walk and do some thinking. I'll either be back in a bit, or I'll give you a call and let you know I'm not coming. It's not a good idea for her to know about me, and I need some time to sort through my thoughts on how to handle things if all of this becomes public."

Jo might have played it cool, but inside she was dying. Of course she wanted to stay and hear what this little tramp had to say. But more than anything, she wanted to stay to make sure nothing happened between Madeline and Natalie. She couldn't explain it, but she felt the sudden need to be assured that she had Madeline's full loyalty and fidelity.

And she had a pretty damn good idea of what was possible when an old flame reappeared.

* * *

Jacquelyn waited by the phone. Surely, Jo would have the common decency to answer her last text or at least give her a call. She needed answers, and she needed them soon.

Her hands shook as she replayed the conversations that had occurred in the course of her investigating. In the heat of the moment, her curiosity had won out over her professionalism. She feared she might have said too much or been indiscreet. With luck, Ian would never find out. She certainly wasn't going to call him up and admit she might have screwed up. In any case, there was nothing to report—all of her questioning had been fruitless.

Whatever was happening was going to hit the press in about fifteen minutes if John was correct in his estimate. She paced back and forth in her living room, flipping through the channels on her TV and repeatedly refreshing her Google news search to check for breaking headlines.

At the ten-minute mark, she decided that she could not wait another minute. She picked up the phone, found John's number in the list of recent calls and dialed it.

"Hello," he answered.

"John, it's Jacquelyn. I haven't heard back from Madeline, and I need to know what's going on. Have things been sorted out?"

"You mean, you haven't heard any of what's happening?" John's voice was amused.

"No, John, I haven't, and now is not the time for games. I'm the press liaison, so if shit is going to hit the fan, I need to be informed ahead of time."

Jacquelyn was beginning to panic. She had talked a big game about being ready to leave, but right now, the truth was that she didn't have anywhere else to go. There was no job waiting for her somewhere else. If this ship went down, she was going to go down with it.

"Well," John said cautiously, but with obvious enjoyment. "Maybe you should ask the pastor's daughter, the pretty brunette who came by the house with Maddie to pick up her things. She might know a thing or two about my Maddie's secrets."

"Jo?" Jacquelyn asked.

"Yeah, they looked pretty cozy," he said, and she heard the gurgle of liquid courage refilling his glass. "I'd say by now she probably knows as many of Madeline's secrets as anyone."

"What are you talking about?" Jacquelyn demanded.

"I'm just saying that things—people, for that matter—aren't exactly as they appear to be a lot of times. Ask Jo. She'll know what I'm talking about."

"I don't have time to ask Jo," Jacquelyn said. The truth was that she didn't want to ask her, but she didn't tell him that.

"Make time, Jacquelyn."

"What exactly should I ask her?"

John laughed. "Why don't you just start by asking her who else my wife has been fucking these days? You know I never was quite Madeline's type. Maybe she's found a pretty little thing with a nice rack and long hair to take my place."

Jacquelyn's phone dropped to the floor, effectively ending the call. Could it be? Or was John trying to retain what little dignity he had by suggesting he was not the only one in the wrong? She had had her suspicions about Jo, but Madeline? None of this made sense. Madeline didn't seem the type. How did Natalie fit into the picture? What did she know?

True or not, if this hit the press, there was no statement to write. Madeline's career as a Republican elected official was over. It was as simple as that.

Picking her phone up from the floor, Jacquelyn again called Jo. Again, there was no answer; it just rolled over to voice mail. Having no other choice, she sent an email to Ian and Gabe.

We have an emergency, need senior staff meeting NOW. Meet in Ian's office in 30 minutes. THIS IS URGENT!

Gabe replied almost immediately.

Still at the office. I'll be there. What about you, Ian?

A few minutes later, Jacquelyn was dressed and ready to head out the door. Ian hadn't responded yet, but this needed to be dealt with immediately. Even if he couldn't get there, she and Gabe could hash out some of the details. Per office protocol, she would wait a few more minutes before giving him an after-hours phone call.

She would fill in Jo and Madeline later—if that was what they all decided. As it was, she didn't want to see either of them. They had made this mess, were forcing everyone else to scramble around at lightning speed to clean it up while continuing to withhold details.

Her BlackBerry beeped with a message from Ian. *I went to grab dinner, but I'll be back in a few. Meet you both there.*

Grabbing her briefcase, she headed to the office. Gabe greeted her at the door.

"What's going on? Is everything okay? What is all of this about?" He shot the questions at her, one after the other, like machine gun fire.

She held up her hands to slow him down. "It's about Jo and Madeline and a phone call I got from John Stratton."

Ian came through the doors then, and Jacquelyn stopped speaking. He took one look at her face and suggested they go to the conference room. The staff had all gone home, but there was less chance they'd be overheard there by a custodian or someone coming back for something they'd forgotten than if they met in his office.

Suddenly, Jacquelyn questioned her judgment in calling them. She didn't want to reveal what she had heard, and even if she did, she wasn't sure she would be able to find the right words. When they got to the room, she seated herself and let out a deep breath.

"Okay, Jacquelyn," Ian said. "What's going on?" He and Gabe were sitting straight up in their chairs, their eyes glued on her.

"That's the thing," Jacquelyn began, "I don't really know. I got a strange call this afternoon from John Stratton. He warned me that if I didn't get a message to Madeline that the woman he had been sleeping with—Natalie—had something she was going to tell the press about Madeline."

Their eyes widened, and Ian held up his hand to stop her. "I thought Madeline didn't know Natalie Longworth. That's what she told us when her picture was splashed all over the press. Is something else going on there? Or was she threatening to go to the press with something new about her affair with John?"

"I wasn't sure at first, but I wanted to avoid a press firestorm. So I called Madeline. I asked her if she knew what this was about. She said she did and she'd take care of it. She must have gotten it all straightened out, because nothing has hit the news yet. When I followed up with John, though, he said something that I think we need to figure out how to deal with."

Jacquelyn's hands were shaking, so she set them in her lap. She was about to throw her colleagues a curveball, and she wasn't sure how it would go over. Their jobs would hang in the balance too.

"What did he say?" Gabe pressed.

"Neither of you are going to like this answer," Jacquelyn warned.

"It doesn't matter," Ian said, now impatient. "Spit it out."

"I called him to ask what issue Natalie was taking to the press, and he said I should ask Jo, the 'pretty brunette' who had gone to the house with Madeline to pick up her things."

"We know that. Jo hasn't been back, has she? Hasn't mentioned anything about having some kind of interaction with John while she was there, has she?" Gabe asked, looking around the table for answers.

"No," Jacquelyn answered. "It wasn't that. He said I should ask Jo whether or not Madeline has been…um, 'sleeping' with anyone else. Apparently, for some reason he believes that she's sleeping with—or…um…has slept with women. I'm guessing Natalie is privy to that information, somehow, and so is Jo. He also insinuated that she and Jo seemed 'cozy' and that by now Jo probably knew all Madeline's secrets. I don't know what's going on, but we need to find out, so we don't get a bomb dropped on us by the nightly news."

Gabe and Ian stared at her, completely perplexed.

"Are you saying Madeline is a lesbian?" Gabe asked.

Ian shrugged, shaking his head in disbelief.

"Is Jo?" Gabe asked, still trying to make sense of it all.

Ian shrugged. "I never would have guessed," he said in astonishment.

Gabe glared at Jacquelyn, demanding an answer.

"I don't know," she finally answered. "But these are some pretty heavy accusations, and John seemed convinced that Madeline was. And I've had my suspicions about Jo. Either way, we've got to figure out how to move forward."

"Do you think that's why she stayed at Jo's place?" Gabe asked, his eyes wider than Jacquelyn had ever seen them. "Are they sleeping together?"

Jacquelyn didn't want to add fuel to the fire. But in light of everything they couldn't afford to give them the benefit of the doubt right now.

"It would make sense, if it's all true," she said.

"If this gets out, it's the end—true or not," Ian said. "Madeline was elected on the basis of being a social and fiscal conservative. She's actively stood against gay marriage and made numerous speeches on traditional family values. If there is even any speculation about her sexuality, she is ruined. Aside from that, while I'd like to steer clear of the gossip mill, if she's accused of sleeping with a staff member, there's no coming back from that."

Ian wasn't usually one to jump to worst-case scenarios, and his doing so made Jacquelyn's heart race. He was voicing her deepest fears.

Ian put his head in his hands, and when he looked back up at them, his face was ashen. "I was going to tell you this at the staff meeting tomorrow, but Jo resigned this morning. It's all making sense now. If all this is true, she could have been doing that to protect Madeline."

Gabe looked as if he had bit into something rotten and Jacquelyn felt like she had as well. As they sat around the conference room, discussing options, Jacquelyn refreshed the news pages on her phone, hoping the news wouldn't drop.

Ian was already on his phone, dialing both Jo's and Madeline's numbers repeatedly. After the fifth try to each, he left voice mails and shook his head.

"They could at least have the decency to answer their damn phones."

Determined to get a jump on things, he decided that a call to the media from the mayor's chief of staff might yield more results than one from Jacquelyn. As quickly as possible, he placed calls to his contacts at the major media outlets in Oklahoma City, requesting that they call him before they ran anything on his boss so they'd have the opportunity to respond.

When he finally set his phone down, he let out a long sigh. "They all said that they haven't heard anything, but gave me their word they'd alert me if they did so we could issue a statement. It roused their curiosity, but I don't think we had much choice. Didn't stop the damn vultures from prying for information, of course."

Jacquelyn texted Isaac again, but got no answer. It was a busy hour of the workday for him, she knew, but she wished he could at least reply and set her mind at ease.

"I guess if nobody's heard anything yet, John and his mistress are holding off," Jacquelyn said, though she couldn't stop the churning in her stomach.

Around the table, they fell silent for a while, all still weathering the shock. Finally, Ian slapped his legal pad down on the desk and began drawing out a timeline. Per his direction, they decided that if something got leaked—which they would desperately try to avoid—there was little they could do at this point. It was impossible to make plans when they didn't know what was going on. If any media queries came to them, they should forward them to him. With luck, they'd find out more tomorrow and be able to put together an action plan.

At the end of the meeting, Ian stood and hugged Jacquelyn. "We'll figure it out," he told her. He shook Gabe's hand. "Either way, know that both of you can expect a solid recommendation from me if this heads south."

He walked out, leaving Gabe and Jacquelyn alone.

"Do you really think she's a lesbian?" Gabe asked, looking like a child who'd had his favorite toy ripped from his hands.

"Gabe, is that all you've been able to focus on tonight? Forget about Jo, okay? Even if she isn't a lesbian, she isn't interested in you. And if she is, well, isn't it reassuring to know that isn't your fault?"

Gabe shook his head, clearly incapable of grasping the concept.

"C'mon. Get it together. We have bigger fish to fry—like the fact that we all may be jobless come election time—or sooner—if this leaks."

"We won't be. This is all a lie," Gabe said. "I have plenty of gay friends—family members even—and Jo just doesn't fit the bill."

"Denial is all very well, Gabe. We need to find out for sure. How do we go about that?"

"Maybe the two of us should just go and ask them," he suggested. "I could go to Jo's house, and you could try Madeline's hotel."

"No," she said. "Only one of us needs to go. If we go together, it'll look like an ambush."

He nodded his head. She was about to let him volunteer, when she remembered the last time she had handed off a task like this. Jo Carson had stepped up to the plate, and now look where they were.

"I'll go," she said. "I'll be the one to ask."

CHAPTER TWENTY-THREE

Since the phone call with Maddie earlier in the afternoon, Natalie had been a bundle of nerves. Which outfit should she wear? She had flipped through her closet, dismissing each choice. *Too slutty. Too grungy. Too casual. Too dressy.* Finally, she had slipped into a pair of jeans and a tight-fitting shirt. She wanted to stay away from clothing that would remind Maddie that Natalie had slept with John, but she also wanted to remind Maddie of the great sex they used to have.

It was a lifetime ago, but she wanted Maddie to remember the good times as well as the bad. She hoped it would help open her to Natalie's apologies.

On the drive over to Maddie's hotel room, all Natalie could think was how out of line she was acting. She had been the one to screw up and the one threatening to go to the press. That was only a tactic to get John to get in touch with Maddie, though. She had promised Maddie during their phone call that she wouldn't go to the press if she would meet with her, and she meant it.

Wouldn't want to mess up John's scheme, after all. He wanted to have the power to go to the press, and she was content to give it to him. As long as she could get what she wanted by dangling her threats over his head. Early on, that had been money—now it was Maddie.

She pulled into the parking lot and sighed. For a brief second, she considered peeling out of the lot, pointing the wheels west, and not stopping until she was a world away in California. Instead, she steadied herself.

"It's now or never," she said, giving herself a little pep talk.

She checked her reflection in the vanity mirror one last time. For an aging mistress, she didn't look too bad, she thought. She got out of the car and walked toward the hotel. It was time to face her past and her future all in one evening.

* * *

Madeline paced back and forth in front of the couch in the living room of her suite. Perhaps they should have chosen a different meeting place, she thought as she looked around. This place was tiny. Panic engulfed her. There would be no way to escape Natalie—or the rush of memories—once she got here.

There was a knock on the door, and she thought her heart might explode. Jo took her hand to keep her calm. She was thankful that Jo had come back, but it was a little unnerving to have her past and her present colliding in such dramatic form.

Jo kissed her on the cheek. "I'll be in the bathroom if you need anything, but for now I'll give you two some time alone." She looked as if she was torn between doing that and staying to fight Natalie, but after a pause she turned and walked away, leaving Madeline more nervous than ever.

She walked cautiously to the door, aware that behind it stood a threat to all the happiness she had so recently found. She took a deep breath and opened the door.

That is one beautiful threat, she thought. Even after all these years, Natalie Longworth was a knockout.

A knockout who slept with my husband, Madeline reminded herself.

For a moment she didn't speak, and neither did Natalie. It was like seeing a ghost. Until the moment passed Madeline allowed herself to relive every bit of their shared history.

"Do you want to come inside?" Madeline asked, breaking the silence.

"If that is okay with you."

Madeline stepped aside, allowing her to enter, careful to maintain as much distance from her as the room would allow.

"What is it you wanted to talk about?" Madeline asked, suddenly regretting inviting this woman into her room. Natalie was not some innocent bystander. She was someone who had wrecked Madeline's life not once but twice. The bitterness that rose in her heart must have shown on her face, because Natalie took a step back.

"You have every right to hate me and never want to see me again," Natalie began. "But I wanted to see you—to apologize to you in person."

"Apology not accepted. Is there anything else?" It wasn't the smart response, Madeline knew, but the unresolved feelings, the fear of being exposed, the plan to mollify Natalie and convince her to remain silent—they had all evaporated. It was clear to Madeline that she had all she needed now and that Natalie was nothing more than a distraction.

"I wanted to set the record straight," Natalie said.

Madeline waited. Natalie would try to sugarcoat it, but she couldn't change the facts. During college, she had wanted to live wild and free. She had "explored her options," unbeknownst to Madeline, and in the process shattered her heart. And now she had destroyed her marriage. She had to have known who John was—everyone in the state did—yet she had slept with him anyway.

Natalie cleared her throat. "I didn't sleep with John to get back at you. It wasn't for revenge or anything."

"Revenge?" Madeline laughed bitterly. "Why on earth would you need to get revenge on me? You were the one who felt the need to sleep around, remember? If anyone was left shattered by our past, it was me. I would have been the one seeking revenge."

"Okay, well, what I'm saying is that I didn't seek him out," Natalie tried again.

"So you wanted to see me in person to tell me that my husband was the filthy cheater, and you were just a poor girl who fell prey to his charms?" Madeline retorted.

"No," Natalie lowered her gaze so she didn't have to meet Madeline's stare. "I am at fault here. I just—well, I did it for the money."

"He paid you?" If Natalie thought that this meeting was helping, she was dead wrong. With every sentence out of her mouth, she was making a bad situation worse.

"No, well, yes..." She hung her head again, searching for the right words. "He didn't pay me for sex. None of them do, but when my career as an artist fell through, I didn't have a whole lot going for me. I had an art degree and a failed dream. What do you do with that?"

When she didn't continue, Madeline threw out, "Fuck for money?"

"Maddie, please let me finish," Natalie said.

"Don't call me Maddie. I hate being called that. My name is Madeline. Maddie was the name of a stupid college girl who was mistaken in thinking that sex meant love. Madeline is a woman who knows what real love is."

"Okay, Madeline." Natalie pronounced each syllable carefully. "What I'm saying is that I made some poor choices. I started sleeping with rich men. Some would pay me to keep quiet, some would pay to keep me around for a while. John paid me to keep my mouth quiet about you and me."

"Yeah, he wanted to keep that secret all to himself so he could blackmail me for my money," Madeline said, irritated at both of them. "Maybe you should just stay with him. You make a good little, deceitful couple." She wanted to drive the knife a little deeper. "You're both whores who would rather fuck someone new and exciting than stick around and hold onto something real."

Natalie reached out and placed her hand on Madeline's shoulder.

"Don't fucking touch me," Madeline said. "I think it's time for you to go. I never want to see you again."

"Wait," Natalie said. "I'm not done."

"Yes. You are. You have nothing to say to me that I want to hear. Whatever you came here for, you can forget it. I want nothing to do with you."

Natalie didn't move.

"Get the hell out of here," Madeline screamed, her body shaking from years of pent-up anger and resentment.

"Why?" Natalie shot back, her frustration showing—and something else Madeline couldn't quite identify. "Do you have someplace to be? That's the way it always was. Little Miss Popular, with all the money and the promising future. You've still got better things to do than sit around and listen to me. Is that it?" Bitterness shone through every word, as she too brought up unsettled fights from decades ago. "Or is there someone else? You've always moved on pretty fast, haven't you? Do you have some new, hot little number waiting to come over?"

Madeline tried to hide the surprise on her face. No one knew about Jo—at least she didn't think there was any way they could. Maybe Natalie was just calling her bluff.

"I don't know what you are talking about," Madeline said.

Natalie smiled a wicked grin. The world had definitely changed Natalie for the worst.

"Oh, I don't doubt that you understand precisely what I'm saying. John said you had a staff member named Josephine—Jo—when he and I talked on the phone the other night. He said she was a preacher's daughter in her twenties. Said he had a hunch there was something going on between the two of you. And whether or not it's true, it would make one juicy story, wouldn't it?"

"He has no idea what the hell he's saying!" Madeline's anger and fear collided. How could he know anything?

As if reading her mind, Natalie answered, "Your reaction told me all I needed to know."

Her eyes narrowed. "I hoped there might still be something…but I guess I'm not young enough for you now.

Maybe I wasn't just a fling after all—an 'experiment' is what you called it when you left. Perhaps you are into women after all, and it might be that I was never good enough for you. That had to have been why you always paraded around—with all of the things I could never have—and didn't stick around to fight for us when I had one night of bad decisions. It doesn't matter, though. It never really did. And John wasn't interesting enough, just like I wasn't. At least that's what he told me," she said, turning on her heels.

"Neither of you knows what you're talking about," Madeline said, hoping Natalie didn't notice the quiver in her voice.

"Let's let the press decide for themselves who they want to believe then," Natalie shouted, slamming the door in Madeline's face as she left.

Jo emerged from the bathroom, wide-eyed. Swallowing deeply, she took Madeline in her arms.

"What do we do now?" Madeline asked, shaken from the whole ordeal.

Jo stroked Madeline's hair. "We come clean—with the senior staff at least. Maybe the whole office. We can't hide out here forever. Not if she's going to be out spreading rumors and prompting more questioning."

"How did John know?" Madeline asked.

"I don't know," Jo answered, shaken by the same mystery.

Madeline's brow furrowed until she hung her head. "The parking garage where we first kissed," she said. "The one we hid in when the press was chasing us. It didn't hit me until just now, but it was the parking garage at his office complex. Maybe he—or someone else—saw something. Or maybe he's just out to cause some trouble and picked up on the tension between us."

"All the more reason to come clean," Jo said, squeezing her hand.

Madeline wanted to argue, but the words just wouldn't come. Jo was right. With a ticking bomb like Natalie around, they couldn't just go back into their world of sweet oblivion.

* * *

Natalie seethed as she sat in the parking lot. How dare she talk to her that way?

Madeline hadn't been wrong about some of the things she had said. But she hadn't even given Natalie a chance to explain. There had been no softness, no chance of forgiveness.

John must have been right about the new girlfriend. She must have been the one who answered when she called that night. After Natalie had hung up, she realized that though the person on the other end of the line had sounded shaken when she gave her name, as Madeline might have been, it hadn't sounded like Madeline. She figured out she had the wrong number when it went to voice mail. That's where she had gotten Jo's name. When she'd asked John he told her that the girl was a member of the staff. He had also triumphantly—as if privy to secret information—let on that Jo was the girl who'd been with Madeline when the press cornered her at the house, the one who'd cut off their inquiries and whisked her away to safety.

Natalie had not planned on broaching the subject, but when things had headed south, she figured she had nothing to lose. The flicker of fear and shock that had passed over Maddie's face when she mentioned Jo's name had sealed the deal. There definitely was a new girl in Madeline Stratton's life, and clearly Madeline did not want Natalie to interfere with that budding relationship any more than she wanted to accept her apologies.

So be it, Natalie thought. *She'll regret this.*

There was nothing that Natalie hated more than rejection. She had gone to Madeline's room and laid her heart bare, only to have it trampled on, and now she was only seeing red. Nothing had changed. Madeline was still as unforgiving as ever. She would pay for it—this time at least.

She fumbled with her cell phone, intending to call John, when she noticed the changing shadows from the third window on the top floor—Madeline's room. There were two figures now where she and Madeline had stood. In the dim light, she could only make out the fact that both shapes were female and one was holding the other in her arms.

"Bitch," Natalie muttered under her breath, wondering why they didn't even have the decency to close the curtains.

The girl had been there the whole time. She screamed in anger, put the car in reverse and sped away, phoning John as she drove. When he answered, she didn't even offer him a greeting.

"That bitch of a wife you have didn't even give me the time of day," she ranted. "And she's got her new little girlfriend there with her at her hotel."

"What did you expect, Natalie?" John asked.

What an asshole. Why was he choosing now to be reasonable?

"Fuck you, John. You know what? I shouldn't have even bothered calling you. I've got other things to take care of." She spewed her words like venom.

"Don't do anything stupid. We had an agreement, remember?" John warned.

"Fuck you and our agreement. I don't give a damn about the money. I already told you that. I wanted Maddie, wanted to talk with her and resolve this whole damn thing. She wouldn't listen, though, because that Jo girl has her under her thumb. I'm going to make both of them pay."

She clicked the phone off, plotting what to do next. She'd had no intention of going public earlier in the evening, but after how she had been treated, she saw no need to cut Maddie a break. Mayor Stratton was going to go down in flames and very publicly.

Her little girlfriend would too. A Google search earlier in the day had revealed most of what she needed to know about Jo Carson. She was, in fact, a preacher's daughter. And not just any preacher—but the high and mighty Michael Carson, a man who regularly condemned the same-sex lifestyle from the pulpit, calling it one of the evils of this world. He would be pretty surprised to hear that his daughter liked to eat pussy and that Madeline Stratton did as well. The rest of the state—hell, the whole country—would be surprised to hear that too.

Using the Google search on her phone, she found the number for Michael Carson's church office. Unfortunately, his home number was not listed, but a call to the church could be equally dramatic and effective, she decided. She tapped the number into her cell phone and saved it. She would give Michael a call shortly, but she had something to do first.

Pulling to the side of the road, she put her car in park. This could not wait even another minute. It had to happen tonight! Before Madeline could figure out some way to talk her way out of it.

She reached into her purse. All of the news stations had given her business cards in case she had anything to add to her story, and now she did. She fished out the first business card she could find. The name on the card was Isaac Williams with Channel 4 News.

Here goes nothing, she thought, dialing the number.

"Channel 4, this is Isaac." His voice came across the line, obviously tired.

"Hi, Isaac. I'm not sure if you remember me, but this is Natalie Longworth."

His voice noticeably perked up. "Of course I remember you, Natalie. What can I do for you?"

* * *

Ever since his discussion with Jacquelyn earlier in the day, Isaac had been waiting to hear about the story she thought was coming his way. He felt now like a dog that had been handed a bone. He wanted to call her and let her know, but he could not just give this information away.

He had the mistress in John Stratton's affair on record saying that she had known Mayor Stratton for years. That they had been old college roommates—and *lovers*. There was a slew of other information as well, including an allegation of a relationship with a staffer. Apparently, if Natalie was correct, Madeline Stratton was sleeping with the daughter of mega-church pastor, Michael Carson.

The story was huge—if true. Michael Carson had written books, had a live telecast of each Sunday's sermon. He was a huge antigay activist—as was Madeline Stratton, supposedly.

His head was swimming. He would let Jacquelyn know he had the information, but not until he confirmed it—and notified his boss. This was huge, so huge that he had personally offered Natalie Longworth a thousand bucks to keep her mouth shut when he learned that she hadn't called any of the other stations yet.

If she kept her word, he would call Jacquelyn tomorrow morning and pay Natalie the money.

An hour later, he had all the information he needed to make a news story. Old school records from Madeline's college days confirmed that she had roomed with a girl named Natalie Longworth. How in the world had the press missed this information the first time around? Simple. Because they had all been looking to the mayor as the real story, not the other woman. Would Madeline Stratton crack under the pressure? Would she offer an on-camera interview? Could they get more of the story of the woman shattered by her husband's infidelity?

The details of Natalie's past had not been closely examined because they hadn't been relevant to the story that the media wanted to tell. Now, though, he had a story that everyone in the state would buzz about for days. He had secured the necessary verification for the main part of the story. They had enough to do an on-camera interview that covered the rest—as long as he remembered to throw in words like "allegedly."

He called Natalie, who agreed to come to the studio right away for the interview. They would tape and edit it tonight and air it first thing in the morning, as people dressed for the day.

Landing a story this big had resulted in his boss not only congratulating him but also promising him that he was safe in his job for a while. For the first time in ages, Isaac felt like he could breathe. He suppressed the nagging in his gut that told him to call Jacquelyn. They needed to get the footage first. Once he had that, he would phone her.

CHAPTER TWENTY-FOUR

Jacquelyn had been considering making a trip to Jo's apartment for the past hour. While she wasn't sure where they were, she figured it was a safe bet. If nothing else, maybe she could catch Jo alone and confront her—which would be safer than facing Madeline with the allegations she had in her arsenal.

What would she say? She wanted to have something planned, not just show up and accuse them of sleeping together. That would only seal her fate as the first to be fired whenever the shit started hitting the fan.

Her phone rang, interrupting her thoughts.

It was Ian. He was probably calling to see if she had heard anything. She wanted to ignore his call. Instead she answered it.

"Hey, Ian," she said.

"I think we might be about to get the answer to our question," he said, forgoing a greeting.

"What are you talking about?"

"I just got off the phone with Jo. She and Madeline want to meet with me. I told her that I would, but that I was bringing the rest of the senior staff with me."

"Did she agree to that?"

"Actually, she said that would probably be best. She seemed upset, but she said this needed to happen tonight—as soon as possible."

"Great," Jacquelyn replied. "Whatever is happening, we need to get to the bottom of it as quickly as we can. I'm in for the meeting. What time? Where? And have you let Gabe know? He will want to be there as well."

"Gabe knows. He will be there. We're all meeting at the office. Come as soon as possible. I think Jo and Madeline are already there," Ian said.

There was a pause. "Be prepared, Jacquelyn. I am pretty sure they're not calling us in for a late night meeting to give us good news."

She knew it could not be good news, but she appreciated his warning anyway.

"Thanks, Ian," she said. Hanging up, she tried to prepare herself. She was pretty certain, though, that she knew why they had called the meeting. It was confession time.

* * *

They had arrived before anyone else. Jo wanted to be the first to the office, wanted to get settled in the conference room and establish some type of normalcy. She flipped on the lights and held the door open for Madeline. Her face was as white as a sheet, and more than anything, Jo wanted to comfort her.

What they were about to do would change the future irrevocably for the both of them, but it had to be done. Natalie was volatile and unpredictable, but she had threatened to go to the media twice now, and this time she had seemed very determined.

There was not a doubt in Jo's mind that her face and Madeline's would be splashed about the news tomorrow morning. It was something she had feared from the very beginning of her feelings for Madeline, something she had known was a possibility the moment they slept together.

Looking at Madeline, she wanted her to know one thing. She squeezed her hand. "It has been worth every minute," she said, a single tear running down her cheek.

She had no idea why she was crying. Since Natalie had left, she had tried to be the strong one, for Madeline's sake, but now she felt as though she might crack.

Confession had never been her strong suit. She knew what everyone was going to say: She and Madeline had put everyone's career on the line—and together they had jeopardized all of the changes that Madeline had worked so hard to implement. Chances were good that none of the anti-corruption measures would matter at all once it was revealed that the mayor had been sleeping with a staff member. It would have all been for nothing.

That was true, but she meant what she had said. It had been worth every minute, and she would do it all over again. Selfishly, she realized that finding something meaningful in Madeline's arms had been worth everything it would cost.

Madeline squeezed Jo's hand in return. She opened her mouth to speak, but no words came out.

"It's okay. You don't have to say anything. I can tell them what has happened," Jo reassured her.

Madeline swallowed hard. "Thank you."

"I'm sorry," Jo whispered, afraid it might be the last time she had the opportunity to speak the words.

"Me too," Madeline said in reply.

Ian came in first. As he opened the door, Jo let go of Madeline's hand. It was too late. He had seen it, and his tightlipped look left no doubt that he understood the reason for their hand-holding.

"As you were," he said crisply and took his seat at the front of the table.

Jo dropped her eyes. She had never felt particularly guilty about being a lesbian—never thought it was a wicked, despicable thing, like her parents did. It was who she was, even if she hadn't lived out and proud. Now, however, she felt as though she should feel ashamed—though more for the sake of whom she had slept with and what she had done. The look Ian had given her said he disapproved—not of her lifestyle, perhaps, but of her actions. After all, she had slept with her boss—a married woman, even if that marriage was over when it happened and she had resigned as soon as was practical in order to mitigate the situation. Still, it was a reprehensible action, and she knew it.

She felt the heat rise to her cheeks. Never before had she shared details of her sexual history with anyone with whom she worked, and she was about to do just that—and come out of the closet—all in one swift move.

As she waited for the others to arrive so they could get this over with, she thought back to all the articles she had read on coming out of the closet. They had all said it was the most freeing experience in the world. Jo didn't feel free. She felt like she was in a living hell. It was like that dream where you showed up to high school naked, except now, not only was she going to be laid bare and naked in front of her co-workers, she was possibly ruining the careers of people she cared about. Her heart pounding, she forced herself to look Ian in the eye.

He just shook his head and looked away from her.

Gabe entered the room, a look of disbelief on his face. He took off his coat and set it on the back of the chair, taking care not to make eye contact with Jo as he did so.

She felt like screaming. Didn't she have an ally anywhere? She knew she didn't deserve one, but she felt hopeless and all alone. She looked at Madeline out of the corner of her eye, noting that she seemed to have checked out. She was sitting still, staring at the ceiling and looking like she thought her life was over. Actually, it was. The life she had known was done. There would be no return to the sense of normalcy she had known before the affair. And while it was possible she'd be allowed to serve out her term, it was more likely that the remainder of her tenure as mayor would be measured in weeks, not months.

Jo forced out a breath, suddenly finding it difficult to fill her lungs. Gabe glanced in her direction and then pointed at his phone. It was a signal they had used regularly during work hours. Gabe had sent her a text message and wanted her to check it.

She pulled her phone out beneath the table and read it.

Why didn't you tell me?

There was no easy answer. She had never made a practice of telling people. That was the reality of living life in the closet. You didn't tell, and when people questioned, you lied. Life was easier that way. He should understand that, having a brother who was gay, something he didn't feel free to talk about in the office. But that hadn't seemed to click with him just yet.

I'm sorry.

It was the only reply Jo had. She truly was sorry—not for being a lesbian, not even for sleeping with Madeline, if she were to be honest. But she was sorry that it had jeopardized all of their work, all of their jobs. Sorry that it had come to this.

These were talented people, though. They would all go out and find new jobs. They would not be damaged by Jo and Madeline's actions. They would be known as former Stratton employees, yes. But they could truthfully say they hadn't known, hadn't had a part in anything that had happened. Not that she and Madeline had broken any laws, no just ones anyway. Whatever they needed from her, she would give. She would put it in writing and sign in blood if that's what was needed.

Jo put her head in her hands, wanting more than ever before to simply disappear. She thought for some reason of those Southwest Airlines commercials. The ones that said, "Wanna get away?" at the end. Right now, her life could be turned into one of those commercials. Jo would lay money that no one in their right mind would want to change places with her right now.

Finally Jacquelyn arrived. Ian cleared his throat, breaking the silence in the room.

"Thank you all for coming tonight on such short notice," he said.

Jo looked around the room. His greeting was really not necessary in this setting. He and the others looked shaken and on edge. Their faces suggested they already knew the truth or thought they did. How they knew, Jo was not sure, but it was clear they knew something.

Ian continued, "Mayor Stratton, Jo, this is our second meeting of this nature today. Jacquelyn, Gabe and I had one earlier. We understand you have something that you need to bring to our attention now. So, I will let either of you—or both of you—speak. Then we can discuss what action needs to be taken."

Jo glanced at Madeline, who simply nodded.

"Okay," Jo said, her voice shaking as much as the rest of her body. "I guess I will be the one to fill you in." She tried to remember to breathe. "I want to start by offering everyone in this room an apology."

She turned to look each of them in the eye. Gabe stared right through her. Jacquelyn's look could have killed, and Ian sat stone-cold at the end of the table.

She swallowed. "I apologize for my hesitation too, but…there's no easy way to jump into this. What I need to say is that I'm…a…lesbian." The sentence was the hardest one she had ever had to string together.

"I'm a lesbian," she had to repeat it aloud to confirm to herself that she had just publicly admitted it for the first time. "And though I am not really sure how or why…things have happened between Mayor Stratton and me."

"What kind of things?" Jacquelyn demanded.

Jo glanced toward Madeline for help, but she was staring at the ceiling again. Jo let out a sigh. She was on her own here.

"We slept together," she admitted. "We didn't do it before she filed for divorce, and we did our best to keep it from public attention, but the truth is, we slept together."

Gabe looked like he might cry. Jo could not bear to look at him. In addition to driving his job into the ground, she had crushed his heart.

"Why are you bringing this to our attention now?" Ian asked.

Jo and Madeline had rehearsed what she would tell them, but even so she felt as though she were betraying Madeline's confidence. "I wasn't her first," Jo said softly.

"We need the whole story, Jo," Ian prompted impatiently.

"Natalie Longworth," Jo said. "You all will remember the name. She was the woman John Stratton was caught with and photographed with. She was the woman who started this whole mess. She was also Mayor Stratton's roommate in college."

Jo hated talking about Madeline as though she was not in the room, but she had little choice, given Madeline's sudden aversion to speaking with staff.

"They were lovers in college. Natalie is now threatening to tell the press about her and Mayor Stratton—and about what she assumes happened between Mayor Stratton and me," Jo finished. She hung her head at the admission, wanting desperately to crawl back into the hole where no one knew her secrets.

No one spoke, and the silence threatened to swallow Jo whole.

"I'm sorry," she said again, wanting to cry.

"Don't apologize." Madeline spoke with such strength that Jo did a double take.

Was this the same woman who had sat motionless through her entire confession? Was she now jumping to Jo's rescue?

Jo met Madeline's gaze and saw a new fire burning within her eyes.

"I want to say to all of you as well that I'm sorry who I am was not who I always appeared to be. I was not straightforward with you all, and I am the one who owes the apology." Madeline took a deep breath. "What Jo has said to you all is true, and it took great courage for her to take that step tonight."

Suddenly Madeline was not some weak victim. She was the mayor again—the strong, confident boss who had led them all thus far—and she was making her power known. Jo felt a tingle of relief go through her body. She would not have to face this fight alone.

"I think you all owe Jo some respect," Madeline added. "To be sure, our actions have not been the most admirable. In fact, they were wrong—not because we are both women, but because of my position and because of the effect that they will have on the work that we have been doing. I apologize for trying to keep this out of the public eye, but I will not apologize for sleeping with a woman. That part of our relationship is not wrong, and neither was my relationship with Natalie Longworth."

The silence lasted for only a few seconds. This time it was Gabe who broke it.

"Why didn't you tell us, Jo?"

"Which part was I supposed to tell you?" Jo asked.

"That you're a lesbian. I think that you know you could have trusted us." Gabe appeared genuinely to be hurt, but his words made no sense to Jo given the tacit warning he'd given her when he'd told her about his brother. He seemed to realize at the same time that he might be on shaky ground with his comment. A look of fear flashed across his face as she began to answer him.

"Gabe," she said carefully, "I think it is unfair that I should have to disclose to my colleagues who I choose to sleep with. You are not required to go around telling everyone that you like to sleep with women. Nor are you required to disclose information about *acquaintances* of yours who date individuals of the same gender. Why should I—or anyone else for that matter—be held to a different standard?"

The question obviously hit its target. Perhaps what they all needed was a little bit of perspective.

"How would you like it?" she asked, turning to Jacquelyn and Ian. "What would you do if your decision to follow your heart made you a criminal in the eyes of your co-workers?"

Ian shook his head. "It is not the same thing, Jo."

"What do you mean it isn't the same?" Jo asked.

Ian was normally calm and collected, and his level-headedness made him a great manager. But now, suddenly, he was transformed. He was enraged.

"I have a wife," he bellowed. "Because that is how it is supposed to be. I am a man, and she is a woman. That is how it is supposed to be. You don't get to decide on a case-by-case basis, and you do not get to change the rules." He shot an angry look at Jo and then turned to Madeline. "What the hell were you thinking to engage in such depraved and unnatural behavior?" he demanded of her.

"Ian," Madeline said calmly but with authority, "I do not demand much, but I demand that you drop the homophobia. We have stated clearly that we know what we did was inappropriate, and we are prepared to deal with the consequences. You will show respect to Jo and me both as people and as lesbians."

At her use of the word "lesbian," Jacquelyn and Ian sat up straight in their chairs looking as if someone had doused them with ice water. The word struck a chord within Jo. She smiled, noting it as the first time Madeline had identified herself so clearly. At the table, Gabe remained motionless, defeated.

"You may disapprove of us, you can fault us for our affair—but be civil, all of you," Madeline continued with unparalleled confidence. "Am I understood?" As she asked the question, she made a point of surveying each individual face.

Gabe nodded and Jacquelyn looked away.

Ian continued to fume in the corner. "I am not going to sit here and listen to the two of you explain this away. You may be my boss, but I will not stand by while you say that you have done nothing wrong by sleeping with another woman. We are *not* going say that to the media, to the public or to the rest of the staff."

"And just what do you expect me to tell everyone then?" Madeline asked. "Remember when you answer that you are not only impacting me and my career, my life and my future, but you are impacting the career, life and future of this promising young woman." She pointed to Jo.

"She forfeited a say in the matter the minute she came to work for you," Ian said. "It is all a part of the job. We accept that when we come to work for a public official. Anything you say or do can be called into question. When it does, we each have to step up and 'take one for the team.'"

He pointed at Jacquelyn. "If something you were quoted as saying in a press release went terribly wrong, if we took a position on something and the 'facts' we based it on turned out to be incorrect, she would take the fall for you. Plagiarism, faulty statements, a spelling error, being misquoted—any of that and she would be the public scapegoat. It comes with the territory."

He pointed at Gabe. "If you miss a meeting, he takes the fall. If you decide not to take part in a charity, an event or a committed engagement, he shoulders the responsibility and says it was his error. The public cannot be upset with you for missing anything, so he takes all the heat."

"Additionally," Ian continued, "if one of them—if any staff member—is caught doing anything inappropriate while working for you, they take the heat. They know that they represent you wherever they go. And that when someone on staff is caught doing something that will garner negative press, they are likely to be asked to leave."

"I know that, and I am grateful to all of you for your service," Madeline said, looking at each of them. "Truthfully, I am. And while I am ashamed of the timing of matters and the fact that they occurred when I was her boss, you have to take her behavior into consideration as well."

Jo could feel all eyes turn to her. "It's okay. I'm prepared to come to terms with whatever the fallout may be," she said. "I don't deserve any special treatment in this matter."

"No, you sure as hell don't," Ian said, turning to face Jo. "You see, we have protocols for this sort of thing."

"The gay sort of thing?" Jo asked, trying to alleviate some of the tension, but also needing to seriously ask the question.

"No," Ian answered. "The sort of thing where you are going to give this office a bad name. When you do that, there are repercussions."

"Let me guess," Jo cut him off. "I'm fired. Is that it?" She emitted a tired sigh. "Ian, I resigned this morning, remember?"

Ian nodded curtly. "I guess that's right. You're no longer a Stratton employee—not that it means much anymore—but it does mean that you are dismissed from this meeting."

She stood, positive that this was no longer worth the fight.

"Well, then, thank you all for the opportunity to work here. I have learned a lot and enjoyed my time with you. Again, I extend my apologies to you all."

Jacquelyn appeared relieved that Jo was leaving. Gabe's expression was torn. There was a part of him, obviously, that was deeply hurt by Jo's confessions tonight and another part that still cared for her. She hoped they could stay in touch after this storm blew over and life went on—in whatever direction it might go for Jo.

Ian cleared his throat. "That'll be all now, Jo."

"Goodbye then." He waved a hand at her, signaling her to leave.

As she walked past Madeline, she leaned down. "I will be waiting in the car."

To her surprise, Madeline reached up and wrapped her arms around Jo's neck, pulling her closer. Right there, in front of her senior staff, Madeline kissed Jo deeply and passionately.

Jo pulled away after a second, but Madeline added a small peck on the lips to finish off the kiss. "I will be out in a little while," she said as Jo walked out of the room.

Standing in the hallway, Jo savored the rush of having kissed Madeline that publicly.

"That is what you are condemning. Do you understand that?" Jo heard Madeline's voice boom. "I care about Josephine Carson, and here you are, shutting her out for returning those feelings."

Jo fought the urge to stay and listen. She had no idea what she was going to do with her future. She had been kicked to the curb, was without a job and was now a step closer to being publicly out once and for all. Very soon everyone—her parents and sisters and most of those living in this part of the nation—would know that she was a lesbian.

The fact that her family would know made her heart pound. She had decided to tell them eventually, but she hadn't been prepared for it to occur almost immediately. Everything she had worked so hard to hide from them her entire life was going to come avalanching out of the closet in a very real, very public fashion. She walked to the car, trying to envision what that was going to be like. Somehow she knew it was going to be exponentially more difficult than anything she was imagining.

CHAPTER TWENTY-FIVE

The fluorescent lights in the conference room hummed, and a cell phone made a muffled vibrating sound under the table. Other than that, everything was silent.

Madeline sat proud and tall, ignoring the judgments being shot at her from every corner of the room. It wasn't easy. With every passing minute, this day felt more and more like one of the Salem witch trials. At one point in history, she recalled, they had publicly dunked women thought to be witches. If they survived, they were said to be witches. If they didn't, well, then that was just their bad luck.

That was how today felt. If you are thought to be a lesbian, you will be put out of office. If you really are a lesbian, you are condemned to live a "life of sin." If you're not, well, sorry about that—you're still out of office.

Yes, she was involved with a woman—but it still felt so unfair. What did that have to do with her ability to govern, to foster important, necessary changes in a city she loved? If the attention were to focus solely on the fact that she had engaged in an inappropriate relationship with a staff member, she could have dealt with that. She knew, though, that her being with a woman would be the focal point of the news stories—more so than the woman in question having been a staff member. The news of her "lesbian tendencies" were likely to create a much greater stir, as they had with her staff. And that was unfair.

It was how things went in politics, she guessed, but it still did not prevent the sting of the rejection she was feeling from each of her most trusted staff members. These were the people she was supposed to rely on most, and, as Ian said, the ones who often took the fall. But most importantly, they had always been the people who were fighting for her, not against her.

It felt as though they had given up, resigning themselves to either watch her be voted out of office next year or tender her resignation at some point in the near future.

After moments of painful silence, Jacquelyn finally spoke.

"I will draft a statement for the media tonight, so we can hit the ground running when this breaks. It isn't really a matter of if anymore. I think it is safe to say that given everything we have heard, the media will catch wind of this very soon. If they haven't already."

Gabe, who had avoided eye contact with everyone since Jo walked out, now looked at Madeline. "What will you say?"

"We will say that the allegations are true—that I did sleep with a woman in college. But we will leave Jo out of it, if possible. We will address the situation, but we will affirm that this does not interfere with my ability to perform as mayor and that I still have the best interests of the citizens of Oklahoma City at heart."

"We will not," Ian interjected.

Madeline cleared her throat. She had always had the final say about the statements she put out to the public. After all, she was the one saying them.

"And what do you propose we say, Ian?" she asked.

"You will say that all the allegations are false," Ian said pointedly. "That there is no relationship whatsoever with Jo, who in any case, resigned recently to pursue other opportunities. That this so-called news story is something cooked up by a source looking to earn another fifteen minutes of fame and a little cash from the news stations and some expiation for having been discovered stepping out with your husband in the first place.

"As for your relationship with Natalie, you will minimize it. You will dismiss it. Lie if you have to. You could say, for instance, that, once, at a party you were dared to kiss each other, and you did. That way if some other *witness* to your actions comes forward, it's out in the open already as some sort of stupid college stunt. Case closed. Nothing else is open for discussion.

"Then you will say that you are sorry for all the turmoil this has caused for your constituents and that even though you are facing a very difficult time in your life, they come first. You hope that they will understand the burden of stress you have been under and that you are committed to serving them no matter what."

Madeline shook her head. Could he be any further off the mark?

"It will likely not be enough to save us in the election, but it will get us out of hot water for at least a little bit," Ian continued. "Jacquelyn, you work up the statement. Gabe, you work on scheduling a public press conference for tomorrow morning, where we will release these statements."

"And you," he said, turning to Madeline, "you will have nothing further to do with Jo Carson. You are not to see her or be seen with her."

Madeline laughed. "Just who the hell do you think you are, Ian?"

"The only one making rational decisions at a time when you are off sleeping with inappropriate people and making a mockery of this office," he shot back.

"I will not stop seeing Jo, and I will not issue a statement full of lies," she said defiantly. It was true. She would no longer lie about who she was or what she was doing. Life was too short to be spent cowering in a corner hoping no one saw through the fabrications.

"Oh, now you are suddenly an upstanding citizen, focused on telling the truth and spreading morality? That's really rich coming from someone pursuing a sinful and disgusting lifestyle," Ian yelled, losing control once again.

"You will lower your voice, and you WILL show respect for me," Madeline demanded in a cold, quiet voice. "I am still the mayor—if only for this very minute. I have apologized for what I have done wrong, and I fully accept what is coming, Ian."

"I will not," he said. "You forfeited all authority in this room the minute you put your desires above the careers of everyone here. You selfishly and foolishly placed us all on the line to fulfill a depraved fantasy. And now you will listen to what we have to say, and you will follow our lead."

"I will not," Madeline echoed. "Sit your high and mighty ass back down on that chair and listen up. My actions were reprehensible, and I have addressed that. You can oppose homosexuality until you are blue in the face, but it does not change the fact that I prefer to sleep with women. Nor does it change the fact that you are a bigot and an asshole."

Ian opened his mouth to speak, but Madeline cut him off. "You want to talk about actions that are sinful and disgusting? Let's think this one over for a minute. Now, you, as I recall, are the one who's always telling me to quote the Bible, so let me quote some scripture for you. How about 'Thou shalt not bear false witness'? Is that anything like filling a press release full of lies?

"Or how about, 'Let he who is without sin cast the first stone'? Do you remember that one?"

He narrowed his eyes at her, clearly not amused.

"Well," she continued, "if memory serves, two years ago one of our staff members knocked up the girl he was dating. Did the media ask about this? Yes, they did, because it happened at the very time when we were advancing our family values campaign. Did I fire this staffer?"

Madeline looked around the room to add to the dramatic effect. "No, I did not. He is now my chief of staff and is married to the woman with whom he had a child."

"Correct me if I am wrong," Madeline continued, looking Ian in the eye. "But wouldn't some church folks call that precious baby boy of yours an abomination, just like you are calling my relationship an abomination?"

His anger, which had dropped down a notch, was quickly replaced by sheer hatred. No one liked being called out on their own issues. It was easy to make a fuss about someone else's supposed wrongdoings, but when the tables were turned, it was harder to digest.

Gabe and Jacquelyn both looked terrified, she saw. And they should be. She had enough on each of them to bury them. As she was about to remind them. She wasn't done, not by a long shot.

"Gabriel," she said. "You had a DWI a year ago, didn't you?"

"Yes, ma'am," he said.

"The press inquired about that too. Yet here you are at this table," Madeline said.

He nodded his head. There were other issues that she could have brought to the forefront of everyone's minds regarding Gabe, but he had been the least hostile, so she decided to let them slide for now.

"Jacquelyn," she said, turning in her chair. "Have you ever been caught red-handed by the press sleeping with inappropriate people and getting fall-down, pass-out drunk in public?"

Jacquelyn's eyes widened in horror. Madeline had been keeping that gem of information pretty much to herself. She had shared with Ian what she had heard. He had cautioned Jacquelyn, but basically it had been swept under the rug. She was never told that Madeline had been informed.

When Jacquelyn did not answer, Madeline decided to dig a little bit deeper.

"You see, an old friend of mine who works for the *Oklahoman* called one night to tell me that he had seen you shooting doubles for an entire evening, to the point that you were about to pass out. Apparently, though, that was not enough to make you go home. Instead, you proceeded to have sex with a stranger in his car outside of the bar. Does this incident sound familiar at all?"

Jacquelyn cast her eyes downward.

"Luckily, my friend the reporter told me he was not going to say anything—he just thought I should know," Madeline said. She swept her gaze around the room.

"As you see, I am not the only one to have tarnished the reputation of this office. Each of you have too. So, having said that, I will write my own damn statement and each of you can go fuck yourselves."

She stood up and pushed in her chair.

"You can expect my statement by email tomorrow morning," she said to Jacquelyn. "Between now and then, I'll be making decisions based on how I want to proceed and on what type of staff I want to surround myself with, should I choose to remain in office or seek another term."

* * *

Jacquelyn felt her heart settle into a normal rhythm, a strange phenomenon, considering everything that had transpired tonight.

It was highly likely that she would be out of a job as of tomorrow morning, and even if she wasn't, there was a shitstorm headed their way that could not be avoided. Nonetheless, she felt free.

Freedom's just another word for nothing left to lose. Jacquelyn suddenly understood the words of the old Janis Joplin song, and she sang them to herself for comfort.

Glancing down in her lap, she clicked on the message notification that had been blinking there for the last twenty minutes. *We need to talk. Call me when you have a minute.* The message was from Isaac. She tried to care about whatever he might say, but all of her energy was gone. Had the news already come out? Was it coming out tomorrow? She hung her head, realizing she didn't care. It was as if the *Titanic* had already hit the iceberg and she was content to go down with the ship.

She had heard colleagues talk about being burnt out, but she had always thought she was better than that. If you stayed dedicated to your job, you wouldn't burn out, she had said. She had been wrong.

She tried to figure out exactly when she had stopped caring. Was it the moment when Madeline chose to lean on Jo rather than her? Was it earlier when Madeline announced she would not hide the truth and she would not apologize, thereby sinking her political career? Or was it a moment ago when she realized

Madeline was right in stating that she had nothing to apologize for—not to the public, not to anyone?

Madeline Stratton was a giver of second and third chances. She always had been and, as a result, over the past few years she had built somewhat of a family in this office. Everyone had their share of baggage and dysfunctional relationships, but when times were tough, they stood together as one.

Usually, that is. This time, they had turned their backs on Madeline, leaving her and Jo out in the cold alone.

She fought the urge to chase after Madeline and apologize. It would do no good now, just as Madeline's confession to the public tomorrow would do no good.

Looking across the table at Ian, she wanted to slap him. What right did he have—what right did any of them have—to judge so harshly? Sure, it had been inappropriate for a mayor to sleep with a staff member—but it happened all the time. The truth of the matter was, had it been a man and a woman, everything would have been swept under the rug.

And what did it matter in the end? Political careers were tumultuous and unstable at best. She and the other staffers would hit the campaign circuit, or they would find another official position. They would be fine.

She took a deep breath and decided that she had to call Isaac back. If only for tonight, she was still communications director for Mayor Madeline Stratton. She fought the urge to laugh. Which one of their titles would vanish first? Would she become the former communications director before Madeline became the former mayor?

"I have a call to make," she announced, making Gabe and Ian jump. Everyone had been lost in their own thoughts.

She stood and walked to the hallway. It didn't really make a difference since she knew pretty much what Isaac was going to say, but at least she would find out when everything was going to all come to light.

She dialed his number. After only one ring, he answered, out of breath. "Hello?"

"Hey, Isaac. It's Jacquelyn. You told me to call," she said.

"Oh, right," he answered, clearly both intoxicated and happy. "I got a bonus today."

"You called to tell me you got a bonus?" she asked. "I mean, congratulations," she added, unsure of why he had bothered to call if that was all he had to say.

"Well, you may not be congratulating me for very long."

"Why is that?" Jacquelyn asked, already suspecting the answer. Of course he had received a bonus at work. He was about to help break the story of the year, possibly the decade.

"We got a tip on your boss today, and man, it was a big one. We've got a story—and an eyewitness who will blow the minds of our viewers," he said, not even trying to disguise his celebration.

"That's what I thought," she said, unable to feel anything about the fact that everything was crashing down around her. "When will it run?"

"So you knew about this?" he asked.

"It's my job to know," Jacquelyn replied.

"Why didn't you tell me?" he asked.

"I didn't think we were at the point of full disclosure yet, okay, Isaac?" She let out a sigh. "Anyway, when is it going to run?"

"Well, I thought we had a deal. Maybe I shouldn't even tell you when it's running," he slurred.

"Cut the crap, Isaac. We slept together a few times. Don't act so hurt. When is it running?" She didn't have the patience to deal with this tonight.

"First thing tomorrow morning," he said, and she heard the phone click dead.

She guessed that settled the question of how long their little fling was going to last. Stretching to the side, she let the stiffness in her neck crack.

Tomorrow morning was the beginning of the end. She knew she should feel something—anything. It took a while, but finally she thought she did. When she tried to define it, though, only one word came to mind—*jaded.*

CHAPTER TWENTY-SIX

An empty bottle of wine sat on the kitchen table, and Jo sat in her living room staring blankly at the walls. She heard the periodic click-clack of Madeline's laptop keys. It did little to silence her fears.

What would her parents think? Would she be cut off from her family for good? And what would she do for work?

It wasn't the financial side of things that worried her, it was the relational side. She was not overly close to her parents, but she loved them deeply. Without them in her life, things would change significantly.

She had contemplated calling them tonight, but she wanted to see what Madeline was going to say first. That would be the true test.

She picked up her phone again and scrolled through her contacts until she reached the one labeled Mom. Her finger hovered over the SEND key, but then, with a sigh, she set the phone down. No amount of explaining could help them understand, not any time soon anyway. She had heard, time and time again, the things they said about the gay and lesbian community.

Abomination. Sinful. Disgusting. Awful. Horrible. Dirty. Despicable. Depraved. Gross.

The words revolved through her head like a carousel. Many of them were words she had heard tonight from Ian's mouth. She knew that they also would be words tossed about by the general public after tomorrow's announcement.

Not ready yet to face their shock and condemnation, she opted to send a text to her mother.

"I just wanted to give you a heads-up that there will probably be something big on the news tomorrow that will affect us all. I can't say more, but I want you and Dad to know that I love you very much. If the press comes to you with questions, give them my cell phone number. I'll call you when things settle down."

It was simple and short on details, but she knew she needed to prepare them. And she hoped it would give them something to hold on to when it all hit—a reminder that their daughter was the same girl they had raised, regardless of what the media might say.

Jo closed her eyes, hoping Madeline was typing out something truthful and meaningful. She had not said anything when she got to the car, but Jo was pretty sure what they wanted her to say—that it was all a lie. If Madeline did deny it, Jo would too—at least regarding her relationship with her former boss. But if she owned up to it, Jo would stand beside her, tall and proud, and make known publicly for the first time exactly who she was.

The part that puzzled her was that she wasn't sure which would be worse, having Madeline stand up and equate everything they shared to a malicious rumor or having her life on display for all to see—and denounce.

At least they now knew when the news was coming. Jacquelyn had emailed to say that Channel 4 would be breaking the story on the morning news.

She heard the typing stop in the other room, and Madeline walked into the living room to stand in front of her. Looking at the deep smile on her face, suddenly Jo had the sense that some way, somehow, everything tomorrow would be all right again.

"Do you want to hear my speech?" Madeline asked, looking like a schoolgirl who had completed a particularly difficult assignment. "I made some edits to the one you drafted."

Jo nodded, curious to hear how many changes she had made and what kind. Was it still a resignation speech, or had she tailored it to hide the truth?

As Madeline read it aloud to her, Jo stared at her, amazed. How could such great strength come from one woman? When she finished, she stood and hugged Madeline. Her intuition had been right. Somehow, something good would come from all of this, and one day in the future, all would be right again.

"I've got a couple of emails to send to my family, my dad's company, and a few others," Madeline said. "They deserve to know something is coming before it hits. Then, it's time to turn off the phones and get a little sleep before mayoral Armageddon."

* * *

The next morning they sat hand in hand on the couch to watch the Channel 4 news. Jo squeezed Madeline's hand in support when Natalie's face came on screen. Lead Investigative Reporter Angie Rhodes sat across from her, her face looking ever so serious.

"I am joined here in studio with Natalie Longworth, who has been in the news off and on for the last month after allegedly having an affair with Mayor Madeline Stratton's husband, John Stratton. This morning, Natalie has unveiled some new facts to the story."

Angie turned to face Natalie. "So, Miss Longworth, is it true that, despite Mayor Stratton's statements to the contrary, you have known her for years?"

Natalie put on her most charming smile. "Yes, that is true. We were roommates in college. Roommates, best friends and a little more." Her smile broadened.

"Would you care to expand on that last part?" Angie asked.

"Sure. We were lovers. It happened during the time that we were living together. You know, it was college. Everyone experimented, but our experiment lasted longer than most."

"How long did your relationship with Mayor Stratton last?"

"Well, from the time we first slept together until we called it quits, I would say it was about two years," Natalie said.

"So was this *two-year relationship* just a *phase* the mayor went through? I mean, after all, she has been an advocate for protecting the sanctity of marriage by defining it as being between a man and a woman. She has actively spoken out against same-sex unions, and she has even had numerous fundraisers with groups that advocate for traditional family values—which is almost always code for antigay political activity. Was this just something she experimented with in college?" Angie asked, setting things up for Natalie's next revelation.

"I have reason to believe it was not," Natalie said. "When John first came to me, he was looking for a friend—someone to talk to. He said he felt like his wife—Madeline—had never actually wanted him. He said that it was like she always hoped he was someone else."

"Someone female, perhaps?"

"That was my first thought," Natalie replied. "I mean, given my memories of Madeline, I had always assumed she would just end up with a woman. It *shocked* me when I heard she had ended up with John, honestly. But now I hear she has gone back to what she loves."

"What do you mean, 'gone back to what she loves'?"

"She has found ways to heal after her very public breakup with John. Just tonight, I mean last night…" They had obviously tried to make this appear live. "I went to her hotel room to talk to her—to apologize about this whole thing. I cared about Madeline Stratton deeply. She was a big part of my life in college, and I wanted to smooth things over. I know what I did was wrong, and I wanted to offer her my deepest, most sincere apology."

Of course, she would put on her sweetest face for the cameras. Jo was getting more pissed with every second of this interview.

"When I got there, she cut me short. I figured it was just because she was angry. But right after I left, I saw someone come out of the shadows of the other room and embrace her. It was a woman. I saw the two of them engage in a very passionate kiss."

Jo tried to remember if they had kissed last night in front of the window. She doubted it, but then again, she had thought she had given Natalie plenty of time to get out of the parking lot when she had come to comfort Madeline. For all she knew, the whole thing could be fabricated—but then again, it could be true.

"You saw the mayor kissing another woman last night?" Angie's face carried an expression of carefully calculated shock.

"That's right. I was curious, so I asked John about it. He suggested I research the people on her staff. I visited the mayor's website, scrolled through the pictures of the staff and there she was, Madeline's new girlfriend. At least the picture matches the person I saw kissing Madeline last night." Natalie turned to the camera. "Can you believe it? The mayor is dating one of her staff members."

"Miss Longworth, would you tell us the name of this staffer?" Angie asked. Jo tensed. This was the moment of truth.

"I believe her name is Josephine Carson. Everyone calls her Jo. She's the mayor's speechwriter. She's also the daughter of Michael Carson—that mega-church pastor in Tulsa." Natalie spit the words out quickly, as if she had been waiting to tattle on Jo. It seemed clear to Jo that she had a personal vendetta against her. She wondered if other viewers were getting the same impression.

"Let me get this straight," Angie said, holding up a hand. "You are saying that our conservative, traditional-marriage-supporting mayor and the daughter of an actively antigay pastor have been having a lesbian affair, all while Jo Carson worked for the mayor?"

"That is correct," Natalie said as a picture of Jo filled the screen behind them.

"Well, that is one side of the story. We have not heard from the mayor yet, but if she issues a statement, you will hear it here first. As for now, we will let you decide," Angie said as a picture of Madeline popped up beside that of Jo. "Are these two women engaged in a relationship that would make the mayor's socially conservative record completely irrelevant to her voters? And if so, what laws, if any, have they contravened?"

Jo clicked the off button on the television and sat back with a loud sigh, knowing that the segment was prompting salacious conversations in households around the city and beyond. The switchboards at Oklahoma City's talk radio stations were lighting up like Christmas trees, no doubt. She reached over and turned off her phone, not ready to take any of the calls that had been pouring in. She was only going to be able to handle so much today. Hearing from friends or family would be more than she could take.

Madeline raised Jo's hand to her lips and kissed it gently. "We're halfway through the battle. Let's get dressed and win this war," she said, standing and pulling Jo to her feet.

Madeline was right. They had more to do. There was a press conference in an hour, and both of them looked unkempt. Jo glanced down at her sweatpants and sports bra and noted that even though Madeline looked great in one of Jo's T-shirts, they should probably hurry and get ready to avoid giving the press even more of a show than the one they had coming anyway.

* * *

Cameras flashed and clicked. The murmur of the press was alive in the auditorium Gabe had secured for the event. He and Jacquelyn had helped facilitate the conference at Madeline's request. As they always did, they had done a fantastic job. It was packed.

Madeline was on edge. This was something she had to do on her own, she knew. Sitting at the front of the room, though, she wished she had someone beside her.

She spotted Jo in the crowd and smiled at her, as much to settle herself as to calm Jo's fears. They had both decided to turn off their phones, and Madeline knew that Jo's emotions must be all over the place, wondering what friends and family had to say in reaction to this morning's news. The pinched look around Jo's eyes was a clear indicator of the toll this whole ordeal was taking on her.

Madeline took a deep breath. The statement Jacquelyn had sent to the media announcing the press conference had informed them that she would not be taking questions. They would try to ask them anyway, of course, but she would simply give the speech she had prepared and then leave the podium.

She cleared her throat, silencing the audience.

"Good morning. I know that by now you have heard the story from the mouth of Natalie Longworth that aired on Channel 4 this morning. I would like to tell you my side of that story now. To tell you all the truth."

She paused briefly to make eye contact with several cameras and to let her words sink in.

"As you know, Miss Longworth made some pretty substantial allegations against me and a member of my staff on the news this morning. Rest assured, I will address every claim she made."

She lifted the index finger of her right hand.

"First, I do know Natalie Longworth. She was my college roommate, and, yes, she and I dated."

A collective gasp sounded throughout the room. This was not the response the press had expected to hear.

She continued. "I was young and exploring, as Channel 4 Reporter Angie Rhodes claimed. But it went beyond that. In the course of my explorations, I discovered who I was, including the fact that I like women more than men. However, due to societal pressures and the stereotypes often imposed upon women like myself, I ran from this discovery. My running led me into the arms of the man I would marry, John Stratton."

"I was never unfaithful to John during our nearly twenty years of marriage, but as Natalie suggested, there was something missing from our relationship. Recently, he was found to be having an affair with her—only one of many such dalliances from what I now understand. After that was brought to my knowledge, we separated and are in the process of getting a divorce.

"I don't stand up here today, however, as a woman betrayed who is looking for sympathy and understanding. I stand up here today in order to shed light on a personal situation that has become very public."

Madeline looked to Jo for strength. She nodded in support. She took a breath and said, "I stand up here today as a woman who loves women, asking only that you hear me out fully and look at the situation from all sides before passing judgment. I stand here today for all the girls and women who have dreaded having their desires and actions being cast in an unfavorable public light. To tell those girls that it is okay to feel what they feel and to be who they are. Hoping that, as a result, there will be more women living authentic lives and fewer women who take the path I took, because it was safer—because it was expected."

She smiled at Jo, allowing her expression to soften as she began the most important part of her speech.

"On the first night after my marriage fell apart, I stayed with one of my staff members who was kind enough to take me in. I didn't have anywhere else to go. Not anywhere that would allow me to be unbothered by the ever-present news cameras anyway, where I might have a minute or two to think things through. That is where Jo Carson comes into this picture. She has been a member of my staff for the better part of a year, but the night she entered my personal life was the night I found out about John's infidelity. Soon thereafter, we became friends. And, as Natalie informed the public this morning, we have very recently become more than friends. I am involved with—and care very deeply for—Jo Carson."

Even as she spoke them, the words tingled through her body. This is what freedom felt like, she was sure of it.

"That is the truth. And I do not make apologies for that today, except to say that though our relationship was—*is*—consensual, as Jo's boss my actions were inappropriate. Had I not been her superior, there would be nothing to criticize in our relationship in my opinion. As mayor, I should be held to a higher standard, though. I am ashamed that I crossed that line.

"Yet, given the chance to do it all again, our timing is the only thing I would change. I would have waited until yesterday morning, when Jo resigned her position, hoping to avoid such a dilemma. However, we cannot change the past—and I would not want to, because it all led me to where I am today. And today I am *happy*. It has been an honor to serve all of you as mayor and to work with one of the finest staffs anyone could hope to have—none of whom, I hasten to add, had any knowledge about or involvement in the personal choices I've made."

She paused for a moment to look to her staff members. Gabe nodded appreciatively at the comment, Jacquelyn shrugged as if she didn't know how to process the moment it was all ending, and one of the interns wore a look of shock and disbelief. Knowing that they would be okay in the end, she took a deep breath and continued.

"I thank you for the opportunity to serve Oklahoma City and its citizens. Although the recent news has not been about initiatives or efforts made to better our city, I hope that years from now, those items—rather than the details of my personal life—will be what you remember about the Stratton administration.

"I hope you remember the hundreds of jobs we have added in the past three years. I hope you remember the great strides we've made in fighting corruption in government. I hope you remember the times I sat down with you over coffee to discuss the future of this great city and of you, your children and your grandchildren. I hope that you remember those times, because I will—and I will cherish the memories.

"Now, however, they must become memories. Due to the notoriety my private life has gained and to the extent to which I have become more of a celebrity than an elected official in the eyes of many, I am resigning my position as mayor effective immediately. Interim elections will be held as decreed by city statute. In the meantime, municipal affairs will be handled by the city council and the city manager, assisted by the experienced and professional staff I am leaving behind. With that, I thank you all."

As Madeline expected, a barrage of questions was hurled her way as stepped away from the podium. Even though she had clearly stated that there would be no questions, this crowd was intent on hearing more. She calmly walked toward Jo without speaking, grabbed her by the hand and exited the back of the building to where Jo's little red sports car waited with a tank full of gas and two suitcases packed with only the essentials.

Once in Jo's car, Madeline let out a long breath.

"You were amazing," Jo said, leaning in to kiss her. "Let's get out of here and get started on that vacation you promised me last night."

"Do you have any calls you need to make?" Madeline asked, remembering Jo's family.

"I do, and I will take care of it all further down the road. For now, let's just celebrate being together and being open," Jo said. She put the car in gear, smiling, aimed the wheels west toward California, and cued up "Hold On" by Wilson Phillips on her iPod, much to Madeline's amusement. It was true. They were finally free to create new dreams—authentic ones—together.

Bella Books, Inc.

Women. Books. Even Better Together.

P.O. Box 10543
Tallahassee, FL 32302

Phone: 800-729-4992
www.bellabooks.com